COUNTER MEASURES
COUNTER MEASURES

A Murder Mystery

By
Eugénie D. West

THE SAMOTHRACE PRESS

This is a work of fiction. Names, places, events, motives, characters, personalities and descriptions in this book are products of the author's imagination and/or are used fictitiously. Any other interpretation is beyond the intent of the author.

No part of this book may be reproduced or transmitted in any form or by any means, electronic or mechanical, including photocopying, recording or through information storage/retrieval systems, without permission in writing from the author.

Gratefully dedicated to the
Pennsylvania State Police Troopers
and to Law Enforcement everywhere,
with respect for their constant sacrifices
and unwavering dedication;
and to their families, whose gift
of their best and brightest
does not go unappreciated.

And to NPC, always.

About the Author

The author of 'Counter Measures,' Eugénie D. West, was a news reporter for a weekly newspaper for more than 15 years. All of the books in her 'Reporting is Murder!'© series, of which 'Counter Measures' is the ninth, are inspired by actual cases the author encountered during her time on the news beat, and from events and cases that occurred in the surrounding area. The treatments given these cases in West's books are fictional, with motives, details and outcomes that are not the same as the real ones. West writes her novels under a *nom de plume* borrowed from a paternal great great great grandmother.

'Counter Measures' features West's protagonist, sleuthing journalist Gracie Barufaldi, along with her on again off again boyfriend Jack and several other intriguing characters, both new and recurring. The ensemble players interact with each other and carry forward their own personal stories against the backdrop of a puzzling murder and its eventual solution.

Like most of the books West writes, the featured murder isn't the only crime in the story, nor is the thread of Gracie and Jack's relationship the only sub plot. As in life, other misdemeanors, dramas and passions intervene, making for a richly woven tale that is satisfyingly blended and concluded.

West is inspired by people she has known and places she has been, but the characters in her books are fictional: amalgams of qualities, characteristics and traits from scores of acquaintances, strangers and other personalities. They are created to fit with and further the story. To read any more into them, or to attempt to identify real people in West's characters is foolhardy.

West holds a Ph.D. in English and enjoys history, languages, music, science and travel. Like Gracie, she lives in a rural part of the northeastern United States, is a bit of a techno-geek, and is an accomplished cook.

Visit West on her Amazon Author Page, and find her on Twitter (@EugnieDWest), Facebook(Eugenie D. West), Pinterest, Goodreads and on her blog, ThebooksofEugnieDWest.blogspot.com.

A portion of the sales of this book will be donated to a nearby cat rescue, where West can sometimes be found cleaning litter pans and giving out treats.

Also in the
'Reporting is Murder!'© Series
by Eugénie D. West:

Baby's Breath
Coercion
Black Card
Where There's Smoke, There's Murder
Spin
Tide's Reach
Natural Causes
Precipice

§

And as
Deborah L. Courville
(historical fact-based fiction):

A River In Time
Treachery in Time
A Christmas in Time

COUNTER MEASURES

COUNTER MEASURES

CHAPTER ONE
CHAPTER ONE

Wyatt McGinley picked up the small brown branch and laid it carefully atop the others he held in his arms. He should be able to carry one or two more, he thought, as he scanned the leaf-fall covered ground. He hoped his father would be pleased, since a couple more branches would make a considerable pile of kindling for their campfire. Eight year old Wyatt was of the opinion that his father hadn't expected him to return with anything like this amount of wood, and he was secretly pleased at having exceeded his exacting parent's expectations.

Mount Greylock State Forest in Western Massachusetts was in its glory now, in the last few weeks of full summer. Conifers and deciduous trees mingled to create a thick and greenly shadowed forest floor replete with layers of past seasons' toffee-colored dried leaves and bronze pine needles atop the hard pan. It was warm during the day, even here, in the deeper shadows. But at night, temperatures dropped to the fifties because of the area's elevation: perfect, Wyatt's father Aaron had declared, for camping.

They had found their site in the small 'primitive' campground just an hour ago, and quickly set up their new, roomy, waterproofed canvas tent. Wyatt had watched as his dad had driven sharp, long spikes into the packed, rock-like earth: the spikes, attached to strategically placed rings around the tent's perimeter, would secure their temporary dwelling against any wind. A tarp tied to tree trunks conveniently if not precisely located at the four cardinal directions would shield the tent in case of rain.

However, the forecast was for fine, dry weather throughout the Labor Day long weekend, so Wyatt and Aaron expected neither rain nor wind to interrupt their camping experience.

It was the first time Wyatt had gone camping; his father had camped frequently as a boy, and then as a young man, but father and son had yet to share an 'outdoor adventure,' as Aaron referred to it. Belinda, Wyatt's mother and Aaron's wife, was deathly afraid of insects, snakes and the outdoors in general. So, although Aaron had loved camping most of his life, family camping as an activity had been a non-starter since his marriage. And honestly, Aaron had been so immersed in his ever expanding career as a securities analyst for Greylock Mountain Bank, he really hadn't had the time.

But this weekend, he was making the time. If he were to be completely honest with himself, Aaron sometimes worried about Wyatt: at eight, the child seemed disinclined towards typical male games and pursuits and more interested in math and music. While Aaron was proud of Wyatt's nearly straight A status at school, he often wished his son would run outside and toss around a football rather than stay in his room, calculating another in a seemingly unending series of mystifying equations. Or playing the flute or piano.

Just the previous week, Wyatt had mentioned at dinner one evening that he might be able to study the harp for a short, six week elective being offered at his elementary school. It was a program that partnered musicians from Tanglewood with local educational institutions, and Aaron and Belinda had thought the project an interesting one.

But, the harp? Why couldn't Wyatt have selected another instrument: *any* other instrument, Aaron had grumbled to his wife late that night.

Despite Belinda's opinion that there was nothing wrong with the harp, and it was only for six weeks, anyway, which would hardly make Wyatt a harpist, Aaron had gone to bed in consternation. Harpists, to him, were women, and he was uncomfortable with his son taking up any more 'female oriented' pursuits: the violin and flute were bad enough.

Aaron had, however, awakened with a plan: he would take Wyatt camping! That should toughen him up, Aaron thought, and get some male bonding accomplished too, something he guiltily acknowledged to himself had been quite lacking in their family. It was the long holiday weekend, the perfect time. And, if Aaron recalled correctly, the primitive campsites at Mount Greylock State Forest would probably be available, even on such short notice. The children were back in school and families had quit their summertime pursuits, turning their eyes towards autumn, and winter.

Aaron had broached the idea the following evening at dinner, and although Belinda had looked unenthused, and then relieved when she realized she wouldn't be required to go, Wyatt had been cautiously curious.

Encouraged, Aaron had dashed to the Berkshire Mall after work the next day and purchased everything he and Wyatt could conceivably need: tent, sleeping bags, tarps, coolers, a small hibachi to supplement the fire ring all campsites featured, and other accoutrements the cheerful clerk at the L.L. Bean store had been only too happy to ring up.

Aaron had raced through the aisles of the local supermarket, too, collecting such campground staples as tinned stews, baking potatoes, lunchmeat, bread, cereal, milk, and apples. All of it could be assembled easily or cooked over their campfire in the new 'all purpose stew pot' he had secured along with the rest of their new camping gear.

A call to Mount Greylock State Forest had reserved a primitive campsite for them, as well. Aaron had scooted out of work a little early that holiday weekend Friday, and by late afternoon he and Wyatt had been unpacking their gear and setting up the new tent.

'A fire is next, Wyatt,' Aaron had told his son. 'We need kindling: small branches and twigs that we can use to get the fire going,' he had explained. The State Forest Office had sold them a cord of firewood when they'd checked in, and Aaron had told Wyatt they would use the larger logs once the fire had made a good start on the smaller ones.

Proud to be entrusted with such an important task, Wyatt had set out to find kindling in the woods across the dirt road bordering their campsite. If the fact that no other campers were nearby, and indeed, the entire primitive area was pretty much deserted, bothered either father or son, neither said. Belinda might possibly have vetoed the task, claiming that sending an eight year old child into the woods alone to gather wood was not safe. She would have at least insisted on accompanying her son. But Belinda was not there.

So Wyatt tramped through the crunchy fallen leaves quite cheerfully, certain that he could collect the wood and return to the campsite safely.

Wyatt's plan was to traverse the strip of woodland until he came to the fresh water lake that was less than a quarter mile away, and where his father had suggested that a good supply of kindling-suitable wood might be found. Then Wyatt had planned to reverse his steps and return to their campsite. It wasn't far, and according to the compass his father had bought him—the one item connected with this camping trip that truly delighted Wyatt—he had walked dead South to reach the lake shore, where he'd loaded up with small branches and twigs, as instructed. To return to camp, he had begun to walk dead North: simple.

Now, Wyatt reckoned that he should be nearly through the woods to the dirt road that bordered their camp. It seemed as though he had been walking about as long as he had on the initial leg of his trip.

He bent his head awkwardly to peer around his armload of branches and twigs and catch a glimpse of his compass' face. Luckily, the instrument had come with a strap, which Wyatt had slipped over one wrist. But still, checking his direction with an armload of kindling wasn't easy.

He had gone a little west of true North, Wyatt realized as he looked at the compass. He turned slightly until the needle pointed straight North, and took a few more steps.

Then he stopped.

The armload of kindling clattered to the ground, and Wyatt set off at a dead run in completely the wrong direction, yelling at the top of his voice.

CHAPTER TWO
CHAPTER TWO

"Whoa, there, buddy, slow down!" Aaron urged his son a few minutes later. He had heard the child yelling from the woods across the road, and then Wyatt had burst through the trees, hollering at the top of his lungs and waving his arms as though the hounds of hell were after him.

Now, Aaron tried to get his son to calm down and speak intelligibly. It had sounded as though he'd said he'd seen 'a monster' in the forest. But that couldn't be.

"Tell me again, what did you see in the woods?" Aaron asked patiently. He stroked his son's dark hair and patted him gently between the shoulder blades in a comforting gesture. Sometimes Wyatt seemed much younger than his years.

Wyatt gulped air; his eyes were very wide and he was making every effort he knew how to make in order not to cry: surely his father wouldn't appreciate that!

"It was a monster. A man. I don't know," Wyatt admitted, his voice shaky. "A monster," he decided.

"And why do you think you saw a monster, Wyatt?" Aaron reiterated, his voice calm. He spared a glance to look around their little campsite: their Ford Explorer, the tent and all their gear, the dirt road, the tall trees extending skyward bordering the roadway. And that was pretty much all. Quiet. Peaceful. Almost deserted. Maybe Wyatt had found it frightening? But he hadn't acted that way, hadn't said a word, Aaron considered, looking at the freckles sprinkled across his son's nose. He got those from his mother.

"Because he was dressed in all black," Wyatt replied finally. "Even his face!"

"There probably are other campers around, Wyatt," Aaron reassured his son. "You probably saw one of them."

Wyatt shook his head vehemently. "No, no: it was a monster!" he insisted.

"Now, look, Wyatt: we don't have time for this silliness," Aaron's voice had lost most of its patient tone. "And where is the kindling I sent you to gather?" he asked sternly.

Wyatt looked down. He scuffed the toe of one sneaker in the hardscrabble of the campsite and shifted uneasily in the folding chair his father had made him sit in; his feet didn't quite reach the ground. "I dropped it," he confessed, his voice nearly inaudible.

"You *dropped* it?" Aaron asked, sounding amazed.

Wyatt nodded glumly. "Yes. And there was a lot of it, too." His addendum was defensive.

Aaron's lips thinned into a line. "Why did you drop it?"

Wyatt looked up at his father, incredulous. "Because I saw the monster! I got—scared. I ran. I couldn't run with all that wood. I dropped it. I'm sorry…" he said, all in a rush. He knew his father didn't believe he'd actually seen a monster, but that was what it had looked like to Wyatt: rising up before him, not ten yards away from where he'd stood awkwardly balancing the armload of kindling while he checked his compass.

The thing—it had had two legs and two arms and a head, but it couldn't have been a man, Wyatt reasoned—had just come up out of the ground, from beneath a couple of downed tree branches. People didn't do that: they didn't just pop up out of nowhere, so it had to have been a monster. And, it had been dressed all in black, what had looked to Wyatt like black leather in the dim late afternoon forest light.

The monster had appeared almost startled to see Wyatt, as though he hadn't been expecting him. But if he had been surprised, his shock had been nothing compared to Wyatt's, who had been both frightened and astonished in equal parts. He wasn't sure if it had been the fear or the unexpectedness of the creature's appearance that had made him drop the wood.

"It should all be in a pile, all together," Wyatt told his father now. "I can tell you where—" he began, but his father interrupted.

"You are going to *show* me, young man," Aaron ordered sternly. "We are going to retrieve that kindling together," he added in a no-arguments voice. "Probably isn't that much, anyway," he muttered as he hauled a reluctant Wyatt across the road and back into the trees. His son's protests had no effect. "I don't see why you couldn't have kept a hold of it, even if another camper *did* startle you, even if you *did* run, like a sissy," Aaron chastised.

A couple of hours later, in front of a cheerily crackling fire that had warmed up their dinner nicely, Aaron had to admit that the pile of kindling his son had gathered had, indeed, been considerable. They had found it right where Wyatt had indicated, and Aaron had been happy to see the boy make good use of the compass he'd bought him.

Together, they had picked up all the twigs and branches and returned to their camp site; a quick scan of the area had shown Aaron nothing remarkable. Even the downed limbs where Wyatt insisted the 'monster' had appeared had just looked like a couple of fallen tree branches and some leaf mold to Aaron.

"See, Wyatt? Everything's fine," Aaron said indulgently now. He stretched out his long legs towards the fire, and shot a look that was more affectionate than he realized at his son.

He was writing in the dog-eared notebook he carried everywhere with him. For a child so clever on his computer, tablet and smartphone, Wyatt had an odd allegiance to paper and pen, manifested by that notebook.

Wyatt had been subdued since their return to camp, but had helped to 'build' the roughly cone shaped pile of sticks and watched raptly as Aaron had lit a match and blown gently on the nascent flame to encourage it to grow.

The child had eaten the chicken stew and canned green beans without complaint, and had finished off an oatmeal raisin cookie and an apple for dessert. Now he sat a couple of feet away from his father, around their fire ring.

"I don't see any other campfires," Wyatt said softly. He had raised that complaint before, to counter his father's insistence that the figure in the woods had been a neighboring camper.

"The Ranger at the Office said that there were very few campers in the primitive area this weekend," Aaron reminded his son. "There are some in the 'improved' campsite section, though, but that's beyond those hills, over there in a completely different area of the forest. And with the leaves on the trees, and the slope of the land, it's unlikely you'd see any campfires, or campsites, anyway, unless they were right next to ours," Aaron theorized.

Aaron gave a covert burp, then tilted his head back to look at the stars. " 'Scuse me," he mumbled. They'd sleep well tonight, he thought, even with just a sleeping bag between them and the hard ground. "What constellation is that, Wyatt?" Aaron asked a second later, pointing to the indigo sky that was dotted with twinkling spots. It was time for the boy to forget about whoever he'd seen—or imagined he'd seen—in the woods that afternoon, and enjoy their camping weekend. He knew his son loved astronomy: he'd bought him a fancy telescope the previous Christmas and Wyatt had it permanently set up at his bedroom window, trained on the heavens.

Wyatt looked up, and began to enumerate the constellations, planets and stars that they could see overhead. Their view was ringed by the dark shapes of trees, and the flickering light and smoke of their campfire made the heavens appear quite magical.

CHAPTER THREE
CHAPTER THREE

Gracie looked out the greenhouse window over her kitchen sink at the guests gathered on her terrace. It was the Sunday of Labor Day Weekend, and Gracie's traditional House Party was in full swing. Her childhood friend, Joey, and his partner Tyler, had driven in Friday evening from Boston, where they owned and operated the trendy, upscale eatery *Mange Tout* on Copley Square. Her best girlfriend Susan had driven up from New York City, bearing a gift for Gracie of a mixed media wall hanging done by Susan's latest artistic protégé. Susan was a research biochemist at Cornell Labs, but in her spare time—and with her spare cash—she supported newly emerging artists in the city.

Gracie had been unsure of where the unique, three dimensional work might look best: for the moment, the yard-square canvas board adorned with deep jewel toned paint bursts, twisted wire and fabric-and-bead accents sat in a corner of the Oak Room. She would figure out a place for it once the hectic weekend was over.

Joey, Tyler and Susan, along with Joey and Tyler's cats, Kenya and Safari, all stayed at Gracie's renovated, 300 year old farmhouse for the weekend. Pumpkin, Gracie's orange female tabby, knew Kenya and Safari—two seal point Siamese cats, well from previous visits and seemed to think that they were *her* special weekend guests.

Joey and Tyler had brought champagne, as they often did: this time, it was a case of St. Hilaire, which Joey told her had been Thomas Jefferson's favorite champagne.

'How on earth did you learn that?' Gracie had asked when they'd presented her with the gift Friday night.

'Tyler read a book about Jefferson's interest in French cuisine, and they mentioned this champagne, and the fact that it was Jefferson's favorite,' Joey had replied.

'So of course, we had to try it,' Tyler had chimed in.

The dozen or so other guests, all friends of Gracie's from the area, had begun arriving about 11 a.m. that morning for the House Party Cookout, always the highlight of one of Gracie's holiday weekends. They all appeared to be enjoying the St. Hilaire, although other libations were also available.

This year's cookout was a bit simpler than most of Gracie's annual events: it had been a long, and very sad summer, and she just hadn't had the heart, or the time, to get really complicated. Jack's best friend, Mike Garnier, had been murdered, and the subsequent months-long investigation had uncovered a corruption scheme whose tentacles had spread throughout much of local government in a neighboring county. The scandal was still big news, and although Gracie's coverage of it had lessened from two or three long articles a week to brief updates for the *Intelligencer*, she still wrote about the aftermath of the entire thing for her local paper.

A Mediterranean theme for the cookout, however, had been quick to pull together and quite easy to source. Gracie had whipped up a large couscous quinoa salad with chopped scallions, peppers and Greek olives; a fresh parsley dip with sour cream and Turkish spices for a crudité basket; platters of grilled summer squash with Feta and mint; and a Provençal green bean salad in an anchovy, caper and garlic dressing.

Joey and Tyler had brought their own fresh, spicy homemade sausage which they used to adorn several large pizzas; Tyler was the pastry guru and rolled out the many rounds of whole grain, gluten free crusts. Joey slathered on Gracie's homemade tomato sauce, sliced the sausage, and added chopped, grilled crimini mushrooms, slivered red onions and smoked Gouda. Although pizza wasn't strictly Mediterranean, no one really cared, since it was a crowd pleaser and one of Gracie's absolute favorite foods.

For dessert, which would come later that evening along with coffee and tea, Gracie had planned a grilled nectarine crumble: the lemon mascarpone topping for the cute little individual desserts was already chilling in the fridge.

She'd invited some of her best friends from Club: Anne, Paula, Jean, Courtney, Maddie, Farida, and Hilda, along with their spouses or boyfriends if they wanted to bring them. Hilda, a widow, was in the Morris Dancing Troupe that Gracie had recently joined. Hilda's friend Maureen, whom Gracie had met in the course of a previous investigation, was also in the Troupe, and also on the invitation list.

Gracie's nearest neighbors, Bob and Anna, and their mutual friends Justin and Ginger, who were all in the musical folk group Gracie sometimes played keyboard for, were also invited. Charlotte, the woman who had proofread Gracie's articles at the *Intelligencer* since Gracie had begun reporting for them, was also invited, along with her husband Pete.

Now, gazing out her greenhouse window at the crowd on her terrace, Gracie realized that except for Farida and Jean —both of whom had had other plans and regretfully declined —everyone she'd invited had shown up.

But not Jack. Gracie had invited Jack, of course. They were close, even closer now, after the trauma of the summer. And so, although she'd known Jack was still mourning his friend Mike, Gracie had asked him to come to her Labor Day Mediterranean Cookout.

He'd looked askance at her terminology, and wondered aloud if Mediterraneans even *had* cookouts, but said he might try to stop in.

Gracie had assured him that grilling was a popular form of food prep in Mediterranean cuisine, and cookouts had caught on a couple decades ago in Europe and the UK, and had urged him to attend.

Tyler rushed into the kitchen just as Gracie was sighing and realizing that she missed Jack.

"I have to roll out more pizza crusts," Tyler announced, slightly bemused. "Don't your friends eat before they come here?" he added with a chuckle. He retrieved the dough he'd prepared earlier from Gracie's top of the line fridge freezer, and cheerily went to work on one of the bluestone countertops, rolling out more pizzas.

"They do, I'm sure they do," Gracie replied, turning from the window. "But they know we serve great food at these House Parties," she reminded him. "That's become a tradition!" she concluded happily.

"Well, it's a good thing you made a vat of the couscous —and people are raving about the hummus, too: is that yours?" Tyler queried, ladling sauce on the pizza shells.

"No," Gracie admitted with a smile. "Farida dropped that off Thursday," she explaining, mentioning her friend from Club. Farida was Syrian, and made the best hummus Gracie had ever tasted: smooth, creamy and with just the right amount of lemon. She had brought over a large plastic tub of the chickpea and tahini spread, along with homemade pita, for the party as an apology for having to decline Gracie's invitation.

"Well, it's fabulous," Tyler declared, finishing off the fresh pizzas, and maneuvering them into the pizza oven next to Gracie's indoor grill.

Gracie heard the sound of her antique front door bell and with a wave to Tyler, dashed off to answer it.

CHAPTER FOUR

CHAPTER FOUR

"Pretty sunset," Jack commented laconically. He was stretched out on one of Gracie's Adirondack chairs on the terrace, and looked the most relaxed she had seen him in weeks. He had arrived, finally, as most of the party guests had been on their second or third helpings of food and drink. Nonetheless, Jack had done justice to the offerings, though he'd eschewed Jefferson's favorite champagne for his own new favorite micro brew: he'd stashed a few bottles of 'Nights in White Satin Ale' from the Blue Canoe Brewery in Pennsylvania at the back of Gracie's fridge when he'd come for dinner a couple weeks before.

Now, Gracie perched on the substantial arm of Jack's chair and nodded. "Yes, it is." She looked around the flagstone-paved space: although a few of the guests had left for other holiday engagements, most still remained, fueled by the food, the champagne, and most of all the friendships. In a far corner of the patio, Hilda and Maureen were showing a giggling Maddie the basic 'foot up and back' step of Morris Dancing. They were probably trying to recruit another dancer for the Troupe, Gracie thought with a smile.

Well, more dancers would always be good. Hilda and Maureen's group currently had eight dancers. Gracie was still learning, not good enough to 'dance out,' or perform, but she made the ninth member. If Maddie joined, at least they could bumble through the practices together, Gracie thought, and when they were ready to perform, there would be an even number of dancers, which is what Morris dances generally called for.

Not naturally graceful, Gracie had to work at being coordinated when performing any dance step more complicated than a shuffle. She found the Morris Dance tradition of disparate but complementary leg and arm movements quite challenging.

A cluster of guests was also chatting together near the dessert and coffee table, and Gracie realized Joey and Tyler were regaling them with tales of being Boston restaurateurs. A real, life, 'Top Chef,' Gracie thought to herself with a grin.

Anna, Bob, Justin and Ginger had pulled their chairs in a semi-circle, produced their fiddles and autoharps, and were playing some Early American folk tunes as a backdrop to the conversations, while the sun sank behind the charcoaled hills and left a crimson-streaked pearl indigo sky as a memento.

"Another successful party," Jack opined, shooting a half smile at Gracie.

"You think so?" Gracie asked, her concern genuine.

"Oh, yeah," Jack reassured her. "Great food and drink, good company, what's not to like?" he asked rhetorically. "Even the animals are enjoying themselves," he added, explaining that he'd seen his wolf-dog Woof lounging on the screened porch along with Pumpkin, Kenya and Safari.

Gracie smiled. "Good. I didn't have a lot of time to think up themes and order exotic ingredients, and I'm still too downhearted to fuss as much as I normally do," she confided softly. "But I'm glad people are enjoying themselves." She paused. "And I'm glad you came," she added, softer still.

Jack nodded. "I am, too." He sighed. "I've realized that while Mike would understand my sadness at his death—and the way he died, too, and the reasons for it—he wouldn't want any of us to mourn forever." He paused. "I heard from Sandy this week," Jack went on, referencing Mike's young widow. "She's doing good: really loving helping her parents run their kayaking business, loving Maine…I guess, if she can go on with her life, so can I," he admitted, giving Gracie another half smile, this one self-deprecatingly wry.

"Well, Jack: you and Mike had been friends since college," Gracie murmured sympathetically. "And both of you ending up in law enforcement, I think that just cemented your friendship. Had the positions been reversed, god forbid, and had it been you who had been murdered, I think Mike would have mourned you just as deeply, and been just as determined to find your killer," she added, her tone certain.

Jack gave her a long look. Because of the semi darkness —it was nearly eight o'clock now, and the sun had just set— Gracie really couldn't tell, but she thought it was a look full of gratitude. And respect.

"You helped a lot with that, Gracie," he told her then, and reached out to enclose one of her hands in one of his.

Gracie looked down at their clasped hands, and heat scalded through her. She shot a look at Jack, and thought that his mind was afire, as well. Perhaps...

From inside her house, the tones of Gracie's police band scanner erupted, shattering the convivial party atmosphere and interrupting conversations, music, and contemplations. Jack's phone began to chime insistently just seconds later; he quickly sat up, let go of Gracie's hand, and fished in his trouser pocket for the device. On her kitchen counter, Gracie's iPhone also began to ring, but that noise was obliterated by the scanner and by the sudden burst of concerned, questioning chatter among the house guests.

'Mount Greylock State Forest Park Rangers report 11-44, times two, probable 187 in the primitive campsite area of the Forest. Requesting backup,' came the 911 dispatcher's voice. The several shrill tones repeated, then the dispatcher's message came again.

Both Gracie and Jack began heading for the kitchen so they could hear the scanner more clearly.

"A 187, that's a homicide, right?" Gracie asked Jack in a whisper as they gained the screened porch door that led to the kitchen.

He nodded grimly. "Greylock again," he said, sounding sick at heart.

Of course: Mike had been murdered while he'd been hiking in the Greylock State Forest. It had been in a different part of the forest, of course, nowhere near the primitive campsites, Gracie realized, but still...

They listened to the scanner as the dispatcher repeated the message.

"And 11-44 times two means—" Jack said, turning towards the driveway where his vehicle was parked. Greylock State Forest was in Berkshire County: as County Detective, his purview included the Forest, even though it was a State Forest, and his job was to report to the scene of a crime such as this.

"Two dead bodies," Gracie finished for him, still whispering.

CHAPTER FIVE

CHAPTER FIVE

Gracie did not leave her guests to report to the scene, as it was not only a holiday weekend, but it would be rude of her, as hostess, to depart. She also knew that she would get the full report from Jack, possibly before the stroke of midnight, and in any case could make a quick trip the next morning to the Greylock Ranger Station to see if they had any news releases on the incident.

But the interruption from the scanner and Jack's abrupt departure had dissipated the party atmosphere and everyone left within about an hour. Maddie stayed to help clean up along with Tyler, Joey and Susan, and Gracie was happy to hear that the older woman had decided to give the Morris Dancing Troupe a try.

"My grandchildren are a delight and keep me on my toes," Maddie told Gracie as she prepared to leave. They were standing in the foyer of Gracie's home; Maddie was slipping into a light jacket, as the evening had turned chilly. "But I enjoy adult interaction and conversation," she admitted jokingly. "The Morris group sounds like good aerobic exercise as well as a lot of fun," she concluded.

Maddie had assumed the upbringing of her three grandchildren—a six year old girl, a toddler boy and a newborn—that spring after a family tragedy that had ended with the incarceration of her daughter. Maddie's son in law had been spared prison, as his involvement in the matter had been mitigated by what the courts had deemed 'diminished latitude of action' but he was still on probation and would only be allowed supervised visitation with his children for a while.

"It is!" Gracie enthused. "Would you like to ride together?" she asked, adding that the Morris troupe held its practices about a half hour away, in a community hall. Since she'd been attending the bi weekly practices for a month or so now, she was familiar with the route.

Maddie agreed happily, and Gracie said she would pick her friend up before the next Morris practice the following Wednesday evening.

Joey and Tyler had loaded the dishwasher and Susan had finished drying all the crystal champagne flutes. Gracie called the animals in from the porch—Jack had left Woof in her care while he had dashed to the crime scene—and everyone settled in the Oak Room with a final nightcap. The animals flopped in front of the fireplace, even though it was not lit; Kenya and Safari were relaxed bundles of fur, as close to 'flopping' as Siamese could get. Pumpkin curled nose to nose with Woof, her buddy. Joey and Tyler commandeered the chocolate leather love seat while Gracie and Susan sat on either end of the matching sofa. Everyone's nightcaps were salted caramel martinis, liberally dolloped with heavy cream: they went down more like milkshakes than liquor.

No one said it, but they were all waiting for Jack. As they'd tidied and washed and dried, Gracie had explained what the scanner jargon had meant, and reminded them of Jack's friend's death just a few months before in the same State Forest although not in the campground area.

"He may be very late," Gracie murmured now, glancing at one of the many clocks in the room. It was just about 10:30 p.m.

"He'll come back here?" Susan asked; there was a subtext to her question, but everyone pretended there wasn't.

Gracie nodded. "To pick up Woof," she confirmed, not answering the unasked question.

"Or to crash," Joey hinted.

"Of course, he could certainly stay here," Gracie commented, still not being specific. Normally she would have already confided in her friends about the state of her relationship with Jack. But somehow, their, well, reunion—if one could call it that—was so tenuous, the two of them hadn't even really discussed it. So somehow, Gracie felt that she couldn't really tell her friends, because she wasn't sure just what to say.

"Well, I still think you and Jack belong together," Susan opined staunchly. She'd always favored Jack, Gracie recalled. "I mean, Ben was nice, but you found out what he was all about—"

"What do you mean?" Gracie interjected, perturbed.

"Oh, come on: Ben was all about making you into his own idea of the perfect wife or girlfriend, you know that," Susan replied flatly. "You told me that you realized he only loved you inasmuch as you fit into his life in the way he wanted you to."

Gracie bit her lip, but she had to admit that Susan was correct. "But I'm not sure that just because I called it quits with Ben and David, that means I 'belong' with Jack," she protested, not very convincingly. "And anyway, I don't think anyone 'belongs' to anyone else…"

Susan just arched one amber brow, and sipped at her drink. Joey and Tyler shared a smile, and then started talking about the autumn menu at their restaurant. Gracie cleared her throat and then sighed.

Susan went up to bed at 11 p.m. and Joey and Tyler stayed with Gracie to watch the start of the late TV news, which had only a scanty report on the incident in the Greylock Forest. Then Joey and Tyler turned in as well, taking Kenya and Safari with them.

Gracie listened to the news through the weather report, which promised a cooler than normal week, and then turned the television off. She got up to flick on the front porch light, and then returned to the Oak Room, calling Woof and Pumpkin up onto the sofa with her, and pulling down a cotton throw to snuggle under. If Jack returned yet this evening, it would only be polite to wait up for him.

CHAPTER SIX

Bright and early Tuesday morning, Gracie was at the Ranger Station at Greylock State Forest, then at the Massachusetts State Police barracks in Cheshire to get their news releases on the discovery of the bodies. Then she arrived at the Courthouse in Pittsfield where Berkshire County DA Peter Paul Popovitch was due to give a news conference on the incident at 11 a.m.

When Jack had returned late Sunday night, he had filled Gracie in on the particulars, facts he knew would be in the news releases and reports she would gather Tuesday. He had also described the scene in detail, knowing she would not divulge anything he told her and needing to share what he'd seen in order to process it.

Therefore, when Gracie, on Tuesday, read the Ranger report, and the State Police report, she was able to vividly imagine the scene described in terse black and white. While she waited for Popovitch's news conference to begin in the large courtroom, she typed a draft of the article she would file within a couple of hours for her paper's web page: this way, she would only have to plug in any worthwhile comments made by the DA, should he make any (which was doubtful), and it would be finished.

'Two bodies, that of an adult male, and a juvenile male, were discovered Sunday afternoon by a group of hikers in Mount Greylock State Forest. The hikers were taking a shortcut through the sparsely tenanted Primitive Campsite area when they discovered the bodies; they immediately called 911.

'Documents found at the scene identify the bodies as that of Aaron McGinley, 37, of Adams, and his son Wyatt, 8, also of Adams. Mr. McGinley is an investment analyst with the Greylock

Mountain Bank. According to his wife, Belinda McGinley, Aaron had taken their son camping for the weekend. She told police that she last heard from them on Friday night after they had set up camp. Because mobile phone service is spotty in the Mount Greylock State Forest, Mrs. McGinley said she did not find it odd that she had not heard from her husband and son since the initial contact. She was notified of their death late Sunday night.

'Crime Scene Unit workers at the scene report that Mr. McGinley and his son appear to have been shot multiple times each with a high powered automatic rifle. Time of death has preliminarily been given as very late Friday night. Both bodies are undergoing autopsies Tuesday, and a definitive cause and time of death is expected shortly after.

'Shell casings and bullets recovered at the scene identify the murder weapon as a black powder muzzleloader, similar to a Thompson Center Triumph type, with a scope. Police report that at this time, it appears that only one shooter gunned down Mr. McGinley and his son.

'Police have not released any word concerning suspects or motives in this case, which is still under investigation.

That was good, Gracie thought as she scanned the article and made a couple of slight changes. Concise, clear, and correct: her journalist's mantra. She shut her laptop as a stir near the Judge's dais signaled the arrival of the DA through the back corridor that lead from the courtroom to the Judge's Chambers and into an interior courthouse hallway. Gracie crossed her legs, straightened her shoulders, and looked expectantly towards the doorway.

First came a couple of Troopers, probably the officers of record, Gracie thought. Then came the county's Sheriff along with two Deputies: Gracie wasn't sure why they were there, unless it were to add *gravitas* to Popovitch's eventual arrival.

Then Jack stepped into the courtroom and made a beeline for his usual spot at one side. He shot a quick glance towards the seats where the press, and therefore Gracie, generally sat for any proceedings in the courtroom, but didn't smile even though their eyes made contact.

Finally, Popovitch blustered through the door—Gracie noted he had to turn at a slight angle in order to fit—and made his way to the ornate wooden divider, or 'bar' that separated the lawyers' and judge's area of the courtroom from the seating for press and spectators.

"Good morning," Popovitch began in a loud and quite commanding voice. Gracie gave him that: he could get your attention. At least initially.

Behind her, hurried footsteps heralded the arrival of Gil Butcher from the Pittsfield *Gazetteer*. Butcher was the editor of the local weekly that was in direct competition with the paper Gracie wrote for, the *Intelligencer*. He was also notoriously late, unprepared, and reportedly a real demon to work for, with a crabby, bitter personality.

"What did I miss?" Butcher asked the stringer from the Springfield daily paper: he knew better than to ask Gracie.

The stringer barely turned her head to acknowledge Butcher, and murmured out of the side of her mouth that they had just started. Butcher, satisfied, sat back and took out a grubby notebook and a much-chewed pencil.

The DA presented his statement then, which contained absolutely nothing that the Rangers' report and the MSP news release had not already made public. Popovitch also did not make any comments that Gracie felt she could turn into any type of meaningful quote for her story. She was just deciding that she probably wouldn't mention the DA's press conference in her piece at all, when Popovitch launched into his last point.

"Given the apparent randomness and violence of this shooting, I have instituted a series of roadblocks surrounding Mount Greylock State Forest and will be expanding those checkpoints, with the help of local law enforcement, to surrounding areas," he said.

Gracie wondered exactly what surrounding areas the DA had in mind: her house and property were quite near the southern border of the Forest, and several towns including Cheshire, Adams, Williamstown and Lanesboro were also close by.

"These measures, as well as further investigative techniques I am not at liberty to discuss, are meant to aid us in discovering and capturing the individual responsible for these horrendous murders," Popovitch was saying next.

Well, good, Gracie thought. But wasn't it a bit late?

"Additionally, I am asking all citizens of Berkshire County, particularly within the areas near the Forest, to be especially vigilant. Note and report anything unusual, anything or anyone out of place," Popovitch urged, adding that an additional police presence in the region would become commonplace until the murderer was found. "And finally, until this matter is resolved, I am instituting a county wide curfew between 10 p.m. and 6 a.m. Residents should remain in their homes during those hours, with their doors locked and any security systems available armed. People found traveling the roadways or walking in the streets during curfew hours will be questioned by police and possibly taken into custody."

This announcement caused quite a stir among the reporters and the handful of courthouse workers who had gathered to hear what Popovitch had to say. Gracie saw Andrew Gaillard, the county's Chief Administrator, shake his head and murmur something to one of the other courthouse staff members standing next to him along the side wall of the courtroom. Maybe she would ask him for a comment when the press conference was over, Gracie thought.

CHAPTER SEVEN

"Can you tell us where the checkpoints will be?" Butcher asked boldly once Popovitch opened the press conference up to questions. " How wide an area will they cover?" he added, standing as he spoke, and giving the DA an ingratiating smile.

Popovitch nodded self-importantly. "Well, now, I can't really tell you exactly where the checkpoints and roadblocks will be, can I?" he replied jovially. "That would take the element of surprise away. But I can tell you, Gil, they'll be extensive." He paused, furrowing his overgrown brow and looking around the courtroom as though seeking something or someone. "We are still working with local law enforcement to hammer it all out," he added, sounding quite satisfied with himself.

Gracie stood. "Gracie Barufaldi from the *Intelligencer,*" she introduced herself. She knew it was unnecessary, since the DA knew only too well who she was, but it was proper form in case another reporter present needed to get in touch with her about something. Plus, she knew it aggravated Popovitch, so she spoke her identification with a sweet smile.

Popovitch glowered at her: he'd never liked Gracie. She was far too assertive, quick and sharp for his tastes. He liked his reporters more like Butcher: a bit slow on the uptake, not too curious, and easy to intimidate. "I know who you are, Ms. Barufaldi," he growled, making her name sound like an insult.

"I was just curious about your statement that you were imposing a curfew," Gracie began quietly, but the room had gone silent and people were listening, hard.

Popovitch nodded. "Yes, I—"

"Don't you think it's a bit late for that?" she asked, echoing her silent doubt of a few moments before. "I mean, the shootings happened Friday night, from what I've read," Gracie continued, waving the Police and Ranger reports in one hand. "Don't you think whoever shot the McGinleys is long gone?"

A reasonable question. As one, the faces in the courtroom swiveled from looking at Gracie to looking at Popovitch, and awaited his response.

"Well. Well, all I can say is that authorities believe the shooter may still be in the area," Popovitch replied, sounding uncertain even to himself.

And with good reason: his statement was a complete fabrication: he'd heard many Troopers and Rangers theorize, in fact, that whoever had shot the McGinleys had high-tailed it out of the region. But no one knew for sure.

Gracie smiled. "Oh, I see. Well, it's good to be thorough," she commented, nodding.

Popovitch looked surprised, then mollified.

Jack, from his spot along the side of the courtroom, looked over at Gracie: she had more up her sleeve, he could tell by her expression. More fool Popovitch to think he'd won that round.

"Just one more thing, Mr. Popovitch, if I may?" Gracie asked, and then carried on speaking, not waiting for the DA's green light. "According to Massachusetts State Law, I believe Title Seven, Chapter 40, Section 37A, I think, it is the purview of each municipality within a county to institute a curfew, is it not? And if a county wide curfew were to be instituted, it would properly be the Sheriff, under direction from the County Commissioners, who would establish such a curfew here in Berkshire County, isn't that right?" she asked in a voice that was steel covered in sugar.

Popovitch looked stunned.

"I do not believe that setting curfews is within the scope of the District Attorney's powers," Gracie added, affecting honeyed regret.

Jack sniggered quietly, and covered it up with a fake cough.

"Uhm—well, the Commissioners are on board with it," Popovitch began, looking wildly around the courtroom as though he were trying to find one of the county officials he spoke of. "And, uhhh, I'm sure the Sheriff will...will be, too," he finished lamely, glancing to one side at that very official. Gracie noted the Sheriff studiously avoided meeting the DA's eyes, affecting vast interest in the condition of his fingernails.

"Ah, so you meant to say that you are *announcing* that the *county* is imposing a curfew—is that more accurate, Mr. Popovitch?" Gracie queried, sounding as though she were relieved to have clarified that point.

Popovitch still looked as though he'd been hit over the head with a brick, but managed a weak, "that would be right," before Gracie sat down, and the Sheriff leaned into the microphone to announce that the press conference was over.

As Jack exited, he shot a crooked half smile over at Gracie, who was biting her lip to keep from grinning.

She hurried out of the courtroom and through yet another little known, and little used, corridor that connected to the second floor commissioners' offices on the other side of the building, and intercepted Andrew Gaillard just as he was returning from the courtroom.

"Care to comment, Andy?" she asked with a big smile.

He gave her a chuckle and an admiring glance. "That was some question, Gracie: how did you know that about the state's curfew law?" he asked as they entered the commissioners' suite of offices. "Sure, I'll comment," he continued happily, not giving Gracie a chance to answer. "Can I say I think the DA is a jerk?" he asked merrily.

Gracie laughed. "I don't think that would be wise," she offered. She had known Gaillard, and the commissioners, as well as their staff, for several years: the entire time she had been reporting for the *Intelligencer*. They all had very cordial working relationships, and she felt fortunate to have such colleagues. She waved hello to the two administrative aides, Linda and Lori, as she followed Gaillard across the reception area. "I meant, would you like to comment on the efforts to apprehend the shooter?" Gracie amended with another smile.

Gaillard thought a moment. They had walked as far as his office and now he took his seat behind the desk. Gracie stayed standing. "Well, I think it's probably too late: if I were the killer, I'd be long gone," the Administrator replied frankly. "And since the murder happened, what, Friday night? And they didn't discover the bodies until Sunday, the guy's probably in Canada or something by now," he noted with a wry chuckle.

"So you disagree with the roadblocks and curfew?" Gracie asked.

"Well, no: I suppose it's worth a try. But I hope it won't go on too long." He paused, and waved a 'while you were out' memo that he'd picked up as they'd walked through the outer office. "Just so you know, there will be an emergency commissioners' meeting at noon today: might want to stick around."

"Don't they have to advertise that?" Gracie frowned. The 'Sunshine Law' was pretty clear about how official government meetings had to be announced.

Gaillard shook his head. "Not in an emergency. We post a notice and make the minutes available after the fact, but in an emergency, no," he corrected her.

Gracie nodded. "I see. Are they going to sign a resolution about a curfew?" she asked expectantly.

Gaillard nodded. "Yup, and the Sheriff is requested to be at the meeting," he added, reading the memo.

"I'll stick around," Gracie agreed.

CHAPTER EIGHT

CHAPTER EIGHT

"How *did* you know that about the curfew law?" Jack asked Tuesday evening. He'd come to Gracie's for dinner at her invitation, and was glad of a chance not only to see her, but to talk about the case with her.

"Hey, hey, hey, now I'm not just a pretty face!" Gracie retorted with a smile.

They were in her kitchen, where she was plating broiled tilapia on rounds of polenta atop sautéed kale with garlic. She finished each dish with a drizzle of Tuscan herb infused olive oil, and put them on the barn board table.

Jack noticed their place settings were autumn-themed, complete with coordinating cloth napkins and stemware. A basket of freshly baked rolls of some kind wafted a warm fragrance from the table. He poured them each a glass of pinot grigio, at Gracie's suggestion, and they sat down to eat.

Woof and Pumpkin had already enjoyed their repast, and were now quietly sitting next to the table, just in case any morsel might drop to the floor and need to be cleaned up.

The rolls turned out to be studded with olives and sun dried tomatoes, and to Jack's surprise were gluten free.

"That's kinda my new thing," Gracie admitted, adding that a couple of her friends including Maddie and Courtney Proulx of the local health food store, had been touting the benefits of a limited gluten diet and she'd decided to give it a whirl. "I can't take credit for baking those from scratch," she added of the rolls. "I bought them frozen at Planet Provisions." She bit into one that she had spread with a dab of organic butter from Wales, of all places. "Pretty tasty though," she assessed.

Jack agreed.

"Oh!" Gracie interjected a minute later, "the curfew thing. Well, I just didn't think it sounded like something a DA would do. Maybe in conjunction with other agencies, but not on his or her own. And every film I've ever seen where a curfew is imposed, it's always the sheriff or something who does it, not the DA. After all, 'DA' stands for 'district attorney,' so basically the DA is just the chief lawyer for the district," she continued, enthused. "In this case, Berkshire County. But lawyers don't impose curfews."

"So you took a shot?" Jack asked, a bit disbelieving. That had taken guts, especially in an open forum like a press conference.

Gracie grinned, chewed a bite of tilapia and explained. "Sorta. I also saw Andy Gaillard's reaction when Poppinfresh said *he* was instituting a curfew," she revealed. "He was protesting it to a couple of other staff members. So I thought something was hinky, so I googled it, didn't I?" she said, sounding smug. "And I was right."

"That's how you were able to quote chapter and verse of State Law," Jack said, realizing.

Gracie nodded.

"Well, it was quite—amazing. And you should have heard Popovitch when we got back to the office," he added, chuckling.

"Was he on a tirade?" Gracie queried, sounding quite happy about the possibility.

"He called you every name in the book," Jack replied, trying to be solemn but not succeeding.

Popovitch, once he'd returned to the relative safety of his own domain, had, indeed, leveled several invectives at the absent news reporter at the top of his voice. Jack repeated a few of them now to an increasingly amused Gracie, who had to stop eating she was laughing so hard.

"He really hates you," Jack concluded.

"He's always hated me," Gracie returned. "And don't worry: Dave knows all about that. As long as I was polite, which I was, and correct, which I also was, he won't worry about Popovitch's reaction to me catching him out," she finished, referring to Dave Tiller, her editor at the *Intelligencer*.

In lieu of dessert, Gracie made 'fancy coffee' with a dollop of organic hazelnut syrup in it, and she and Jack went into the Oak Room for the balance of the evening. Woof and Pumpkin followed.

They discussed the efficacy of road blocks and check points, a couple of which they had both run into during the course of their travels that day. They did agree finally that the curfew might not be a bad idea, at least for a few days.

"Whoever this guy is, the shooter I mean," Jack theorized, "he is probably staying out of sight during the day, and moving around at night. If he's even still in the area."

Gracie agreed, filling him in on what Gaillard had said, that he thought the murderer was likely long gone by now.

"But, Jack, who would want to kill McGinley?" Gracie asked. "That's the key to the whole thing. He was an investment banker: any leads there?" She paused. "And who besides Belinda knew her husband and son would be camping?"

Jack sighed, and ran one hand through his hair in an habitual gesture Gracie knew signaled frustration. "I only spoke very briefly with Mrs. McGinley," he began. "She said that as far as she knew, only she herself knew about her husband's and son's weekend plans. But, she also said that it was probably very likely that Aaron McGinley had told people at work what he was doing with Wyatt."

"So you'll be speaking with them?"

Jack nodded. "Yup, and Aaron McGinley's clients, too. I ran the family's financials: everything looks on the up and up," he told her.

"What about his banking activities on behalf of his clients?" Gracie asked. "Anything there look weird? Any investments that lost money for people? That would be a motive," she suggested.

Jack nodded. "Sure, it would. But I haven't finished all of that yet and I'll probably contact a forensic accountant to go over everything, too, and be sure I don't miss anything," he added.

Gracie reached over and touched Jack's cheek. "You won't miss anything, Jack. You'll figure it out," she assured him softly.

A short while later she asked, "what about Belinda? I mean, don't you always look at the spouse?"

Jack gave Gracie a skeptical look. "I thought you said that Belinda was beyond reproach, because she's in Club?" he asked, reminding Gracie of what she'd said Sunday night when he'd told her who the victims were.

Gracie shrugged. "Well, there's always the exception that proves the rule. And I don't know Belinda that well," she hedged.

Jack smiled slightly. "Well, even with that ringing censure of Mrs. McGinley's character, I still would have to wonder where she got a black powder muzzle loader rifle, and learned how to use it."

Gracie nodded. "There is that. I take it the murder weapon hasn't been recovered?" she queried.

"Nope."

She paused. "Exactly what is a 'black powder muzzleloader,' anyway, Jack?" Gracie asked. "I know we've had black powder muzzle loader Rendezvous near Greylock

Mansion, on the grounds, but those are antique rifles," she continued. "I don't think that's what you guys meant when you said that was the murder weapon. Or did you? Are we talking about an antique rifle of some kind?"

Jack chuckled. "Not really, Gracie, no. They call it that because of the design. But the gun that killed the McGinleys was something anyone can get at any good sporting goods store. They're pricey, of course, especially with a scope, which we believe this one had."

"How pricey?" Curious.

"Around a thousand bucks, I'd guess, maybe a bit less. The one we think most likely to be the murder weapon is a Thompson Center Triumph brand."

"I googled that once I got the police report," Gracie put in.

Of course, Jack thought, she would have done that.

"It sounds like a really nasty rifle: it's trademark name is 'Bone Collector,' " she added with a shudder. Then: "do you think they will find him? The murderer, I mean. Could the police check sales of rifles like this one? Even if you do identify, say, a client who might have wanted McGinley dead, if he's gone missing…"

Now it was Jack's turn to shrug. "I don't know, Gracie. I've already got someone tracking down sales of rifles like the one used, but that weapon could have been purchased anywhere, not necessarily near here. And I think it will worry me more if we don't find a client of Aaron McGinley's with a plausible motive."

"Why?"

"Because that will mean the shooting was in all likelihood random. And that would mean anyone could become this guy's next target."

CHAPTER NINE

"You have all of Aaron's records now," the Greylock Mountain Bank Branch Manager told Jack Wednesday morning, indicating the several folders and short stack of CDs she had just given him.

Jack thanked her, and asked if she had a few minutes to speak with him.

"Of course, Detective," Daphne Colquhoun said cooperatively.

"I'd like to speak to your staff, as well," Jack put in: it wasn't really a request, but he phrased it more as a suggestion than a demand.

"Of course," Colquhoun repeated, her smooth face troubled.

She ushered him from Aaron McGinley's office where she had retrieved the records Jack wanted, through the bank's open plan lobby, to her private office, and closed the door. Then she sat behind her desk and folded her hands on her blotter. Jack noticed the blotter held a myriad of scribbles and notations.

"Tell me about Mr. McGinley," Jack began evenly. "How long had you worked together?"

Colquhoun sighed. "Three years and a few months," she replied.

Jack asked about their working relationship, and Colquhoun replied that it had been 'cordial.' Jack sensed a discomfort, and so probed. He was rewarded when the Branch Manager hooked a lock of blonde hair behind one ear and sighed again.

"I'm not sure Aaron had much, well, much confidence in me at first," she admitted. "He was well-schooled, experienced, he had a lot of authority," she explained. "And he let you know that right up front," she added, characterizing McGinley's style as 'assertive.' "Me, on the other hand, well, I prefer a different, more oblique approach," she admitted.

"More oblique?" Jack asked, echoing her terms.

Colquhoun nodded. "Maybe because, as a woman in what had been strictly a man's position until rather recently, I've found that both genders respond better to a female who doesn't come on too strong, if you know what I mean, Detective."

She pointed at a button on her lapel: it was a name tag, but its border said, 'I'm a proud Panther Mom!' referencing the Pittsfield Area High School's girls' soccer team. It was ranked number one in the state, Jack knew, and a serious contender for the national title.

"It has nothing to do with banking, but it gives people a frame of reference, and at the very least a platform to open a discussion with me, and that can put them at ease," she explained. "I may take more of the 'soft sell' approach, but I know my stuff, and I get things done," she concluded with a smile.

Jack nodded. "I see: as opposed to a female whose style would have been more like Mr. McGinley's?" he asked. "More direct, no nonsense?"

Colquhoun looked relieved that Jack understood her. "Exactly!"

"Did people take offense at McGinley's, erm, forthrightness?" Jack queried.

The Branch Manager looked undecided. "I certainly didn't," she hedged. "And I don't believe his clients did: they were happy and grateful to have someone who obviously was very capable and in control. Particularly since Aaron was male, and his attitude fit most people's perceptions of what an Investment Analyst should be like."

"Well, then, who <u>did</u> take offense at McGinley's attitude?" Jack asked, pouncing on what had been unsaid in Colquhoun's response.

She sighed. "I think Bobby resented Aaron," she replied, low. "But that doesn't mean he killed him!"

"Belinda McGinley?" Maddie Jesperson queried, surprise evident in her voice.

Gracie nodded. "Yes."

"But—she's in Club!" Maddie protested.

Gracie smiled and recalled Jack's comments the previous evening about the status conferred by Club membership. At least in the minds of other Club members.

"Well, yes, Belinda is, but of course Aaron wasn't," Gracie said gently. "I don't know her too well, did you?"

Maddie shook her head.

"But I'm still going to the funeral, to support her," Gracie returned. "Whenever they set that date."

"I will, too," Maddie agreed. "I think most of Club will, if they can."

"The police are still working to discover what, if any, motives might be out there to make someone want Aaron McGinley dead," Gracie said then.

"I can't imagine," Maddie replied in a subdued tone.

The two were on their way to the Wednesday evening Morris Dance Troupe practice; as she had promised the Sunday before, Gracie had collected Maddie at her home a short while before, and was driving them both to the practice.

"There was some fancy footwork with the jurisdiction, I can tell you," Gracie continued as she drove. "I mean, Mr. McGinley and his son were killed on State Forest property so technically the case belongs to the Forest Rangers. But they aren't equipped to investigate murders. I think they're more used to handling poachers and trespassers, that kind of thing." She sighed. "So anyway, the case has been transferred to the DA's office. Since the Forest is in Berkshire County, it's our DA."

Maddie snorted. "Well, at least Jack's there," she murmured, and Gracie smiled over at her friend.

CHAPTER TEN
CHAPTER TEN

The autopsy report had come through early Wednesday morning, and a copy had arrived in Gracie's email folder. The report had noted that both Aaron and Wyatt McGinley had sustained several shots to their torsos; the CSU team had done a reconstruction, and confirmed that all shots had come from a single AK 47, and from a single shooter. It appeared, however, that the killer had not really aimed, as such, but had just opened fire and kept shooting until he had been certain his quarries had been mortally wounded.

Shell casings as well as bullets had been retrieved both at the scene and in the course of the autopsy. The DA's office's report, which Jack had written of course, stated that given the condition and position of the bodies when they had been found Sunday evening, it appeared that Aaron and Wyatt had been shot while sitting at their campfire. The autopsy report pinpointed time of death to between 11 p.m. and midnight on Friday.

The bodies were released on Thursday, along with the effects, which had been returned to Belinda McGinley. The double funeral was swiftly scheduled for Friday morning. There were to be no viewing hours, and the caskets were, of course, closed.

Gracie had typed an update containing the new facts on Thursday morning, and emailed it into the *Intelligencer*; her original article had gone live online and would be the lead story in the printed Friday edition of the paper.

Meanwhile, she'd spent Thursday afternoon speaking with Aaron McGinley's co-workers at the bank, much as Jack had done the day before. Gracie's objective was to gain a fuller picture of the deceased, and possibly identify anyone who could have had a grudge against the dead man, and thus have had motive, at least of a sort.

Thursday evening, she and Jack met in Great Barrington, about an hour's drive south of Pittsfield, at a relatively new restaurant Gracie'd heard of, called Ampleksajn. She had overheard someone raving about the place one day when she'd stopped for lunch at the Olive Branch. The name had intrigued her, and the speaker's review had encouraged her, so Gracie had googled the eatery and discovered that Ampleksajn was Esperanto for 'wide ranging.'

According to the restaurant's website, they chose the name to emphasize the fact that they sourced their foods from all over the world, with strict freshness and organic quality guidelines. It had sounded like a great place to try and so on Thursday, Gracie and Jack went there to have dinner and to discuss the case: both felt it would be smart to be at a distance from Greylock Forest and the tragedy it had most recently contained.

Ampleksajn was on the first floor of a former estate: the owners lived on the second floor of the brick mansion that a plaque noted had been built in 1875. The restaurant and kitchen occupied the entire first floor, with the original drawing room, dining room, library and parlor forming four distinct yet congenial dining areas.

Gracie was charmed by the architectural features of the place, including crown moulding and pocket doors: the owners had changed very little, at least in the public spaces, and the antique fixtures shone to perfection.

"You're limping," Jack said, concerned, as Gracie and he met in the restaurant's reception area—what had once been the foyer of the mansion. A gracious staircase rose up to the private quarters on the upper floor, but the foyer itself held the Reservations desk and a small coat check area that Gracie suspected had once been a hall closet.

"Oh, I just came down wrong on my foot at Morris practice last night," Gracie replied with a wave of her hand that indicated the injury was not important. "It's no biggie."

Jack watched her walk, though, as they were shown to their table, and although the limp wasn't pronounced, it was there.

"You should get that checked," Jack advised her, frowning with worry.

Gracie grinned at him and shook her head. "Nah, it's just a sprain, it'll heal. Don't worry!" she admonished, and gave him a quick kiss on his cheek.

They studied the menu once they were seated: it was different from a typical restaurant's menu, because it listed four methods of preparation, including an Asian inspired one, a Southwestern type, a basic prep with minimal spicing and accoutrements, and a Middle-Eastern themed prep. As the menu and their server advised, the best way to order was to peruse the restaurant's protein list first, and choose the meat, fowl or fish you would like. Then the manner in which your protein would be prepared could be selected. Appetizers, side dishes and desserts rounded out the menu.

Ampleksajn's 'protein list,' as it called the entrées, was unusual, too. Selections like Great Plains Bison, Australian Emu, South African Cape Gurnard—a fish—, and Northern European Yak made Gracie smile happily and Jack raise his eyebrows. Tamer selections like organic chicken and wild caught salmon were more familiar, if no less pristinely sourced.

Both Gracie and Jack were glad to see the restaurant didn't offer the meat of endangered species, even if they were ostensibly 'farm raised,' and they agreed that the choices were, as the eatery's name implied, wide ranging.

Jack couldn't resist the Bison although Gracie tried hard to get him to order the Yak.

"You order it, then," he replied, feeling resolute about his selection. Bison was close enough to Beef to be a comfortable choice for him, yet exotic enough so that Jack felt he would be participating in the restaurant's intended experience.

"No, I want to try the Gurnard," Gracie insisted. She ordered hers done in the minimal style, so she could really taste the unusual fish. Jack asked for his Bison to be cooked with the Southwestern prep.

Gracie's side was a melange of grilled squash in a tomatillo and onion sauce while Jack ordered roasted corn and tomato brûlée. They decided to share an appetizer of pretzel dusted home made kielbasa chunks in a wasabi horseradish sauce. Gracie asked for a glass of the house white while Jack had trouble deciding on just one beer from the scores of micro brews available. He noticed they even stocked his current favorite from Pennsylvania's Blue Canoe Brewery, but he wanted to try something different, in keeping with the spirit of the restaurant. He decided on a Vidalia Onion and herb infused stout called 'Black Mambo.'

"They don't call this a 'gastro pub' for nothing," Gracie grinned as their server took their order and left. She leaned over the table and whispered, "what's new with the case?"

Jack chuckled, and told her about his visit with Daphne Colquhoun.

"Did you talk to Bobby Foulard?" Gracie queried eagerly once Jack had told her that Colquhoun had said she thought the teller had resented the deceased.

Jack nodded that he had, but before giving his impression, asked Gracie what she had thought when she'd spoken to the staff at Greylock Mountain Bank that afternoon.

By the time they'd devoured the kielbasa and started on the entrées, Jack and Gracie were politely disagreeing about their impressions of Robert 'Bobby' Foulard. Jack felt the teller, who was in his mid 20's with a bad case of acne, was too 'wimpy' to actually kill anyone, much less with an AK 47. Gracie, on the other hand, pointed out the way in which resentment could grow until it coerced a person to overcome his, in this case, 'wimpyness' and commit terrible acts.

"It's like adrenaline," she theorized. "You know, when you're psyched, you can do stuff like lift cars and boulders and so on, things you normally can't do," she explained, chewing a forkful of fish and then sampling the squash. "Yum," she judged.

"I know what adrenaline can do," Jack agreed. "But that's a physical, chemical response. I don't think resentment has the same effect on a body," he countered.

"Well, I'm going to run a background on Foulard, see what pops up," Gracie concluded firmly. "I didn't have time when I got back from the bank this afternoon. How's your bison?" she asked, changing the subject.

Jack replied that it was delicious and very tender, and asked about her fish.

"It's great," she replied. "Tastes a little like grouper, but different," she murmured, taking another small bite.

"I *am* going to speak to Foulard again," Jack admitted, noting that he'd asked the young man to come into his office on Friday afternoon. "He's got an alibi, but you're right: something's off about him," Jack finished solemnly.

"You're going to the funeral tomorrow morning, right?" Gracie asked, referring to the McGinley funerals.

Jack nodded somberly.

"You think the killer will be there?" Gracie sounded almost eager.

Jack shrugged. "You never know. But it's worth a shot. Plus, I want to go out of respect for the McGinleys," he added.

"You've already talked to Belinda?" Gracie asked.

"Yes, but we have another appointment set up for next week," Jack revealed. "I always think it's wise to speak to the surviving relatives after some of the emotion and activity surrounding the death and the funeral has diminished," he added.

CHAPTER ELEVEN

On Friday morning, Gracie sat with about a dozen of her fellow Pittsfield Junior League members, two rows behind Belinda McGinley and her family. The show of support from Club was strong, and Belinda, who looked dazed, still seemed very grateful at the sight of so many of her 'sisters' in attendance.

"I think she's on a sedative of some kind," Anne whispered in Gracie's ear as they watched the recent widow navigate to her place in the first row.

"I'd have to be, wouldn't you?" Gracie whispered back.

Anne nodded.

Gracie's friend Paula, who had sponsored Belinda for Club membership and who had known the family well, sat one over from Anne; her eyes were red rimmed, and a well-used tissue was wadded up in one hand.

Gracie spotted Jack, at the very back of the large Methodist church; his eyes were scanning the crowd, and his face was somber.

She wondered if the forensic accountant he'd hired had uncovered anything that could go to motive for the killing. Finding a suspect with a reasonable motive was top priority.

Foulard's background check, which she'd run late the evening before when she'd got home, had been interesting. The young man had been in and out of foster homes and had not done well in school. His position at the bank, however, had been the result of a 'study to work' program for underprivileged and underserved students and it appeared that he'd worked hard to succeed since being hired.

None of that made Foulard a murderer, and Gracie had finished her day feeling dissatisfied.

Everyone fell silent now, as the minister walked to the podium and began the funeral service, and Gracie's thoughts returned to the present.

"I just don't get why anyone would want to kill Aaron, or Wyatt!" Paula said in a low voice.

She, Anne, Gracie, and most of those who had attended the funeral were now at The Fireside, a large restaurant on the outskirts of the Pittsfield business district. It was where Belinda had chosen to hold the luncheon after the service. A lovely buffet had been set out, and round tables of eight were set in maroon linen with small centerpieces of alstroemeria, sunflowers, and mums in coordinating shades. The flowers were from Budz in Cheshire, and they'd also done the flowers at the church, and at the cemetery.

"Maybe it was a case of mistaken identity?" Anne proposed. They had claimed a table along with some other Club women who had been able to attend the lunch, and were now seated, waiting for everyone else to arrive and for the opening prayer, and for the meal to begin.

"Maybe, but there were very few other campers," Gracie hissed quietly. "I know Jack's looking into Aaron's work, but I have never heard anything remotely questionable about him, or about Greylock Mountain Bank, have you?" she continued.

Maddie Jesperson, also at their table, shook her head.

"They were such a lovely family," Paula repeated. "I can't imagine what Belinda will do now," she added sorrowfully.

"You're still limping," Jack pronounced as he watched Gracie cross her kitchen to greet him Friday evening. She had invited him for dinner again, to celebrate the weekend and to continue discussing the case.

She kissed him soundly and gave Woof a pat on his head. "I told you: it's just my stupid ankle. It'll heal. Maybe not in two days, but it will," Gracie insisted. She had noticed the swelling Thursday morning, but had basically ignored the injury.

She returned to the countertop, where she had been arranging a *mis en place* for that evening's dinner.

"Does it hurt?" Jack queried, concerned.

Gracie shrugged. "Not really. It's swollen, though, and I hate the way it looks! I have a square foot!" she joked, and stuck her right leg out to show Jack. Her ankle and the top of her foot were, indeed, swollen so that the joint had all but disappeared. "It's not bad in the morning, when I wake up, but after walking on it all day…" Gracie went on, then shrugged as if to indicate that the injury was not important.

"You should get it checked out," Jack advised solemnly. "There could be something broken."

Gracie shrugged again. "I doubt it. If it were broken, it would hurt, and also it would probably be black and blue. I don't even remember doing anything in particular to it. I think it's just a bad sprain, and it'll heal eventually." She paused, and hobbled over to the sink to wash a bunch of scallions. "You forget what a klutz I can be: I'm used to stuff like this. So for a while, I'll walk funny. And I won't be doing any Morris Dancing," she added, sounding more glum.

Jack didn't seem amused, but he let the matter drop since he knew how much Gracie hated it when he became what she would consider 'over-protective.' However, he resolved that he would keep an eye on that ankle himself, and if it didn't get better in a week's time, he would again urge Gracie to go to her doctor.

He knew it was an inconvenience, and he knew she disliked bothering her doctor for inconsequential illnesses or injuries that would resolve or heal on their own. 'If the doc can't do anything except tell me to rest and take over the counter meds, what's the point?' she had often protested to Jack when she'd suffered some minor ailment, like a cold, or a minor burn or scratch or a pulled muscle. While he understood Gracie's opinion from a logical standpoint, from an emotional one, Jack preferred that she at least check with a medical professional if something went wrong.

"So, did your forensic accountant turn up anything?" Gracie asked as she plated dinner: black pepper rubbed braised venison filet with sautéed spinach in garlic and cocoanut balsamic, and red quinoa with scallions.

Jack sighed. He would much rather talk about the fabulous looking dinner Gracie had just put before him than talk about the case, but he knew Gracie was curious, and he also knew from previous experience that talking a case over with Gracie usually helped his own investigative process.

"Well, Aaron was an investment banker," he began, slicing a piece of the venison and bringing it up to his mouth. "Wow," he commented after a couple of chews: the flavor of the tender meat had burst onto his palate. "This is amazing, Gracie," he noted with a smile for her.

"And it's all natural, and quickly killed," Gracie added happily.

"I'm sure," Jack commented, just a bit wry. He shook his head. "I'm not saying I don't care about that, Gracie: I just don't care about it as much as you do," he commented.

Gracie put her fork down. "I couldn't eat something if I knew it had suffered unduly, or lived a horrible life," she murmured. "And I don't think it would taste very good, either," she added with a touch of sanctimoniousness.

Jack just kept eating, and nodded. "The spinach is good —what's that vinegar?"

Gracie explained about her recent trip to The Olive Branch in nearby Windsor: it was a balsamic vinegar and olive oil 'tasting tap room' with a small eatery attached. Gracie had discovered numerous intriguing types of infused olive oils and vinegars, and had loaded up.

Jack nodded again. "Sounds interesting. Is it a new place?"

Gracie affirmed that The Olive Branch had just opened the month before, adding that she'd seen the ad in the *Intelligencer*.

"I'll have to get there: maybe a gift card would be a good present for Mom," he commented, and looked at Gracie for her opinion. The holidays were only a couple of months away, and it never hurt to shop early, Jack thought.

Gracie nodded. "I think it would be," she agreed.

They ate for a while in relative silence: Gracie's many chiming clocks made a soothing, if somewhat jumbled, ticking with the occasional quarter or half hour chime, and over by the unlit gas fireplace Woof and Pumpkin each snored lightly as they napped.

"So—your accountant?" Gracie prodded, laying down her fork and knife. She took a sip of the Apothik Red she had poured, and sat back in her chair as though waiting to be entertained.

Jack finished the last bite of venison, spinach and quinoa all together, took his own sip of wine, and did the same.

"Well, I'm not a finance guy, but according to Indira," he began.

"Indira Patel?" Gracie interrupted. "Deanna Zimmerman's partner?" Deanna had done Gracie's taxes for years and had recently expanded her accountancy firm and taken on Indira.

"Yes. Her expertise is forensic accounting," Jack explained, and named a well known firm in Boston specializing in that area as the woman's previous employer.

"She's in Club," Gracie put in, nodding. "So's Deanna."

"Right." Sometimes, Gracie's frequent invocation of Club got a bit irritating. Jack knew she was acquainted with a number of people from many different social strata, and he knew that the Junior League of Pittsfield, or 'Club,' was a worthy institution. But it occasionally seemed to Jack as though *everyone* they talked about was either in Club or connected to someone who was.

"Well, anyway, according to Indira, Aaron McGinley's investments were pretty much standard: he did as his clients asked. If they wanted very low risk, that's what he did. If they were willing to take a little bit of risk, Aaron chose companies that would produce more, but which could also bottom out and fold."

"Did any of those companies do that?" Gracie asked, curious. "That could be a motive for murder."

Jack nodded. "Right. But no, none of the companies Aaron invested in went bankrupt." He paused. "But there was one interesting, well, a couple of interesting things."

Gracie waited.

"Aaron was running a higher risk/higher return investment trust for a few select investors who didn't mind taking a risk with some of their money if it could mean big returns," Jack began.

"That's legal, though, right?"

"Oh, sure: Aaron didn't do anything illegal, at least not from what Indira could see. Anyway, this particular trust was invested in derivatives linked to an index in the Japanese stock market whose companies didn't include any from the U.S."

"Uh-huh," Gracie nodded encouragingly.

"That's not illegal, *per se*, but the derivative was set up to profit if and when the dollar fell against a particular group of foreign currencies," Jack continued.

Gracie frowned. "Is *that* legal?" she asked.

Jack shrugged. "Indira says yes, but it's not very patriotic, is it?" Jack queried rhetorically.

Gracie was silent.

"Also, this same investment trust also invested in Rosneft," Jack went on.

"The Russian oil company?" Gracie put in.

Jack was taken aback: he had had to ask Indira to explain what Rosneft was. How did Gracie know?

"I just read that the Russians agreed to sell a ten percent share to the CNPC to help Rosneft pay its debt," Gracie continued by way of explanation. "It owes something like $30 billion due in two years or something, but with oil prices going down, they don't have as much money on hand. In effect," she continued, warming to her subject, "their debt has gone up. I don't think the sale to CNPC will wipe it out, but it'll help a lot. Though I couldn't find how much the sale actually was worth. "

"You read about Russian economic strategy?" Jack asked, not sure whether he should be impressed or intimidated. Maybe a little of both, he decided.

"I read anything that grabs my attention," Gracie replied with a grin. "I remembered reading that earlier this year the Chinese CNPC did a deal with Gazprom, the Russian gas company, for $400 billion, so I thought this second financial, erm, alliance between those two countries was pretty interesting."

Jack nodded. "Agreed. Then you throw in that oil's fallen from $115 a barrel to less than $85 this past week…"

"And it gets even more interesting!" Gracie pronounced cheerfully. "So what did all of this mean for Aaron McGinley's risky investment?" she queried, returning to the subject at hand.

Jack sighed. "Well, his investment in Rosneft was high risk, but could have paid off extremely well. Now it looks as though, while the investors won't lose money, they won't make much, either. At least in the short term. If oil goes up again, Rosneft's profits will, too, and if they can pay down, or pay off their debt, their financial picture will be rosier. And so will McGinley's investors'," Jack explained.

Gracie got up and cleared the plates. "Coffee?" she asked, knowing the answer.

Jack nodded.

"How about some Rumchata in it?" Gracie offered, naming a creamy Mexican liqueur they both liked.

"Great."

"But—if the investors didn't lose money, there's no motive for murder," Gracie said from the sink, talking over the noise of the running water as she washed the dinner dishes.

"No, it's not," Jack agreed. He picked up a tea towel and began to dry the plates and utensils. This tea towel, one of hundreds Gracie had in her collection from her travels, said 'You'll find there's never a dull moment in this house.' While that was true, Jack wondered where the quote was from.

"Was there any other odd investing or funny accounting?" Gracie asked.

Jack shook his head. "No. Indira said that while a couple of investments might have been high risk, or ethically questionable, everything looked legit to her."

Gracie sighed, and switched on the coffee maker. "So now what? Why were Aaron and Wyatt murdered?" she reiterated the question that plagued Jack.

"Unless it was a random shooting, or a case of mistaken identity," Jack murmured, unknowingly echoing Anne's suggestion of a few hours before.

"But who would just open up and shoot campers?" Gracie objected. "And I don't buy the mistaken identity thing: there were so few campers at Greylock last weekend, and one of the Forest Rangers who works there told me that the McGinleys were the only father and son on site: everyone else was couples, or groups, or large families."

"A Ranger at Greylock told you that?" Jack queried.

Gracie nodded as she watched the brewed coffee spew into the glass carafe. "Yes: Victorine Hanson. She oversees all of the volunteers at Greylock Mansion," she explained, mentioning the historic home she helped out at when she could. "I called her this afternoon, and asked her if she could tell me who had been registered at the Forest campsites that weekend," Gracie continued. "Not names, but types of campers: old, young, groups, families, you know…to eliminate the mistaken identity possibility. Anne mentioned that at lunch today, and I thought it was worth following up," she added quietly.

They fixed their coffees and Jack hung up the tea towel to dry before they headed for the Oak Room.

"But why would a Ranger at Greylock tell you anything about the campers, even if she does know you from the Mansion?" Jack queried, still puzzled.

Gracie sighed. "She's in Club," she said as they settled on the chocolate brown sofa.

Jack gave a good natured grimace. "I should have known," he commented wryly. "Well, it's good to know that, even though I had planned to get around to inquiring about that very thing," he added, chuckling. "Mistaken identity seemed kinda far fetched to me, anyway."

Gracie nodded. "It was a vicious attack," she murmured, sipping her coffee. "Really awful. I think that means that the killer knew the victims: it seems personal to me somehow," she added.

Jack sighed. "Well, it could be: extreme emotion in a killing can indicate that," Jack admitted. "But it could also not be that..." he trailed off. He was tired of talking about the murder: it was all he'd thought about or spoken about for days, and his brain needed a rest. "Where'd you get that tea towel?" he asked Gracie suddenly, changing the subject completely.

Gracie smiled. "Down in Delaware, at Winterthur," she replied, and reminded him that she had made a weekend excursion there in August with her friend Susan. "The *Downton Abbey* Exhibit?" she prompted.

Jack recalled that both Gracie and Susan were huge fans of the British period drama that their local PBS station was airing. He also recalled that the Winterthur mansion in Delaware had displayed costumes from the series for a limited time, and that Gracie had secured tickets long ago—before she'd gone to England, if he recalled right. He remembered that she'd been away for a long weekend in August, and now that she reminded him, he remembered her trip to Winterthur.

"But what does that tea towel have to do with Downton Abbey?" Jack asked, frowning into his coffee.

"It's a quote from the Duchess of Grantham," Gracie explained. "And since you don't watch the program, it's kinda pointless for me to explain who that is," she added with a *moue.*

CHAPTER TWELVE

CHAPTER TWELVE

Monday morning, Gracie got an email from her editor, asking if she could possibly interview Mrs. McGinley for a follow up to the coverage on the shooting. Since nothing new on the investigation was being made public while everything was still being checked, her editor explained, a profile on the widow and the family would keep readers' interest.

Gracie never liked doing intrusive interviews, and she considered her editor's request a bit on the intrusive side. However, what Dave Tiller didn't know was that Gracie was in Club along with the widow, Belinda McGinley. Gracie was Vice President this year, too, which meant that she was in charge of new members, inductions, and hospitality. So although she didn't know Belinda well, she had spoken with her on several occasions.

It would probably be easier for her to get an interview with Belinda than it would be for anyone else, from any other news outlet. Although she found it slightly distasteful, Gracie picked up her iPhone and called Belinda's mobile number. It was just after 10 a.m. and a cloudy day with a stiff breeze that seemed to portend the autumn weather that would shortly arrive.

Belinda answered, clearly having seen Gracie's caller ID on her phone's screen: she sounded friendly, if weary.

Gracie quickly asked how she was, listened to a brief but telling answer, and then explained what her editor had asked her to do.

Belinda was gracious and understanding, and told Gracie she could certainly come and speak with her, and was this morning a good time?

Gracie replied that she would be there in about half an hour, and disconnected so she could get herself dressed and prepped for the interview.

The McGinleys' home was on Grove Street, which was also Route 8, about two thirds of the way between Cheshire and Adams. The area was shifting from rural to residential, and their house was a two story brick and pale green vinyl-sided home with a slated 'Dutch kick' roof and a small portico held up by Doric columns over the front door. A considerable tract of land stretched around and behind the home, and Gracie could see what looked like a four car garage with a loft at the rear of a long, wide back garden.

Gracie parked in the paver-covered driveway and walked up the manicured brick path that sliced through a velvet expanse of green front lawn. Rhododendrons no longer in flower flanked the three shallow steps leading to the front landing; junipers and boxwoods extended along the home's front and around its sides.

A mat on the landing said 'Welcome' in coir printed with crossed Irish and US flags in each corner, and Gracie noticed an umbrella stand and a UK style letter box near the front door. Over the green-painted door was a professionally painted wooden sign that read, 'Fáilte Roimh don Bhaile Mag Fhionnghaile.' Gracie's Irish Gaelic was practically non existent, but she figured the sign said something like 'Welcome to the McGinleys',' although she couldn't quite work out how Mag Fhionnghaile translated to McGinley.

As she was pondering the Gaelic pronunciation, Belinda opened the door.

"Hi!" Gracie said with a smile, and pointed to the sign over their heads. "You'll have to explain that one to me," she suggested.

Belinda gave a faint smile in return. Her rounded curves were clothed in faded jeans and a black short sleeved T shirt; her blonde hair was brushed but not styled, and she wore no makeup. Gracie thought Belinda lucky to have naturally rosy lips and cheeks: even though she looked drawn, Belinda still looked quite pretty.

As Gracie stepped inside and Belinda shut the door behind her, the widow gave her answer. "Aaron was very proud of his Irish heritage," she began, keeping her voice steady. " 'Mag Fhionnghaile' is McGinley in Irish, and the rest is 'welcome to the home of…' " she elucidated, pronouncing the Irish like, 'Ma-GHOON-lach,' and with more post-alveolar fricatives than Gracie could imagine enunciating.

"Oh!" Gracie nodded.

"I'm just a plain old mongrel American, so I went along with Aaron's ethnic passion," she added, and her smile broadened at the recollection.

Belinda led Gracie through the small foyer and into the living room; the pale yellow box pleat draperies were drawn, no doubt to discourage what Jack called 'lookey-loos,' both curious neighbors and the media. Because of the dullness of the day, the room was shadowy, so Belinda switched on a table lamp, then indicated that Gracie should have a seat on the upholstered sofa.

The room was carpeted in a thick medium grey pile, with the walls painted a pale and somehow warm grey the color of putty. Yellow accents from the draperies and pillows, as well as the grey and yellow chintz print on one wing chair pulled the room together. Prints of still life paintings of fruits and flowers hung on the walls, and on the mantel over the fireplace were family snapshots: Aaron and Belinda's wedding photo, a baby picture of Wyatt, a recent school photo of him, and a picture of the three of them, obviously taken at a professional studio.

"May I bring you something to drink?" Belinda asked graciously.

Gracie sighed and shook her head. "Belinda, I so appreciate you being willing to talk to me, you don't have to be on your best behavior or anything, or go to any trouble, and I promise not to take up a lot of your time," she told her, all in a rush.

Belinda shook her head, and sat down next to Gracie on the silver grey sofa. "I don't mind," she murmured. "Now that —now that it's all over, the funeral, I mean, and everyone's gone, well—there's nothing for me to do, really."

Gracie recalled that Belinda had volunteered with the local Red Cross chapter, but had not worked outside the home. Apparently, Aaron had made enough money that she hadn't had to. Gracie suspected that Aaron had left his wife well placed, financially: Jack had mentioned that there was a substantial life insurance policy, although he'd also said the payout would be delayed until the murder case was solved.

Gracie knew that if the investment angle didn't produce any viable motive or suspect, Jack would next turn to investigating the spouse, i.e., Belinda. Even though Gracie would never imagine the woman who sat just a few inches away from her as a murderer, stranger things had happened.

"Well," Gracie began consolingly, "maybe you should just take care of yourself for a little while," she suggested, her voice gentle. "This has all been so dreadful, Belinda," Gracie continued, and put a hand on the other woman's. "And it will be 'till they find who—who did it," she finished lamely.

Belinda shrugged.

"Maybe you could get a massage, or something, help relieve the stress? I can give you the name of my masseuse, if you like: she's amazing," Gracie offered, still smiling.

Belinda blinked tears away. "That would be really nice," she said, her voice breaking.

Gracie knew it wasn't the idea of a massage that was making Belinda so emotional. Maybe it was just a kindness from someone she didn't know really well. Maybe it was a transference of the emotion surrounding the deaths of her husband and son. Maybe it was all of that, and more.

"Well, I'll write that down for you before I go," Gracie said, her tone brisker. "Now: I've come here to do a profile on you, and Wyatt and Aaron. Do you think we can just talk for a while about what their interests were, and what kind of people they were?" she asked. "I'll take notes, and I'd like to borrow that picture of the three of you if I could," Gracie added, referencing to the snapshot on the mantel.

Belinda nodded her agreement, and they began.

CHAPTER THIRTEEN

CHAPTER THIRTEEN

"You know, that man from the *Gazetteer* called over the weekend, asking for an interview," Belinda told Gracie in a tone that dripped disdain. They had finished the interview, and Belinda had taken Gracie upstairs to Wyatt's bedroom so she could see the kind of things the young boy had been interested in.

Gracie had been impressed: Wyatt, she thought, had been not just smart, as she'd heard, but brilliant. A large telescope had pride of place near one window, and a white board against one wall held a series of equations that looked vaguely familiar to Gracie from her college Physics course. She couldn't make heads or tails of the other writing on the board, though: what looked like sentences—but in a script and language Gracie didn't know—were written at one side. When Gracie asked Belinda about it, the boy's mother shrugged and smiled and said that her son was always inventing 'secret languages' that had been a mystery to everyone but himself.

Books on all manner of scientific subjects, some quite esoteric, were neatly lined up on shelves against another wall, and a model of the solar system hung from the ceiling.

"The police returned their things," Belinda said softly, fingering a little brown paper bag-covered notebook that sat on one side of Wyatt's small desk. "Once the crime scene people had finished with them."

Gracie suddenly understood the reason for the sleeping bag, pillow, and other camping accoutrements, piled up in a corner of the otherwise very neat room.

"This was Wyatt's notebook," Belinda continued, fanning the pages quickly, a regretful smile on her face. "He took it with him everywhere. Even though he had a smartphone, he said he enjoyed the feel of paper and pen," she reminisced, her voice soft. She put the little notebook back on the desk and shrugged. "Wyatt is—was—very bright," she explained. Gracie thought it was quite an understatement.

Now, they had returned to the ground floor, and Belinda had insisted on making some tea for them both, so they were now in the kitchen. Several many-paned double-hung windows let in the cold light of the grey day, but Belinda switched on a warm, bright, overhead light as she moved to the counter to fill the kettle. Gracie had the feeling that, even though she was there as a professional to do the interview, she was thought of more as a friend, and suspected that Belinda might be reluctant for Gracie to leave, and for her to be left alone once more.

"He did?" Gracie asked, referring to the rival paper's editor. "Did you—"

Belinda put the kettle on the range top, and shook her head. "I told him, no." Then she shrugged. "I didn't have any particular reason, I just didn't want to talk to him." She paused. "I don't like his paper, much, but I do like your paper, Gracie. And of course, I know you, so…"

Gracie gave a wry grin as she took in the kitchen's country-inspired decor. An abundance of gingham in brick and cream colors adorned rustic-looking signs with expressions of love and family on them. A large print of several kittens on a bed, called 'Bedfellows' by Randy McGovern hung on one wall, and made Gracie smile. Another wall held a 'Café Chat Noir' poster; when she looked, Gracie noticed several cat-themed items including a cookie jar, napkin holder, and oven mitts. On the refrigerator were drawings, report cards, photos, and awards, all from Wyatt's school.

"He'll probably be really pissed when he sees my article, then," Gracie told Belinda, referencing the *Gazetteer's* editor, Gil Butcher. Gracie bit back a giggle.

"Well, so what? I have the right to speak—or not speak — to whomever I wish," Belinda replied, sounding stronger than she had all morning.

"That's right, you do," Gracie affirmed. At least, she thought, until she retained an attorney and was advised to speak to no one. But that hadn't happened yet, and in any case, the subject Gracie was writing about wouldn't have any impact, really, on the murder investigation. It was just a profile on the family.

Belinda brought over two mugs of tea and the cat-shaped cookie jar. "I baked these," she commented as she lifted the lid of the jar. Aromas of nutmeg, molasses and cinnamon wafted into the air. "Just last week," she added, opening a zip lock plastic bag in which some of the treats had been stored.

"Hermits?" Gracie inquired. "My favorite!" she exclaimed, and accepted a generously sized square from her hostess. "I remember as a kid going to Sturbridge Village with my Mom and Dad," Gracie continued. "And at the end, we would always have hermits at the little coffee shop there. Of course now, it's quite a fancy lunch place, but they still have hermits," she murmured, biting into one.

"This recipe is my own version," Belinda explained. "I happen to like the hermits they bake at the Publick House Inn better than the ones at the Village," she added, also nibbling on one dark, chewy square. "So I based mine on theirs. More cocoa I think," she added, sipping at her tea.

"These are great!" Gracie agreed.

They were silent for a few moments, then Gracie asked about the cats. "I see a lot of cat decorations, but no cat," she said with a smile.

Belinda shook her head. "Aaron is terribly allergic," she explained. "I had two kitties when we met, and every time he'd visit my apartment—this was in Methuen, up north—" she added, referencing her home town and providing attribution for her distinctive accent, "it was a sneeze fest."

"You had to give the cats away when you got married?" Gracie asked, hoping the answer would be a happy one.

Belinda nodded. "Yes. I was a veterinary technician, so I posted their pictures in our clinic, and they found a good home, together, pretty quickly," she said, sounding satisfied, but still sad.

Gracie thought it would be the height of insensitivity to suggest that now that her allergic husband was dead, Belinda could adopt a couple new kitties, so she didn't. But she thought it, and also thought that having a couple of cats to look after might help Belinda fill the void she seemed to be having difficulty adjusting to. She hoped her friend might come to that conclusion herself, in time.

Instead, Gracie asked Belinda if she thought she might go back to work, even just part time, to help fill up her days.

Belinda looked as though Gracie had just given her the answer to her prayers. "Why, I hadn't really even thought of that, but you know, I just might!" she replied happily.

Gracie typed up her article on the McGinley family when she returned home that afternoon. She thought it was a good piece: sensitive, not maudlin at all, and it paid homage to Aaron McGinley's Irish heritage, which Gracie thought would have pleased the dead man. It would run in Friday's

Intelligencer. On Tuesday, Gracie would head into Pittsfield to do her regular courthouse and police 'rounds' and type up the rest of her coverage for that week.

Her ankle was still swollen, and she instinctively found herself limping as she walked. Belinda had noticed, and expressed concern, just as Jack had several days earlier. Although Gracie was convinced that no major damage had been done, and that the muscles around her ankle just needed time to heal, on Monday afternoon once she'd filed her article, she found herself in her Jeep, headed for the Urgent Care Clinic in Pittsfield.

She could have called and booked an appointment with her regular physician, but it was unlikely that appointment would be any time soon. Besides, any tests and such that might be needed could be done at the UC Clinic, and the results sent to her doctor, to keep her in the loop.

"How long since you noticed the injury?" the young doctor at the UC Clinic asked her in his lilting accent from the sub-continent of India.

"Almost a week," Gracie answered, and explained about the Morris Dancing Troupe.

The doctor sent Gracie for both an X-ray and an MRI, the results of which showed no fractures or breaks, but significant muscle injury and some fluid in the joint.

"That is what is causing the swelling, and any pain you may have," the doctor explained.

When Gracie asked about treatment, the doctor said that the fluid could be aspirated, which would bring the swelling down, and then said that Gracie would be put in a soft 'walking' cast to minimize movement while the muscles healed. He estimated six weeks.

Gracie made a face, and caught the eye of the nurse practitioner who was assisting the doctor with her case. The nurse practitioner's expression seemed to indicate that Gracie should not opt for the aspiration/cast solution.

"Erm—and what if I just try to stay off it, elevate it, ice it, you know," Gracie asked ingenuously.

"You mean, RICE?" the doctor replied, using the acronym for 'Rest, Ice, Compression, Elevation,' the classic treatment for sprains and similar injuries. "Well, you could wear a support brace, an elastic bandage," he began, still sounding doubtful. "And rest it, and elevate it and ice it, as you say," he continued.

"But you think—" Gracie began.

"I think," the doctor overrode her, "that aspiration and a walking cast would be a faster resolution to your injury," he concluded.

Gracie told him she would think it over and let the Clinic know, once she'd spoken to her regular doctor.

"Your doctor is not an orthopedist," the Clinic doctor said with a mild hint of disapproval. He, of course, was an orthopedist, and had been specifically assigned to Gracie's case because of that.

"I know. I'll be in touch," Gracie said firmly.

She wasn't a sissy, far from it, but the whole idea of a needle aspirating the fluid from inside her ankle really made her uneasy.

The doctor left, and Gracie stood from the chair she'd been sitting in. "May I have copies of the X ray and the MRI?" she asked the nurse practitioner, who was still in the room.

"Of course," the woman said. "And, you didn't hear this from me, but take them to your chiropractor, if you have one," she murmured in a low tone.

"I used to go to Dr. Grist, over by Whole Foods," Gracie answered back, her voice matching the nurse practitioner's in volume. "I haven't gone in a while, though," she added. She'd gone to the chiropractor when she'd first moved to the area, and had been doing massive renovations on her house. The unusual and strenuous activity had wreaked havoc on her back and muscles. Dr. Grist had made her feel much better, she recalled now.

"He's the one I go to," the nurse practitioner replied with a grin. "I tore my ACL last year, and the docs here said surgery and eight weeks in a cast. No offense to them, but I have to work, so no way that was happening," she continued, punching a few keys on the exam room's computer and handing Gracie a CD in a paper sleeve a couple of minutes later. "But I went to Dr. Grist, and in three weeks, I was walking, back to work. I never had surgery, and you see me: I'm walking fine."

Gracie smiled. "Thanks for the tip," she said, and resolved to call Dr. Grist the minute she got out of the Clinic and could use her iPhone.

CHAPTER FOURTEEN

CHAPTER FOURTEEN

"Where have you been, I've been trying to call you!" Jack asked late Monday afternoon when Gracie finally answered her phone.

"I went to interview Belinda McGinley, and then, you'll be happy to know, I went down to Urgent Care," she answered sarcastically. "They make you turn your phone off."

"You were there 'till now?" Jack returned, sounding worried.

"No—" and Gracie explained about the nurse practitioner's tip about the chiropractor, and her subsequent visit to Dr. Grist's office. "They were really great, squeezed me in, but by the time he finished with me, and then I was right near Whole Foods so I stopped in there to pick up a few things, well, I had my phone off in his office, too, and just now turned it back on, when I got home," Gracie answered, all in a rush.

She could have predicted what Jack's response would be.

"You went against medical advice and went to a chiropractor?" he asked, his tone making it seem as though she'd gone to a snake oil salesman.

"I took into account what both the doctor and the nurse practitioner said," Gracie returned, trying not to sound angry, but knowing her words were clipped nonetheless. "And I took into account the fact that the X ray and the MRI showed no physical damage other than pulled muscles and fluid. It's the fluid that has to be worked out of the joint, that's what Dr. Grist explained to me. The body will, over time, get rid of it by itself, but with his manipulation of the joint—'active response therapy,' I think he called it—the fluid will disperse and the muscles heal, much faster."

She could sense Jack's disapproval even though he was silent.

"You'll see," she insisted, defending herself. Then she wondered why she felt the need to do so: Jack wasn't her guardian, or her father, or even a medical professional. She had the right to choose whatever course of treatment she felt was correct for her own body, and her own injury. "Why were you trying to reach me?" she asked, keeping her tone sweet. "Has something happened in the case?"

Jack made indistinguishable noises on the other end of the connection, and finally said, "I'd be really interested to hear what Mrs. McGinley had to say to you."

Gracie frowned. "Why? It was just about her, and Aaron and Wyatt: kind of a family portrait type of piece," she hedged.

"Mmmm…well, I'm still running financials on all the investors Aaron McGinley had, just to be sure, and on the McGinleys themselves. But I've set up an interview with Belinda McGinley for tomorrow morning."

"Oh?"

"Yeah. We talked to her, of course, once the bodies had been identified, right after they were found, but she was in shock then and honestly, I never like to do interviews when people are under that kind of stress," he explained. "I'm hoping she will be calmer now, and better able to tell me about, well, everything."

"What do you mean, 'everything?' " Gracie queried. "You don't suspect Belinda, do you?" she asked, her tone withering.

"I suspect everyone until they alibi out or are proven not to be culpable," Jack retorted firmly. "You know I always look at the spouse, even if it seems really unlikely," he reminded her.

Gracie recalled her friend Maddie, whose husband had been killed earlier that year. She remembered that Jack had included Maddie in his list of suspects, although over time he had begun to think she was innocent. It had turned out, of course, that she had been innocent.

Gracie did not feel like sharing what she and Belinda had spoken about, even the 'on the record' things said in the formal, sit down interview. And why would Jack need or want details from her interview, anyway? He was completely capable of making his own observations and drawing his own conclusions.

Maybe he just wanted to see how Belinda had impressed her, and see if it were markedly different from the impression he would get.

Well, no matter.

The prickliness between them persisted as they explained to each other how much work they both had to do and said they'd get together 'later in the week.' Then they hung up.

Gracie sighed.

Pumpkin came into the kitchen, where Gracie had unloaded her Whole Foods bags onto the kitchen table to answer her phone. The large orange tabby cat wound herself around Gracie's ankles and sniffed at the swollen one, appearing concerned.

"You just smell the stuff Dr. Grist put on my ankle," Gracie reassured her, hobbling over towards the cupboard where she kept the cat food. She knew that was what Pumpkin really wanted, regardless of her apparent solicitousness: food. "You'll see: he said he'll have me dancing a jig in three weeks," she told the cat as she poured kibble into a clean bowl and added a couple of dental health treats on top. She put the bowl down on a paw-print decorated placemat on the floor and watched as the cat began to crunch in satisfaction. "I'll be fine," Gracie insisted.

"DRAPER!" hollered Popovitch from his office. There was an intercom, which he never used. There were also phones, so he could dial Jack's desk directly; he never did that, either. The Berkshire County DA preferred to yell at the top of his lungs to summon his staff. And that's exactly what it was: a summons.

Across the DA's suite on the third floor of the Courthouse, Jack heard his boss yell his surname, and sighed. It was 4:25 p.m. Not that he punched a clock, but this day he had managed to get several of the 'pending' folders stuffing his in-box cleared, and had thought he had a shot at getting out of work more or less on time. Although there was still one thing that had come up today, as he'd worked his way through case files, that he wanted to check out.

Resignedly, Jack rose from behind his desk, and walked out of his office, into the main reception area where the secretaries worked, past the office of the DA's paralegal, Phyllida, past the small conference room, and to the doorway of Popovitch's lair.

"Yes, Peter?" Jack asked mildly, using his boss' given name, largely because he knew Popovitch found it annoying. Well, Jack thought to himself, if Popovitch was going to be rude, he would at least be informal in the way he addressed him. Such a bully didn't deserve to be called 'sir.'

The DA glowered over at Jack from behind his desk. He was apparently finishing up for the day also, as he was gathering papers and files and stuffing them into a briefcase that was already bursting at the seams—much like Popovitch's suit.

"You arrest the McGinley widow yet?" he asked gruffly. He tried to fasten the catch on the worn brown leather case, but it wouldn't quite reach, so the DA looked expectantly at Jack as he stood and hefted the briefcase under one arm. The motion caused his suit jacket to ride up on one side, exposing a large expanse of rather dingy shirt, and a black belt that didn't match his dark teal trousers. Of course, the trousers didn't match the tan suit jacket either, so Jack supposed it really didn't matter.

Jack shook his head. "No, Peter. I don't have probable cause," he returned mildly.

"Whaddya mean, no cause?" Popovitch blustered, looking affronted. "She's the widow. She inherits all the money, the house, everything. And the dead guy, the banker —"

"Aaron McGinley?" Jack put in, offended on the deceased's behalf at Popovitch calling him, 'the dead guy.'

"Yeah, him: he had a life insurance policy, didn't he?"the DA asked.

That showed how little Popovitch knew about the case. The basic financial printout on the McGinleys was the second or third document in the investigative file: clearly, the DA hadn't read that far, if he'd even read beyond the initial police report.

Jack nodded. "Yes. But it wasn't a huge amount of money: just $20,000, enough for burial and to clear any debts." He paused. "They did have some savings, IRA's, CD's, that sort of thing. About a half a million dollars, that's all," Jack added. Half a million was nothing to make light of, but it wasn't that much, not for a life-savings.

"I've known people to kill for a lot less," the DA returned, lumbering around his desk as he spoke. The effort caused him to catch his breath. "Bring her in."

"On what grounds, Peter?" Jack asked sternly. He wasn't going to tell the DA he had just such an interview scheduled for the next morning.

Jack's position blocked Popovitch's doorway, and Jack didn't move to let his boss pass, either. Not until the DA gave him a reasonable answer to his question.

"Oh, I don't know, Draper, you're the detective!" Popovitch whined in response, and looked much aggrieved. "Question her about her husband and son again, what they were doing in the woods, why they went there, what they were like in the days just before the trip…" Popovitch continued, reeling off the basics of interrogation.

"All those questions have been asked, and answered, by Belinda McGinley," Jack reminded his boss. Sometimes, it was fun to play with the DA, he thought, just to see what he'd do.

But Popovitch was so close to him now, in his effort to get out of the door, that Jack could smell the DA's stale breath. It mixed with a sourly gamey odor of unwashed, morbidly obese body, and Jack instinctively moved away, giving Popovitch the room he needed to maneuver out of the doorway, to freedom.

"Well, then, ask 'em again, Jack!" the DA called out, not even bothering to turn his head over his shoulder as he barged away from Jack, out of the suite and towards the Courthouse's central elevator.

CHAPTER FIFTEEN

Tuesday morning, Jack stopped into the County's Probation Office before arriving at his own. The Probation Director, Lance Melling, was at his desk, and Jack asked if he had a moment.

"Sure, Jack: have a seat!" Melling offered affably. Melling had been the PD for more than 20 years, and he was a fixture at the Courthouse. A recent re-structuring of Probation to merge both Juvenile and Adult under one Director had seen Melling ascend to that position; he now made nearly twice what he had been earning, but he also had at least twice the work. Luckily for him, a handful of experienced Deputies and Officers kept both the Juvenile and Adult divisions running quite smoothly.

"I was reading through some case files yesterday, making sure I had all the upcoming court dates on my calendar, and that everything was in order," Jack began, sitting in the square vinyl and wood chair in front of Melling's desk.

"Unh huh?" Melling offered encouragingly.

"Well, I noticed an irregularity in one of the files, and that led me to do some checking, and, well, Lance I think there's a situation that needs to be addressed," Jack continued gravely.

"Whose file?" Melling asked, turning slightly so he could see his computer screen.

Jack gave him the name, and Melling typed it in. He scanned the document that loaded on his screen a moment later. "And?" he asked Jack expectantly.

"The guy's probation officer is Dennison," Jack pointed out.

Melling verified this, and nodded. "Yes."

"But Dennison is also the one who qualified the client for the Public Defender," Jack said.

Melling checked the document again, scrolling down to the appropriate page and noting the information typed in, and the signature.

"Right you are, Jack:," he agreed, his pale, roundish face still affably composed. "That isn't supposed to happen," he added confidentially, dropping his voice. "My officers know they're supposed to get another officer to do the eligibility eval." He sighed. "Must've been an oversight. I'll have a word with Dennison and have someone else re-do the eligibility," he added.

"That would be great, Lance, thanks," Jack replied, as though that would resolve the issue.

Melling nodded and smiled.

"Can you tell me, Lance, how that's set up? The evaluation process for eligibility for the PD?" Jack asked, feigning innocent curiosity.

"Sure, Jack: two of my Probation Officers in each division are tasked with doing evals. They are supposed to give their cases to each other to do, or to one of the other evaluators, even if they're in the other division, you see?" Melling replied.

Jack nodded.

"That avoids conflict of interest," Melling explained, sounding just a bit self righteous.

"Mmmm…" Jack nodded in agreement. "And—who are the officers you have who do the evals?" he asked lightly.

Melling responded with the four surnames: "Dennison, Hatch, DiGiacomo and Abbarito." They were all senior officers, and Jack knew and liked them.

"Oh, well, that's fine then, Lance: thanks for clearing that up," Jack responded.

He still thought there was a problem, but he needed to check a couple more things, first. And he wanted to talk to each of the four officers separately as well. If, as he suspected, the evaluation process was being handled incorrectly, Melling appeared to know nothing about it. Jack wanted to see if any of the officers directly tasked with doing evaluations suspected anything, either.

Jack and Melling shook hands, and Jack hastened up the back flight of stairs to the DA's suite. It was just before 8:30 a.m and while the rest of the staff was there, Popovitch, of course, was not.

Quickly, Jack said good morning to everyone, grabbed his messages, and settled behind his desk. He booted up his computer and pulled up the budget for the Probation Office. Money, he thought: it always came down to money. But how, he wondered, had this whole thing begun?

While reviewing the files on his desk the day before, Jack had noticed the conflict of interest when Dennison had done the eligibility eval on his own client. Before asking the PD Director, Melling, about it, this morning, Jack had researched the law on the eligibility evaluation for the Public Defender, to be sure he wasn't seeing a problem where there was none. Maybe it didn't matter if a PO evaluated his own client, although to Jack it seemed like it should.

His investigation the previous afternoon had brought him to a very interesting statement in Massachusetts law that Jack had wagered to himself few knew about, and fewer still really cared about.

Section five of the statute regarding court-appointed attorneys dealt with the appointment of the Public Defender in the case of indigent defendants. It read, 'the indigence of a client applying for counsel is determined solely by the Public

Defender's Office or by an agency so qualified and appointed by the Public Defender's Office for this task.'

Jack had read this twice to be certain he wasn't missing any exceptions. Then he had sat back and made certain that his conclusion was a valid one. If the statute said that eligibility for the Public Defender could only be made by the Public Defender's Office or an agency appointed by that office, what was Probation doing determining eligibility? Even if they generally did not have officers evaluating their own clients, if Jack had properly understood what he'd just read, the Probation Office wasn't supposed to be doing evals at all.

Now, Jack ran his eye down the budget sheet for Probation: Juvenile Probation and Adult Probation each got $10,000 a year for the eligibility evaluations. Each officer doing the evals received $4000 a year, and Melling received $2000 per division for 'administration.' That meant it cost $20,000 a year for the Probation Office to do PD evaluations. And of that $20,000, each officer tasked with determining eligibility received $4000 a year, and Melling himself received $4,000 a year.

Not a fortune, Jack considered, but a nice little annual bonus: enough for the down payment on a new car, or a great vacation. He wondered if Probation, who crafted their own budget of course, and set the amount for each line item, was performing the eligibility as thriftily as possible. Never mind the suspicion that the Probation Department shouldn't be doing eligibility evals at all.

The phrase in the statute, 'or by an agency so qualified and appointed by the Public Defender's Office,' was a possible rationale for the way things were being done, Jack thought to himself as he flipped through the venerable and well thumbed rolodex atop his desk. He'd have to investigate some more to find out when, by whom and how Probation had been given this task—and the corresponding budget item.

But right now, he wanted to find out if $20,000 a year was a reasonable amount for handling the eligibility determination.

CHAPTER SIXTEEN
CHAPTER SIXTEEN

Felicia Laurenti answered her own phone, something that Jack admired. He said good morning to the county's Public Defender, and then bounced his question off her.

"If your office were to take over determining eligibility for Public Defense, Felicia, how much would you charge a year?" Jack asked casually.

"Hmmm…let's see…average number of clients… paperwork, secretary, telephone, copying…"

"You can get back to me," Jack suggested. It was a lot to ask her to drop whatever she'd been in the middle of and answer his question out of the blue.

"No, hang on…" Felicia ruminated a couple of moments longer and then replied, "probably about $10,000, give or take. Why?"

"Ten thousand?" Jack repeated. "You're sure. We have a lot of people entitled to counsel who can't afford it," he reminded her.

Felicia Laurenti had been Berkshire County's Public Defender for more than a couple of years, and she knew the needs and requirements of her county, and her clients, well.

"I know that, Jack, but yes, that's about right," she returned. "As I said, give or take. Some years it could be a little more, or a little less, depending on how many and who come through the door," she elaborated. "Why?" she asked again.

Jack didn't answer her directly. "I'm just checking into something, and wondered. That's all. Erm—Felicia, keep this to yourself, ok? Don't tell anyone I asked you this, please," he added.

Felicia laughed lightly. "Sure, okay, Jack. It'll be our secret." She paused. "But I'm counting on you to tell me why, at some point," she added with mock sternness in her voice.

Returning her laugh, Jack agreed, and hung up. But his conversation with the Public Defender had sobered him. Granted, it had only been an estimate, but Felicia had just indicated her office could do the evaluations for half of what Probation said it cost them. Could that be possible?

Before he could contemplate the issue further, however, his intercom buzzed and Millie, the office secretary, told him that Belinda McGinley was here to see him. Jack told her to bring Mrs. McGinley in.

"Thank you for coming down this morning, Mrs. McGinley," Jack begin with a kind smile. The widow gave him a tremulous smile in return, and settled herself in one of the chairs that flanked Jack's desk.

"I'm happy to help in any way I can," she replied. "And please, Detective, call me Belinda," she added.

Jack nodded. "Okay. Belinda." He sighed. "I am sorry to ask you to go through this all again, but would you mind telling me about your husband and son, and their decision to go camping?"

Belinda frowned. "How do you mean, Detective? I mean, I don't think there's much to it, really."

"Maybe not," Jack agreed. "But: you'd never gone camping before, as a family, had you?" he asked.

Belinda shook her head. Jack noticed that her wavy blonde hair just brushed the shoulders of the dark grey short sleeved cotton top she wore with black linen trousers. A single strand of pearls that lapped at her collarbone stood out against the somber tones. She was what his mother would call 'pleasantly plump,' with a naturally rosy complexion and clear hazel eyes. "I am not much of an outdoorsy person,"

Belinda admitted. "Aaron was, though: had been his whole life. But after we got married, no, we never camped."

"Did Aaron camp?" Jack asked. "Maybe, with friends or something?"

Belinda nodded. "A couple of times, early on, he did. But then we got pregnant and had Wyatt. And Aaron seemed to concentrate on his career more, you know, wanting to get ahead." She related the way in which Aaron had moved from a Branch Manager at Pine Tree Bank to an Investment Analyst with Greylock Mountain Bank, after taking some courses in investing. "He earned his MBA in Financial Investment Strategy," Belinda added proudly.

Jack recalled that Aaron had earned a B.S. in Finance from Northeastern and wondered if his MBA had come from there, too.

Belinda answered that question by explaining next that Northeastern offered an online MBA track curriculum to its Finance graduates. That was what Aaron had done, she said, and he had been steadily gaining in both reputation and clients since moving to Greylock Mountain Bank.

"Did Aaron ever have any problems with his investments?" Jack asked. "Anyone ever unhappy with something he did?"

Belinda shook her head and then looked Jack squarely in the eyes. "You're looking for motive, Detective," she said quietly, but firmly. "I don't think you'll find it among any of Aaron's banking associates."

Belinda went on to relate that between helping her bring up Wyatt, whom they realized early on was extremely bright, and his growing career at the bank, Aaron had really been too busy to think about resuming the outdoor adventures he'd spent his leisure time in as a younger man.

"We had also bought the house," Belinda concluded. "And you'll know what I mean if you own a home, when I say that there is always something to be done: painting, minor repairs, and then there were the improvements to the garden and deck...we never lacked for projects to do!"

"So what you're saying is that although your husband had enjoyed camping and hiking and so on as a young man, by the time he had married you, and you'd had Wyatt and bought your home, he was essentially concentrating on his family, his home and his career, and didn't camp any more," Jack summarized. "Is that right?"

"Yes."

Jack nodded, but frowned. "Well then, what made Aaron suddenly decide, after what—about eight or so years? — to go camping two weeks ago?" he asked, confused. "And to take Wyatt?" He paged through the file in front of him and lifted a couple of documents that contained copies of all of Aaron's charge slips. "He bought a lot of gear and equipment, all new," he added.

"Aaron thought that camping would maybe create an opportunity for some male bonding between him and Wyatt," Belinda confessed. "He did buy a lot of stuff, as he didn't have any of his old equipment, but he said he hoped he and Wyatt could go camping again in the future. If Wyatt liked it."

This was new, Jack thought: this hadn't come up in earlier interviews. "And why did Aaron think he needed to do that, I mean, the bonding: why now?" Jack continued. "Any particular reason?"

Belinda nodded almost eagerly. "Yes, of course." She sighed. "Aaron was—intensely proud—of Wyatt. We both were." She paused. "He was so very bright: tests at school put his IQ at 169. That's higher than Einstein's!" she added in a near-reverent whisper. "Wyatt was a good boy, but he was, well, different. He would spend hours and hours in his room, calculating long mathematical equations or devising his own languages and writing systems," she told Jack. "Or he'd play his violin, even composing songs. And he enjoyed it! He was never bored. We tried to get him interested in doing things outside, because it's healthy: fresh air, sunshine, you know… A counsellor at school suggested that if we asked Wyatt to help us in the garden by making labels for all the plants with their full Latin names and care requirements, that task would intrigue him, and get him outside. She also suggested that, because Wyatt didn't seem the least bit interested in shooting hoops or tossing around a softball, we explain the physics of those sports to him so he could relate more easily. Then maybe he'd be more interested."

Jack looked slightly bemused. "Did it work?" he asked flatly.

Belinda shrugged. "More or less: Wyatt did help us in the garden, and he really seemed to enjoy that. And he would go play ball with Aaron if Aaron asked, all the while analyzing his throws," she chuckled a little. "But his favorite thing was just doing his own stuff, in his room."

Jack recalled the whiteboard in Wyatt's room with the unintelligible symbols and equations on it, and nodded.

"But Wyatt was happy?" he asked.

"Oh yes, I think so. His counsellor at school explained that music, language and math are all closely related, which is why Wyatt enjoyed them," Belinda added, warming to her story. "He'd even begun to teach himself Latin after the plant project: said he loved conjugating verbs." She shook her head.

Jack smiled.

"Wyatt begged us for a violin for his seventh birthday, so we got him one, and he taught himself how to play. This year, he's—he was—" she faltered, "in the school orchestra, playing the violin because he's one of three who play well enough. The other two have been studying since they were toddlers, I think," she laughed. "But it just seems—seemed—natural for Wyatt."

Jack nodded and smiled some more. "And he and Aaron had never gone camping before two weeks ago?" he asked again.

Belinda shook her head. "No. As I told you, Detective, getting Wyatt to do outdoors stuff, well, you had to give him a reason to be interested in it. He wouldn't have hiked or camped just for the sake of hiking or camping, or even just to see beautiful scenery or wildlife," she continued. "You'd have had to make it a puzzle or a challenge he understood. "

"Like physics with the sports," Jack confirmed.

"Yes."

"And Aaron had never done that with his son: the camping or the hiking I mean."

Belinda shook her head again. "No. Not really. A few walks now and then in the forest nearby where Wyatt identified trees and categorized fallen leaves by shape, that kind of thing, " she murmured.

"So—what made Aaron decide to take Wyatt camping?" Jack asked for the third time. "Why now?"

CHAPTER SEVENTEEN

"A couple of weeks ago at dinner, Wyatt told us about some new six week courses being offered at his school. They're strictly enrichment courses, not for credit or anything, no grades. But Wyatt thought he'd like to take harp lessons."

"Harp?" Jack echoed, looking mystified.

Belinda nodded. "That was my husband's reaction," she commented a bit sadly. "I told him it was just something that had caught Wyatt's fancy and not to worry, but Aaron seemed to think that Wyatt was becoming too—introverted, perhaps? Too much involved in his own solitary pursuits: violin playing, his equations, his Latin and his languages, and now the harp. I think Aaron, although he was proud of Wyatt's intelligence, often wanted him to be, well, more like a regular boy," Belinda theorized. "More, um, male, if you know what I mean."

"He thought Wyatt might be gay?" Jack asked, frowning.

Belinda made a face and shook her head. "I don't think it was 'gay' exactly, although that might have been part of it. It's probably tougher for a father to accept a gay son than it is for a mother," she added thoughtfully. "But anyway, I think it was more that Aaron was afraid Wyatt's introversion would make him an object of ridicule in school. Make him different: odd, a geek, an egghead," she added, pronouncing the monikers with distaste and a little embarrassment.

"And he thought camping…"

"He thought camping might combat that, a little, anyway. It was a shared activity, and it was outdoors." She paused. "Aaron didn't want Wyatt to become a sissy," she summed up. "Even a genius sissy. Already there had been some bullying at school," she added, noting that the school administration had clamped down tightly and aggressively on the perpetrators. But it was still a worry. "So he thought, well, maybe camping would—"

"Toughen him up?" Jack finished for her. He could understand Aaron's feelings, and his fears. He wondered momentarily what it would be like to have a child who was so much smarter than the parents were. Then he thought about Gracie and the fact that he sometimes felt at a loss with her, for the same reason. Although usually Gracie could sense when she'd left him, or anyone else, behind, and had the good manners to back up and re-phrase whatever she was talking about in terms more easily comprehended. But you couldn't expect a child to do that.

Belinda nodded. "Yes."

"Do you—you probably don't—but do you know if Wyatt enjoyed it? Camping, I mean. Did Aaron call you, or text you to tell you how it was going that Friday when they set up camp?" Jack urged. Someone, somewhere had to know something about what had happened to that father and son in the forest. They had only been at the campsite a few hours: what could it have been, that resulted in their murders? Maybe Belinda had had a conversation with her husband or son that in retrospect could provide a clue.

"Aaron texted me to say they were fine, had set up camp, and that they were going to cook dinner soon," Belinda answered. "We'd agreed that they wouldn't text or call except to say they were set up and okay," she added. "Trying for the authentic camping experience," she continued, her tone just slightly ironic. "And anyway, the signal strength isn't very good out there, so texts were about all that would go through."

"What time was that, do you remember?" Jack asked. "That your husband texted," he added. He knew this had been gone over before, but…

"I can tell you exactly," Belinda replied cooperatively, and pulled her iPhone from her handbag. She touched the screen a couple of times and then handed the device to Jack.

On the screen was a text sent by Aaron from his iPhone to his wife on the evening of the Friday he and his son were murdered. 18:34, which was 6:34 p.m. The text read just what Belinda had paraphrased: 'Arrived, set up camp, Wyatt and I got firewood and we'll be cooking dinner soon. All is well. See you Monday afternoon. Love, A'

Jack had to agree that the message didn't seem obscure in any way and didn't give any clues about what would happen to the father and son in fewer than six hours from the time the text had been sent.

"Believe me, Detective, I've gone over and over it in my mind, everything, wondering," Belinda said now, and the calm of her demeanor began to waver. "I even looked through Wyatt's diary—you saw it, that notebook he writes in all the time?—she reminded Jack, who nodded. He recalled having seen the item among the things confiscated and examined by CSU from the crime scene. "But it's all just his usual gibberish, or numbers, nothing about anything out of the ordinary at the campground. Nothing."

Judge Joseph Norcross hung up the phone, a troubled look on his face. He sighed. Ever since his election to President Judge of Berkshire County after Judge Cranston resigned, he had never enjoyed phone calls from families of the incarcerated. But this one had been more emotionally difficult than usual: a young mother crying on the phone because her husband had been arrested the week before on DUI charges but she had not heard from him in four days.

She had just told the Judge that her husband Steven Starling had called her late Thursday, using his one phone call to tell her he had been picked up for DUI but would probably be home by morning, and would she call his boss and let them know he wouldn't be in on Friday?

Lisa Starling had done that, and her husband's boss had been very understanding; Steven Starling worked at Lee Lime on the production line. His absence, while it would be felt, could be accommodated for. And since Lisa had called him off duty in a timely fashion, no punishment was attached to his absence.

But when Steven hadn't returned home at all on Friday, Lisa had assumed he had been detained for some reason. All weekend, she told Judge Norcross, she'd thought that her husband's bail hearing would not happen until Monday morning.

Lisa Starling told Judge Norcross that she had called her husband off work again on Monday, then waited all day Monday for his return or for information. When nothing happened, however, she said she had begun to call the Courthouse to try and find out what was going on.

'I have a two year old and a four year old here at home,' Lisa had told the Judge in between sniffles. 'I can't exactly go looking for Steven, I'm stuck at the house and he's got the car. Or he did. I need to know where my husband is, and no one seems to know!' she had exclaimed, sounding desperate and nearly hysterical.

Judge Norcross had reflected that if his wife had called to tell him she'd been picked up for DUI and would likely be home the next day, and then hadn't returned for four more days, he would be more than just desperate and nearly hysterical.

So Judge Norcross had told Lisa Starling that he would personally get to the bottom of the matter and find out what was going on and where her husband was.

Now, he called the Jail, a direct line to the Warden's office.

"Yes, we have a Steven Starling," confirmed Warden Mick Jones. "He's on A Block. Why?"

The Judge explained.

"Let me pull his file," the Warden said.

Judge Norcross heard a drawer open, then the sound of files being shuffled. Then Warden Jones came back on the line.

"Unh…your Honor, I need to investigate this further and get back to you," Warden Jones said, his tone guarded.

"What's amiss?" Judge Norcross pounced. Something was wrong, he sensed it.

Warden Jones swallowed hard before answering. "There's a file with Inmate Starling's name on it," he answered, "but there is no intake paperwork in it."

"No paperwork in it?" echoed the Judge. "What do you mean? There has to be something."

"Well, there's the list of his belongings, and the list of the uniforms and shoes and bedding we issued him," the Warden explained. "Result of the strip search, Public Defender document, all of that, but no body receipt, no Criminal Complaint and no commitment form."

"Is it possible that paperwork is somewhere else? One of the secretaries might have it, perhaps?" the Judge asked quickly.

The Warden answered in the negative. He shifted in his office chair and pulled up the weekly schedule for the county jail. "When did you say Starling was supposedly arrested for DUI?" he asked the Judge.

"Thursday night, around nine or ten p.m. I think," Judge Norcross responded.

"Second shift last Thursday: shift supervisor was Corporal Hengist," the Warden informed Judge Norcross. He checked his office clock and the schedule again. "Hengist's due in today at three, he usually gets here about two thirty. I'll call him now, and find out what happened."

"Call me back the minute you've talked to him, and meanwhile, I want you to allow inmate Starling to call his wife, is that clear?" Judge Norcross asked, sounding very much like the former Marine he was.

"Yes, Sir," Warden Jones replied, and Judge Norcross disconnected.

CHAPTER EIGHTEEN
CHAPTER EIGHTEEN

"What do you know about a Steven Starling?" Gracie asked Jack without preamble. It was lunch time on Tuesday and Jack had taken her call as he'd been eating at his desk. He'd ordered a chicken club from the Sub Shop; they called every day to see if anyone in the courthouse wanted to order a delivered lunch, and the main switchboard operator kept a list. It was a convenient service Jack took advantage of at least once a week.

"Uhm…nothing. Why?" Jack asked, frowning as he tried to recall if the surname meant anything in particular to him. It didn't.

"Well, I just got a weird call from the *Intelligencer*," Gracie replied, sounding mystified. "Some woman called them, Lisa Starling, and said her husband is missing. Last she heard he'd been arrested for DUI, and he'd called her to tell her that, and said he was being taken to jail but would probably be home the following morning once he had his bail hearing," Gracie elaborated. "I guess he thought it would be ROR," she mused. 'ROR' stood for 'released on his own recognizance,' and was most usual in the case of a first offense with a low blood alcohol level.

"When was this?" Jack asked quickly.

"Thursday night. He didn't come home Friday, so Mrs. Starling thought he would probably have to spend the weekend in jail and be home Monday, but he never came home. Today, she's panicking, and apparently called Judge Norcross."

"She called the Judge?" Jack interjected, swallowing a bite of chicken and tomato.

"Yes, because she didn't make any headway at the prison: I guess they wouldn't tell her anything, which I don't understand, because the Inmate List is public information, isn't it?"

"Well, usually, Gracie, unless there's a high profile prisoner or something…" Jack replied, thinking. Starling? He did not recall that name at all.

"Well anyway then she called my paper. She probably called the *Gazetteer,* too," Gracie added sourly. "So, I wanted to see if you knew anything about him," she explained.

Jack sighed. "Gee, Gracie, no I don't I'm sorry," Jack answered honestly. "I'm as confused as you are." He paused. "I can call the Judge—I wanted to ask him about something else, anyway."

"Oh?" Gracie sounded relieved. "Okay. I'll see if the Warden will tell me anything," she added. She'd known Mick Jones for years, even done an undercover piece on the jail when she'd first started with the paper. They had always had a cordial working relationship. And the Inmate List was, after all, not private. If Jones refused to give her the List, she could always ask her friend Paula, the Prothonotary. Her office had a list of all the inmates, and it was updated daily.

Jack decided, upon hanging up with Gracie, to finish his lunch and then see if Judge Norcross were free. A few minutes later, he found himself buzzing the Judge's outer office door. He presumed someone inside ID'd him from the camera mounted over the door, because two seconds later the lock clicked open.

"Afternoon, all," he said, entering the large, airy space where the court reporter, a general secretary and Judge Norcross' paralegal/executive assistant worked at large desks separated by plexiglass dividers. "How is everyone?" he asked, smiling.

The three women of varying ages, all smartly attired and equally quick of mind, gave Jack cheery hellos.

"His Honor in?" Jack asked.

"He is—let me just see if he's free," Alma, the EA, told Jack, still smiling.

Jack was a favorite with the ladies of the Judge's Chambers, and always had been. He had also been instrumental in convincing the commissioners to approve the budget request from their office to have the new security system installed. The support staff as well as the Judge were grateful for Jack's no-nonsense testimony on their behalf, citing numerous incidents in other counties where enraged individuals had physically attacked members of the Judge's staff, and in one case, a Judge himself. Now that they had the security cameras, they could see who was outside the office complex door, and choose to allow entry, or not. Additionally, the walls surrounding the door had been reinforced with steel bars, and the door itself was solid metal, impervious to bullets, with a lock that couldn't be shot away.

Alma gave Jack the all clear seconds later, and Jack knocked lightly, once, on the inner sanctum door, then entered Judge Norcross' chambers.

The Judge was barely 45 and looked even younger than that, something he sought to counteract with a fairly stern mien. However, he had no need to do that with Jack, and so gave the Detective a broad smile and extended a hand.

"Jack! What brings you to my eyrie?" he asked jokingly.

Jack smiled back, shook hands, and sat in the proffered chair as the Judge sank back into his own black leather desk chair. "I have a question I thought you might be able to answer," Jack told the Judge, and explained the way in which he'd come across a Probation Officer evaluating his own client for the Public Defender. He added his research into Massachusetts State Law, and the Judge stayed his hand, which had been reaching for his thick copy of the Statutes.

"Melling said he would take care of it?" Judge Norcross asked, his light grey eyes keen.

Jack nodded. "Yes. But I thought you should know about it, since Probation is technically your purview," Jack replied. "And, if you want my opinion, I think the way we're doing things needs to be, erm, brought into line with the statute," he finished diplomatically.

Judge Norcross nodded, and Jack noticed the man's fine dark blond hair was freshly trimmed and still shorn in the traditional Marine Corps style. Maybe it was true that there was no such thing as a 'former' Marine.

"I agree," the Judge concurred.

"Good...any idea how this got started?" Jack ventured. "I mean, with Probation handling the evals?" he clarified.

The Judge shook his head. "It's been that way as long as I can recall—before my time, too." He paused. "I could ask Judge Cranston," he suggested, and Jack smiled. "But it was done that way in his time, too," he murmured.

"I could ask my Dad," Jack offered. It had not occurred to him before now to do that, since he had expected that Judge Norcross would know the history of the practice. But since he did not, Jack thought, his father—who had been the county's Senior Judge about a decade before—would probably know.

"Of course, Probation could, in effect, have been appointed as the designated entity tasked with evaluation," the Judge cautioned.

Jack agreed. "But even if that is so, I think it would be good to know who made that appointment, and why, and perhaps review whether or not the current method is the — erm—most expedient one," Jack added.

He had confided in the Judge his conversation with Felicia Laurenti, the Public Defender, and her claim that her office could do evaluation for about half of what Probation was costing the county. The Judge had looked surprised, but then eager to set the situation to rights.

CHAPTER NINETEEN
CHAPTER NINETEEN

The Warden had refused to take Gracie's call, something that she had to admit to herself could have happened at any time, and for any reason. However, given the whole Starling situation, she was suspicious.

She jumped in her Jeep and decided to drive into Pittsfield again, even though she'd already completed her 'courthouse rounds' and had been happily at home, typing up her articles for this week's paper when the call about Starling had come. Viewing the Inmate List was only done in person: telephone inquiries were not honored: a reasonable policy, Gracie thought, because otherwise the Prothonotary's office might do nothing all day but answer queries about the list.

It was inconvenient, but it wasn't the end of the world. And this way, she thought, maybe she could run up to Jack's office and see if he wanted to grab an early dinner. By the time she got to the courthouse and saw what she needed to see at Paula's, it would be nearly dinner time.

Gracie did just that, arriving at the DA's suite just as Millie was turning out the lights, ready to leave.

"Is Jack still here?" Gracie asked as she exited the elevator. She normally took the stairs, but with her ankle being, as she put it, 'stupid,' she chose the easier method of gaining two flights.

"He just left, Gracie," Mille said, sounding sad about it. "I'm surprised you didn't see him!"

"He probably took the west staircase," Gracie said, thinking aloud. "While I—" she gestured back to the elevator and then down at her ankle; below the hem of her jeans, the swollen joint encased in beige elastic was easy to spot.

"Oh, my!" Millie exclaimed, concern furrowing her brow. "Whatever did you do to yourself, Gracie?" she asked.

Gracie explained about the Morris Dance troupe and how she had come to sprain her ankle, but reassured Millie that it was just a sprain and would heal in a couple of weeks.

"Is it painful?" Mille asked, still tut-tutting and shaking her head.

Gracie shrugged. "Not really, unless I try to jump or run on it," she replied cheerfully. "I was hoping to catch Jack and see if he wanted to do an early dinner," she confided to Millie. "But I don't move as quickly as I normally do—I'll have to adjust for that until I'm all better," she ruminated, sounding annoyed.

"I think he said he was stopping at his parents' home before going on to his own," Millie informed her in a whisper.

Gracie grinned and put a quick hand on the woman's arm. "Thanks for that, Millie: I'll try to catch up with him there!"

She hobbled back into the elevator, Millie joined her, and they rode down to the ground floor together. There, they parted, and Gracie limped out to where she'd parked her Jeep, got in, turned over the engine, and headed off to the Drapers' home, just a few streets away.

The residential neighborhood surrounding the courthouse was quite upmarket. Venerable houses that had been built one or even two centuries before had been lovingly kept up or restored. Interspersed were newer dwellings, but even these were designed with the area's historic pedigree in mind.

Gracie passed faux Tudors, dark wooden Colonials and 'Salt Box' homes, and a few brick Federal style houses as she drove. She noticed that the trees were definitely turning; some early deciduous types were even dropping yellow leaves on the dark macadam, making whirling patterns that caused Gracie to smile as she piloted through them.

She signaled, then turned, making a quick right and another left, and was soon rolling up to the Drapers' gracious Federal house, complete with Palladian window over the porticoed front door. Ionic columns flanked the entrance and topped the three curved brick stairs leading up to the landing. Pots of brilliant scarlet geraniums alternated at the edges of the steps along with colonial lanterns she knew automatically switched on at dusk.

And parked just beyond all of this, on the long curving paved driveway, was Jack's navy cruiser. Seconds later, Jack himself exited the vehicle. When Gracie's Jeep pulled up behind him, the look of surprise on his face was worth every painful hurried hobble Gracie had had to make on her way to follow him.

"How did you know where I was?" Jack asked with a crooked grin. He was squinting in the early evening light.

"I have my sources," Gracie replied in a tone of affected mystery. She jumped out of her Jeep, trying very hard not to limp as she walked towards Jack.

He leaned down and bussed her quickly on the lips.

"I'd never doubt that, Gracie," Jack responded, still grinning.

She jutted her chin towards his parents' house. "You going to dinner?" she asked.

Jack shook his head. "Hadn't really planned on it. I have something I want to ask Dad, so I thought I'd stop by on my way home: why?"

"I had to go back to the Courthouse to check the Inmate List in person, so I thought I'd see if you wanted to do dinner," she murmured.

Together they walked up the path towards the front door.

"I need to talk to you about that Starling business," Gracie added.

"Did you find something out?" Jack asked quickly.

Gracie didn't have time to answer, because as they mounted the front steps, Jack's mother Marilyn opened the front door.

Several minutes later, Jack, Gracie, Jack's father Elton and his mother were all seated in the Drapers' gracious sea foam green and white living room, and supplied with drinks: 30 year old scotch for Jack and his Dad, and gin and tonic with a lot of freshly squeezed lime for Gracie and Marilyn.

Although they had protested that they were only there to ask a question or two, and had no intention of disrupting the Drapers' dinner or evening plans, Marilyn had insisted that now they were here, both Jack and Gracie stay.

'I can easily broil two more orange roughy filets,' she had said happily. 'And as always, there are tons of vegetables. Let me go set two more places!' she had offered merrily.

Jack and Gracie had just looked at each other and grinned. While initially Marilyn had disliked Gracie quite a lot, in the past few months her attitude had softened. Jack and Gracie both had sensed that Marilyn, for whatever reasons, was making a real effort to be cordial to Gracie. More than cordial, really: friendly. And Gracie was making efforts, too, which made the atmosphere whenever the elder Drapers were with Jack and Gracie much more pleasant.

Elton Draper, on the other hand, had always liked Gracie. So when his son and his girlfriend presented themselves this evening, the Judge had immediately welcomed them in and eagerly settled in to conversation.

Both Elton and Marilyn exclaimed as they watched Gracie hobble across their threshold, and tut-tutted and shook their heads as Gracie explained about her injury.

"I'm not especially graceful to begin with," Gracie confessed.

"In fact, you're a bit of a klutz," Jack put in with a crooked grin.

Gracie play punched his upper arm. "Shush!" She continued, referencing Morris Dance practice, and concluding by reassuring Jack's parents that there was no permanent damage to her ankle, just a bad sprain according to the X ray and the MRI. "I'm going to Dr. Grist, the chiropractor, three times a week, and he says he'll have me walking normally in three weeks," she finished.

Elton and Marilyn looked relieved, but Marilyn solicitously asked Gracie if she'd like an ice pack for her ankle —Gracie refused with a smile—and insisted that she at least put her foot up on an ottoman.

They sat in the Judge's study, and were given drinks, and without more delay, Jack asked his Dad about the set up with Probation making their own evaluations for Public Defender eligibility.

Elton Draper looked concerned for a moment, and repeated Jack's query. Gracie just looked dumbfounded and shut her mouth, which had popped open in surprise at Jack's revelation.

"You're sure that's still being done?" Elton asked Jack, frowning. He sipped at his scotch.

His son nodded.

"Hmmm…well, I recall when I was Senior Judge for the County, about ten years ago, Gracie, a bit before you moved out here, I'm guessing," he added in a polite aside.

Gracie smiled.

"At any rate, I was Senior Judge, and our PD suddenly died. You remember him, Jack: Donald Prestwick?"

Jack nodded. "I do. He was wonderful," Jack noted. "I was still the Pittsfield PD Chief, then," he added by way of orienting Gracie to this past history of their county.

She nodded, and sipped at her drink. What Jack and his Dad were discussing sounded like a huge red flag to her: conflict of interest, anyone? she thought, but kept silent and listened as the elder Draper spoke.

"Well, Prestwick's protégé, what was her first name? I don't recall. But her surname was hyphenated: Cowens-Mitchell," Elton Draper informed them.

"I remember her," Jack said in a tone that suggested he almost wished he didn't.

"Anyway," the Judge chuckled at his son's tone. "She was specially appointed to fill out Prestwick's term." He sighed. "She didn't do a—well, a stellar job, I would agree with you there," he noted wryly.

"And Felicia Laurenti beat her in a landslide at the next election for County Public Defender," Gracie crowed. She'd been around for that: it had been the first election in Berkshire County that's she'd been assigned to cover, and it had been fun. She'd always liked the current PD, and admired the way she argued on behalf of her clients in court.

"Right," Elton Draper said. "But go back to the time right after Prestwick died. Someone had to carry on with all the duties of the PD office, and there weren't boatloads of people from whom to choose," he noted wryly. "Cowens-Mitchell was selected; I am honestly not sure why, or how," he admitted. "But I do know that while people were, well, comfortable with Cowens-Mitchell, they knew her limitations and didn't want to overwhelm her. So some of the duties of the Public Defender were temporarily outsourced to other departments."

"That's when Probation got the job of doing the evals?" Jack surmised.

"Exactly. I forget now, but there were a couple of other things that got farmed out to other offices: nothing major, just an effort to streamline, so Cowens-Mitchell could get up to speed as quickly as possible."

Jack snorted derisively.

"And it was supposed to be temporary," his father repeated. "A few months, I think, at most," he added. The Judge finished his scotch and held up his empty glass in a silent invitation to Jack to have a second.

Jack, who had only drunk half his first glass, shook his head. "Well, didn't anyone think to mention to Cowens-Mitchell that the evals needed to be resumed by the PD's office?" Jack asked carefully. He didn't want to make accusations, but it seemed someone, somewhere in the Judicial Branch, should have written themselves a memo about this, to be dealt with at the appropriate time. "And who made that arrangement in the first place? Was it you, Dad?" he asked flatly.

His father shook his head. "Not me. It was Judge Cranston's idea. And it made sense, to a point. But as I say, it was meant to be temporary."

"And Judge Cranston never remembered later, to change it back?" Jack asked, trying not to sound accusatory.

His father sighed. "It appears not, Jack. I think Judge Cranston quite possibly had his hands full just then. If you recall, he adjudicated a number of high profile cases in his day, and this relatively minor administrative hitch probably just slipped his mind. And apparently, none of his staff or the Public Defender's staff made note of it, either, to change it back, I mean." He chuckled. "I can see why Probation would keep quiet about it, and hope it would continue: nice little chunk of change in their pocket, doing the evals."

Jack agreed, and filled everyone in on how much Probation made for doing the evaluations, and how the money was apportioned each year.

"But I'm surprised Laurenti didn't pipe up about it: she ought to know it's her purview, and she's been PD for a while now," Elton Draper suggested.

"Frankly, I think Felicia just thought that it had been set up that way. The law does allow for an 'entity' to be appointed by the PD's office, to do the evals. She probably thought that Prestwick had set it up that way. How was she to know that he hadn't, and that it had been a temporary measure instituted to make the transition easier on Cowens-Mitchell?" Jack asked. "She was practicing law here but also over in Hampshire County when all that happened, too. And, as you just said, Probation wasn't going to mention it if no one else did," Jack finished.

His father nodded. "Makes sense. And maybe I should have remembered about it, too, but honestly, I was Senior Judge: it wasn't my decision, and it wasn't my place to interfere in the way Judge Cranston ran his ship," Elton Draper finished calmly.

"But—what does this all mean, exactly," Gracie asked, concerned. "Does it call into question all the PD evaluations for the past few years?"

The Judge shook his head. "No, no. Except in a case like the one Jack mentioned, where the probation officer evaluates his own client for the PD. And Melling seemed to indicate that almost never happens, right?" he asked his son.

Jack nodded. "Yes, but I think I'm going to check into that, too," Jack murmured. He didn't know when he'd get the time to go back through years of Probation's paperwork, but he wanted to do it, just to be sure no mistakes had been made. "And, I'm also going to ask Judge Norcross to reverse the measure, effective this coming January, so we're back in line with state law," he added grimly. "Not to mention the fact that the PD's office will do the job for half what Probation is."

CHAPTER TWENTY

CHAPTER TWENTY

Dinner was out on the patio. As Marilyn said, they wanted to take advantage of every pleasant, warm evening while they could. "Winter's coming, even if tonight it doesn't feel like it," she reminded everyone as she served the dinner.

Gracie had asked to help, but Marilyn had looked scandalized.

'It's just a sprained ankle, I'm not infirm,' Gracie had joked. But the older woman had insisted that Gracie just sit with Jack and the Judge and 'relax,' and keep her ankle elevated. Gracie wasn't sure about relaxing, but she did as she was told and sat with Jack and his dad at the cast iron table, set with pumpkin colored placemats and coordinating linen napkins.

She was excited about the whole evaluation debacle, as she was calling it to herself, and was thinking about whom she could talk to for a story. The head of Probation, for starters. Then the Public Defender. And maybe even Judge Cranston, although she would have to be careful not to sound as though she were accusing him of anything.

She wasn't really: this had clearly been an oversight. But it was an interesting one. And if she could pull all this together in time for this week's edition, she'd have a nice scoop, as she was certain the *Gazetteer* knew nothing about this yet.

"You wanted to talk to me about Steven Starling, didn't you?" Jack asked Gracie at one point.

His father was pouring a light, crisp chardonnay and Marilyn was bringing out the plated dinners. She served Gracie first, then her husband, then her son, and then herself, and sat down.

"Who is Steven Starling?" Marilyn asked, curious.

Gracie sighed, and gave a fast explanation of what appeared to be the situation.

"You mean someone booked him into the jail with no paperwork?" Jack asked, quite shocked. That kind of sloppiness generally didn't happen at their county jail, not under Warden Jones, at any rate.

"Looks like it. I'm working on getting the names of the arresting officer and the booking officer," Gracie added. She tasted the fish. "Mmmm…this is really good, Marilyn: did you use a particular spice rub?" she asked. The fish was just a bit spicy and had an oriental tang.

Marilyn nodded and told Gracie what she had used on the fish, and Gracie smiled and said she would shamelessly copy the recipe. Marilyn looked very pleased.

"Is it possible the young man has—what's the phrase? —'done a runner?' " Elton Draper suggested as he ate. With the tilapia, Marilyn had served sautéed green beans and mushrooms, and a brown rice pilaf with garlic.

Gracie thought everything on her plate was delicious, and said so. Then, "well, he could have, of course, but his wife seems to think he's been lost in the system," she explained.

"The wife is always the last to know," Jack put in darkly, but with a half smile over at Gracie, who grinned back and shook her head.

"Yeah, yeah. Maybe. But I want to hear what the officers have to say about it," she insisted. She turned to Jack. "Did you ask Judge Norcross about Starling?" she asked, referring to their conversation earlier in the day.

"I did mention it," Jack replied, "but he said he had talked to Mrs. Starling already and was handling it. He didn't sound like he wanted to elaborate, and I didn't ask," Jack admitted.

Gracie had scraped her plate clean, and now drained her wine glass. When the Judge asked if she wanted a refill, she refused, reminding him that she had to drive home. She sat back in her chair, frustrated about the Starling case.

If the Warden didn't return her second call to him, asking about the schedule this time and not the inmate list, by tomorrow noon, she decided, she'd ask Jean if she could check the schedule at the jail and tell her who had been the shift supervisor when Starling had been brought in. Gracie thought she'd start there.

As for the arresting officer, well, it was the Pittsfield PD. Technically, their files were public record except in certain cases involving juveniles, or special circumstances. She'd have to make a point to stop by early the next morning.

"I heard you interviewed Belinda McGinley," Judge Draper said to Gracie as Marilyn served coffee and little biscotti.

"I did," Gracie agreed, happy to have something else to think about, and gave them all an outline of what the widow had said. She noticed Jack listening intently. "The sense I got was that Aaron wanted to share something that he had always loved as a boy and a young man, with his son," she concluded. "It all seemed perfectly normal, and pretty harmless." She paused. "I also think Aaron maybe wanted Wyatt to experience something different from his, well, his indoor and rather scholarly pursuits," Gracie added diplomatically.

Jack chimed in, saying that was more or less the impression he'd got from Belinda McGinley's interview with him that morning. He gave Gracie a very warm smile.

"Anything else jump out as a possible motive?" Judge Draper asked, "that you can tell us about, I mean," he added gravely. He was of course cognizant of the fact that his son, the County Detective, could only reveal so much about an ongoing case, even to him. He knew Jack and Gracie were scrupulous about what they shared with each other, as well.

Jack looked frustrated and shook his head. "Not yet. Their financials look clean, and despite having Aaron McGinley's investments for his Greylock Mountain Bank clients gone over with a fine toothed comb, nothing there looks like it would be motive."

"C'mon back, Gracie," Lindsey, one of Dr. Grist's techs, invited cheerfully. It was bright and early Wednesday morning, and Gracie was at the chiropractor's for another treatment. She was getting into a three times a week regimen now that the initial consult and treatment had been completed.

Gracie obediently hobbled after the young woman, who moved with enviable swiftness and ease.

"How's that ankle?" Lindsey asked as Gracie sat on the cushioned treatment table in the small room she'd been led to. Several such rooms made up the practice's office, and Dr. Grist was able to rotate among his patients efficiently.

Gracie made a face. "It's okay."

"You got to be patient," Lindsey counseled with a grin. "It'll heal, and a lot faster here than what the orthos were telling you," she added confidently.

Gracie nodded. "I am sure of that." She paused."Those are cool sneakers,"she noted, changing the subject and pointing to the multi colored footwear that Lindsey was sporting. "What brand are they?"

Lindsey told Gracie the brand.

"I'll have to get a pair: they will go with everything," she said with a grin. The sneakers were black, but covered in brightly colored streaks and dashes of fluorescent green, pink, red, aqua, yellow and purple. Even though Gracie didn't wear sneakers, or 'trainers' as she called them, a lot, she did have a couple of pair. But these were truly eye catching, and unusual: right up Gracie's street!

"Well, they sure let people see you coming," Lindsey returned with an answering grin.

Lindsey said they were going to do the ice/electrical muscle stimulation on Gracie's ankle first, and then Dr. Grist would be in to work on range of motion in the joint. Positioning her leg so Gracie's ankle was not under any stress, Lindsey placed electrical leads in a few key spots, then plopped a soft ice pack over the joint.

She switched on the electrical stimulation unit and adjusted it until Gracie said the pressure was good, then left.

Gracie sighed. Between the ice and the 'stim,' which she always said felt like little alien fingers massaging her, she felt relaxed, so she lay back on the table, closed her eyes, and let her mind wander.

Her next stop was the Pittsfield PD where she hoped Ms. Wolter, the secretary, could give her a copy of the Starling arrest report. She'd had a short, curt message from the Warden that morning, who must have called her when he knew she wouldn't be answering her iPhone: the call had come just after six a.m. His message had just said that he couldn't reveal details of the jail's staffing to her.

So Gracie had texted her friend Jean, and asked her if she could check to see who'd been on second shift the previous Thursday when Starling had allegedly been booked in. With a bit of luck, Jean could get her that information, and identify the shift supervisor and the booking officer. Gracie would then contact each of those people personally, and ask them if they knew about the Starling incident. She would not, of course, reveal Jean as her source, and just to make it look good, she would call a couple of other people who were 'regulars' on second shift.

Meanwhile, Gracie wanted to identify the arresting officer, and she needed to get the report from the Pittsfield PD to do that.

Then, with both the booking officer and the arresting officer identified, Gracie would interview the latter if he or she would speak with her, and file a story for the *Intelligencer*.

About a half hour later, Gracie limped into the Pittsfield PD. The building, which housed a law library, several offices, a small 'night court' style courtroom, and a few holding cells, dated from the early 1800's. The front door was accessed by six shallow granite steps flanked by old fashioned globe lamps with the word, 'POLICE,' stenciled across their fronts. Gracie had always loved the architecture.

"Good morning, Ms. Wolter," Gracie said cheerfully to the matron who staffed the front desk.

The generously proportioned older lady looked up, her fine dark brows raised in expectation. The brows didn't quite match the tightly crimped hair, which was a soft shade of suede brown, and neither dye job did much to fool anyone about Ms. Wolter's age, which was nearer 70 than she would admit. However, the woman ran a very tight ship and Gracie had often thought that the Pittsfield PD would be a shambles without her.

"Why, Gracie!" she exclaimed. "Weren't you just here yesterday? Shouldn't you be staying off that ankle?" she asked in quick succession, concerned. A thin vertical line appeared between her brows and she looked sternly at Gracie.

Gracie shrugged and smiled. "Yes, I was, and yes, I will do exactly that, but first I need to see if you can find a file for me," she answered prettily, and explained what she needed.

The secretary gave Gracie a long look. "I've seen that report," she murmured. "But the arresting officer, Mike Bondino, says he hasn't finished with it," she added, choosing her words carefully. "So it's not on the news board yet," she finished, referring to the clipboard containing OTNs available to the press and the public.

"What's he doing, writing 'War & Peace'?" Gracie asked skeptically, plopping into a hard wooden chair to wait. "It'll be a week tomorrow. Surely that's enough time to write out, what, an affidavit of probable cause?" she queried, impatient.

"One would think that, wouldn't one?" Ms. Wolter returned, one half of her mouth quirking up in an odd smile. Gracie noticed that the older woman's lips were colored in an attractive coral shade, and that she wore discreet pearl earrings with a summer weight suit in a muted plaid seersucker. Ms. Wolter had quite the sense of decorum, and sense of 'place,' as it were, Gracie thought to herself. She wondered idly if Ms. Wolter knew Millie, the DA's secretary: they seemed of about the same vintage. It was likely, she thought.

"Yes, erm, well, hmmmm…" Gracie stalled. "It's just that I'm on deadline and I'd really like to get this story filed for this week's paper…" she offered. Then on instinct, "what do you think of the curfew and roadblock situation?" she asked conversationally. "Have you had any issues with it?"

Ms. Wolter chuckled. "At my age, young lady, I don't stay out past 10 p.m. much, and certainly not during the work week," she returned cheerily. "However, I have seen a couple of roadblocks up north of here," she admitted, "the other afternoon when I went to my sister's for dinner. She lives in North Adams."

Gracie nodded.

"What about you?" Ms. Wolter asked then. She began tapping at her computer as she and Gracie chatted.

"Well, last night after dinner at Judge Draper's with Jack and of course Mrs. Draper," Gracie began, just a bit formally, and thinking that a little name dropping couldn't hurt, "I did run into a road block on my way home!" she finished merrily.

"No! Really?" Ms. Wolter was fascinated. "What did they do? Did they actually stop you?" she queried.

"Yes," Gracie replied. Then she explained that the roadblock had been set up on Outlook Avenue, south of the Forest where the murders had taken place. "My driveway is off Bluff Road, which is off Outlook," she went on. "There's really no other way to get to my house other than Outlook to Bluff, with a vehicle at any rate," she clarified. She added that after showing her ID to the police, they had done a cursory search of her Jeep, with her permission, and she'd been allowed to go on her way.

"Well, it appears they are being thorough, at any rate," Ms. Wolter noted, sounding satisfied. She pushed a key on her computer and a moment later the printer began clicking and whirring to life. A single page shot out seconds later and the secretary handed it to Gracie. "This is what we have on that arrest so far," she said in a circumspect tone. "It's in the computer, so technically, it *is* public record. It's not much. But I've known you to make a story out of far less, Gracie," she added kindly.

Gracie took the report, which had 'PRELIMINARY' in large letters across the top, and which was indeed quite scant, and nodded. "Thanks!"

CHAPTER TWENTY-ONE

As Gracie was driving home from Pittsfield, Jean called. Loathe to drive and talk on the phone, Gracie pulled over to answer.

"I was off that night, so Hengist ran the shift," Jean said without much preamble. Burt Hengist was the alternate Corporal/Shift Supervisor on the evening shift. "I called him and told him I'd heard a rumor about some guy being jailed without paperwork, and he said a trainee had booked Mr. Starling in."

"Didn't Hengist notice there was nothing in Mr. Starling's file?" Gracie asked.

"Hengist is saying that Dinkelaub, that's the trainee, Norman Dinkelaub, never gave the file to him. He was still booking Starling in when the shift ended at 11 p.m."

"But—didn't Hengist ask for it?" Gracie asked, frustrated.

"Well… he says he did," Jean replied. "But then he said he told the next shift supervisor, on third shift, about the issue and was told that he would handle it."

"Oh, and who was that? Third shift supervisor, I mean," Gracie asked.

"It was Greg Simon," Jean replied. "He's the regular Corporal on third," she added informatively.

"So I should call him?"

"I would," Jean advised.

When Gracie arrived home, she gave Pumpkin a perfunctory greeting and settled down at her desk with the OTN Ms. Wolter had given her, and her phone. The OTN, or Official Tracking Number, listed Starling's vital statistics and personal contact information, and gave 'routine traffic stop for moving violation' and 'suspicion of DUI' as the cause for the traffic stop and then the arrest.

The four sentence notation accompanying the OTN—Gracie would hardly call it an Affidavit—said that the officer of record, Mike Bondino, had been in his patrol car and in uniform, doing regularly scheduled traffic monitoring when he had noticed the defendant, Steven Starling, failing to stop at a stop sign. Bondino had added that one of Starling's tail lights had not been illuminated, and so the officer had pulled Starling over.

Upon approaching the vehicle and the defendant, Officer Bondino wrote that he smelled a strong odor of alcohol and asked Starling if he had been drinking. The last sentence noted that Starling had freely admitted that he had been at a local bar and had had a couple of whiskeys, and that he voluntarily took a field sobriety test which gave his BAC at about twice the legal limit.

As far as Gracie knew, there should have been a copy of the commitment order signed by the Magistrate on call, a receipt for the 'body' as they termed the defendant taken into custody and remanded to the jail, and a printout from the field sobriety 'breathalyzer' machine in the file as well, to supplement the skimpy OTN.

Her first call was to Officer Bondino. Luckily, Gracie had his number from long before, when Jack had still been Pittsfield Police Chief. She hoped it had not changed, and was delighted with Mike Bondino answered on the second ring.

After apologizing for contacting him at home and explaining that she was on deadline, Gracie began her pitch. "I'm hearing rumors all over town about this guy Starling being arrested and sent to jail without paperwork," Gracie told Bondino. She added that the *Gazetteer* had been contacted, as well as her own paper, and was gratified to hear Bondino groan at the thought. "Well anyway, Officer, I just wanted to get the truth of the matter from you, the arresting officer, so my paper can print what really happened and put this silliness to rest," she told him sympathetically. "It seems people are so quick to jump on the bandwagon, criticizing the police," she added, "when really, they should be thanking them for being willing to put their lives on the line to keep us all safe!"

She really did feel that way, of course, but thought that mentioning her opinion at this juncture might put Bondino at ease and also in a good enough mood to speak with her.

Her approach was effective.

"Yeah, Gracie, I'll tell you, we aren't the most popular people in town at the best of times," Bondino admitted grumpily. "And this curfew and roadblock stuff doesn't make it any better."

Gracie put in that she'd been stopped at a roadblock the other evening, and that it had only been a couple of minutes and she'd been on her way.

"Well, that's you, Gracie—I can call you Gracie, right?" Bondino asked anxiously.

"Sure."

"Well, as I say, that's you. But I tell you, I can't wait to see what kind of shit—pardon me—uhm, flack, we get once the thermal imaging flyovers start," he added, grumbling.

Gracie had been unaware that the manhunt for the shooter of Aaron and Wyatt McGinley had expanded in such a high tech way. Certainly Jack hadn't made reference to any thermal cameras coming on board. Maybe he didn't know, since technically the Sheriff's Department was handling the search. Gracie shook herself out of her contemplation and focused again on what Bondino was saying. But she made a mental note to check into the thermal camera tip as soon as she could.

"I remember you from when Jack Draper was the Chief," Bondino was reminiscing. "You still with him?" he asked chattily.

Gracie noted that she and Jack were still 'very good friends,' which was all she was telling anyone at this point, and returned to the subject at hand. "So—tell me about the traffic stop with Starling," she urged.

Bondino told her exactly what she had just read on the OTN. This meant that, although Gracie had the OTN as backup, she could write her article using Bondino as her source and quoting him: no need to involve Ms. Wolter, who had been operating firmly in a grey area when she'd given Gracie an OTN that had not been marked 'complete.'

"So, when you brought Mr. Starling to the jail…did you have a commitment order from the magistrate on call?" Gracie asked.

Bondino said that Magistrate Robertson—the one the Courthouse staff called 'wonder boy'— had said he would fax the order in to the Pittsfield PD, but that so far no such order had arrived. "I keep calling him every day," Bondino said of the magistrate. "His secretaries say they haven't seen hide nor hair of it. That's why I marked the file 'incomplete,' " he clarified, sounding frustrated.

"I see," Gracie told him. "Is it usual to commit with just the promise of an order being faxed in?" Gracie asked ingenuously. She knew it was pushing the limit of the law, but wanted to hear what Bondino would say.

A veteran of nearly 15 years on the force, Bondino sighed. "It's not usual, but if it's the middle of the night, we will just call the Magistrate and if it's a routine thing, we let him fax the paperwork in the next morning. I've never known it to be a problem before," he added morosely. "Just my luck."

"So, because this was a routine stop and a fairly straightforward DUI," Gracie summarized, "I mean, no doubt Mr. Starling was intoxicated, and there was good cause for the initial traffic stop," she explained, "you felt that it was within reason for the Magistrate to say he would fax the commitment order in the next morning."

"That's about it," Bondino agreed. He sounded marginally cheerier. The way Gracie had phrased it, Magistrate Robertson was mostly to blame, a fact not lost on the Pittsfield Police Officer.

"So then you brought Starling to the jail," Gracie coaxed.

Bondino said that the 'kid' who was doing the book-in was really flustered. "I explained to him that the jail would get a faxed commitment order in the morning, but he didn't seem to know what I meant," Bondino said.

"Didn't he give you a receipt for Mr. Starling?" Gracie asked, eliminating the 'body' terminology. She knew the police officer knew what she meant.

"Nah, he couldn't even find one," Bondino returned, sounding mildly disgusted. "They oughta have book-in files all ready to go, with all the paperwork you need to fill out," he opined. "That's how they do it at the State Pen. But they don't here: you have to know what forms you need, and then assemble them yourself."

"Oh!" Gracie was surprised: that sounded quite inefficient, not something she thought of when she thought of Warden Jones. She'd have to make the suggestion to Jean and ask her to bring it up with the Warden.

"And this kid, he wasn't even sure what forms he needed. So I told him, just send over the copy of the receipt when he got it done."

It was after noon and Gracie needed sustenance, so she took time out to grab a quick lunch. A few salad greens, sliced tomato and hummus in a spinach wrap and a cup of coffee would do her very nicely, and it took her less than fifteen minutes to make it and eat it, and then she was back at her desk with the coffee steaming fragrantly at her elbow.

Before finishing up her research into the Starling incident, Gracie wanted to confirm what Bondino had most likely let slip about the thermal imaging 'flyovers.' She called the Sheriff's office, and was pleased when the Sheriff himself, Ned Shermayne, answered.

"Your secretary's gone to lunch?" Gracie queried sympathetically.

"Out sick with a really bad cold, and I think she gave it to me," Shermayne replied with a lugubrious snort of his sinuses.

Gracie made sympathetic noises. "I always swear by chicken soup, plenty of garlic, and rest," she advised, adding that she also used two holistic immune system boosters at the first sign of a cold or 'flu. She gave Shermayne the brand names and waited while he wrote them down.

"Thanks, Gracie: I'll pick those up on the way home and take them tonight," he snuffled. "Hope they work," he added grimly.

"I do too, Sheriff. I don't want to take up too much of your time, but I was just checking up on the search for the shooter in the McGinley murders," she explained. "I know the roadblocks and curfew are still in place," she continued.

"Anything else being tried in efforts to locate the guy?" she asked innocently.

Shermayne sighed. "We contacted Springfield and got a thermal imaging camera sent down," he informed her, and Gracie did a silent fist pump on her end. Pumpkin, who was waiting near the alcove where Gracie worked, hoping to be served an early dinner, gave her mistress a peculiar look.

"Now I'm contacting local pilots to see if anyone has ever used one, or is at least willing to fly over Greylock State Forest in a grid search while someone else operates the camera," Shermayne concluded, sounding aggrieved.

"Are you having trouble finding someone?" Gracie asked, surprised. There were several private pilots who used the Pittsfield Municipal Airport. It was a Class G facility, and was fairly busy for a small place. It was where Jack had done much of his training for his pilot's license, which he'd achieved a few months before.

"They're all pretty expensive, and while this manhunt is a priority, I don't have an unlimited budget," Shermayne explained.

"Jack's a pilot," Gracie offered. "Why not ask him if he'd be willing to do it? At least that would mean you'd only have to pay for the plane rental," she suggested. Of course, that was the most expensive part of the deal, but at least if Jack did the flying, the Sheriff's department would save some money.

"I didn't know Draper was a pilot," Shermayne commented. He sounded a little in awe. "I'll ask him! Thanks, Gracie."

After confirming that the thermal imaging search was something she could put in the newspaper, Gracie hung up and returned to the Starling story. It was time to call the third shift supervisor, Greg Simon. She had a momentary pang of guilt about calling when he might be sleeping, but then realized she had one hour and five minutes to file her article and dismissed the pang.

Simon answered on the second ring, and sounded remarkably chipper. After asking if she'd awakened him, and hearing to her admitted relief that she had not since it was his day off, Gracie explained the reason for her call.

"Dinkelaub is new," Simon began. "Only been working at the jail for a couple weeks. This was his first book-in, and yeah, I'm sure he was nervous: everyone is. When we came on shift, he was still trying to find Starling a uniform and canvas shoes," he chuckled. "And he'd been down in the booking room for almost an hour."

"So did your officer take over?" Gracie queried.

"Yes."

"What about the receipt for the body?"

Simon sighed. He'd gone over this with the Warden just that morning when he'd been going off shift and the Warden had been coming in for the day. "My officer, Kent, says Dinkelaub told him the body receipt had been sent with Officer Bondino, who would send back our copy."

"But Bondino said—" Gracie began.

"Yes, I know: Bondino says Dinkelaub couldn't find the body receipt form, and said when he did he would fill it out and send Bondino's copy to the Pittsfield PD. CO Kent says that Dinkelaub told him he'd given the form to Bondino who was going to send back our copy. I don't know whether Kent misunderstood or Dinkelaub mis-spoke, but somewhere wires got crossed," Simon admitted.

"And were you told that the magistrate was going to fax his commitment order along with the Criminal Complaint in to the Pittsfield PD?" Gracie prodded.

"Yeah, that message we got." Simon sighed again. "Anyway, I put a letter in Kent's file because he should never have let a new inmate come into the blocks without any intake paperwork." Simon didn't sound happy.

"Off the record, did you get a reprimand from the Warden?" Gracie asked sympathetically. To her, this whole thing seemed like a series of stupid mistakes and mixups, but in a situation where the alleged criminal had been charged with something more serious than a DUI, like burglary or murder, even a run of the mill defense attorney could get the whole case dismissed on the strength of errors like these.

"I did," Simon admitted. "Letter in my file, too."

"Well, I'm sure Dinkelaub will be spoken to about it, as well, even though he's just a trainee," Gracie said calmly. "And maybe some good will come of all of this," she finished.

She didn't tell Simon that Officer Bondino had shared with her that he was being given a day off without pay for his laxity about the commitment paperwork: that wasn't her tale to tell. However, she hoped to herself that someone—maybe the Judge?—would also take Magistrate Robertson to task for his laziness. If he'd got out of bed and gone downstairs to his home office's fax machine, and taken care of the commitment form right away, it was possible that some of this debacle would have been averted. At least the jail would have a commitment form, if nothing else.

After saying goodbye and thanking Simon, Gracie took a deep breath and put a call in to the Warden. She had 45 minutes now to write her article: the Warden's confirmation of what she'd been told by Bondino and Simon was the last thing she needed.

CHAPTER TWENTY-TWO

"That was some article!" came Jack's voice early Thursday. Gracie's iPhone had issued its current ringtone—a trumpet voluntary she was fond of—and she'd rolled over in bed and grabbed the device. It was 7:30 a.m., quite early; even though Jack usually called her every morning, he generally called at least an hour later than this.

"What article?" came Gracie's sleepy answer. She yawned.

"Still in bed?" Jack teased, but he felt his heart rate speed up at the thought.

"Mmmmph," averred Gracie.

Pumpkin, who had been at the foot of the bed in her customary spot, had padded over to say good morning, as well, and was presently sitting on Gracie's bladder. Good incentive to rise, Gracie thought as she chivvied the cat off, flung the duvet aside, and stretched before swinging her feet to the floor. Her ankle was a lot less swollen, and she felt cheered.

"The one on that whole Starling thing," Jack answered.

Gracie walked carefully towards the bathroom, still favoring her right ankle, as she answered. "Well, Warden Jones confirmed everything," she told Jack. "I don't think he was happy about it, but he didn't want to outright lie to me, so he kinda had to confirm what I'd found out, and been told," she explained.

Her article had gone live on the *Intelligencer*'s website late the evening before, and would appear in the print edition on Friday.

"It really makes everyone look, well, sloppy," Jack commented. "Especially Robertson."

Gracie chuckled, shrugged into her terrycloth dressing gown, and headed downstairs, two-footing the steps. That was getting old, she thought as she clumped down, but at least she was getting better at it. Pumpkin escorted her, tail high, and waited at the foot of the staircase. Then the long haired orange tabby trotted on ahead, down the parquet floored hall and through the green baize door, which separated the kitchen area from the rest of the house. It seemed as though Pumpkin was convinced that her mistress had forgotten the location of her food bowls. "Yes. I hope the Judge disciplines him somehow for his laxity," Gracie continued as she followed her cat and pushed through the swinging door.

Arriving in the kitchen, she switched on the coffee maker, which she'd set up the night before, and put fresh food and water down for Pumpkin, who began crunching away quite happily.

"You're calling early," Gracie told Jack as she opened her fridge and reached for the bottle of organic vegetable juice she'd begun to drink in the morning: it was good to wash down her multi vitamin.

"Oh, I must've forgotten to tell you, what with everything else going on," Jack replied, "I'm spending the morning at the Pittsfield Elementary school."

Gracie chuckled again. "Really? Why?"

Jack explained that there was a new bullying prevention initiative in the schools, and part of the program was to involve local law enforcement. His part was to speak to third and fourth graders about bullying, and how the law addressed the issue.

"No, you never told me about that," Gracie replied, somewhat annoyed. "That would be a great article for the paper," she continued, finishing her juice and glancing at the clock. It was quarter to eight. "Who's the initiative sponsored by?" she queried, and as Jack gave her the particulars, she poured her coffee, added organic half and half, and began slurping it down.

She would email her editor about the new program at the schools—maybe there had been a press release on it, maybe not. The initiative was from the Massachusetts Commission on Crime and Delinquency, and it provided funding to local elementary schools across the state to have special speakers and programs on bullying during this week. The goal was not only to give students information on and tools to deal with various kinds of bullying, both emotional and physical, but also to help teachers and staff identify children who might be victims of bullying.

At any rate, Gracie thought she could get to the school, snap some photos of Jack with the kids and teachers, get some basic info, and write something up. It wouldn't be in time for this week's issue, which was already at the printer's, but it would be great for the following week.

"I'm at the school from 8:15 a.m. through the lunch period," Jack told her now. "Are you really coming down?"

"Yes, of course: as I said, it's a great story for the paper," Gracie repeated. She finished her coffee, put the mug in the sink, and grabbed an apple: it was one of the first ones from her favorite local orchard, R&J Orchards, and it was tart and sweet and juicy. She munched it quickly as she and Jack discussed a couple of other things—weekend plans, the McGinley case—and then said goodbye. She said she'd see him in an hour or so, and, tossing the apple core in her composter container, Gracie once more two-footed it upstairs to shower and dress. She hoped that in a few more days, perhaps, she'd be able to go up and down stairs 'like a grownup,' but for now, she would be careful and do everything she could to help her ankle recover and heal.

Not exactly what she'd planned for today, she considered as she washed her hair with vanilla scented shampoo, but stopping at the school would just push her errands into the afternoon instead of the morning, and the garden work she'd set out for herself into the late afternoon or early evening. Fortunately, in September, it stayed light late enough for her to get some things done, even into the dinner hour. Even though, she grimaced, she moved more slowly than usual right now, thanks to her ankle.

Gracie was able to explain to the Elementary Office staff why she was there and was given permission to sit in on part of Jack's session with the fourth grade classes. She was impressed with the way he handled some of their questions and got a couple of good shots to use with her article. Her pictures showed Jack and one or two of the teachers, but showed only the backs of children's heads, to protect their privacy.

At the break, Gracie took a moment to speak with a couple of the teachers about the bullying initiative and then approached Jack.

"You're really good at this," she said quietly, but with a big smile.

"Thanks, Gracie," Jack answered, looking a bit embarrassed.

"Have you had training?" Gracie asked with a gesture that encompassed the multi purpose room where the children had been seated for the program.

Jack answered that he had done a couple of seminars offered by the MCCD on bullying. Of course, he was also familiar with the way the problem manifested itself in

Berkshire County, since he investigated any cases that came to court.

"I was worried that the kids would be too young to really understand what we were talking about," Jack said, low. "Or that they were too young to be told about stuff like this. But they know all about it—"

"Some first hand, I think, from what I heard and saw just now," Gracie put in, her tone solemn. "And it can be so cruel," she went on. "And really nasty, physically," she added with a moue of distaste.

Jack just sighed. "I don't remember it being like this when I was in grade school," he commented as they started for the door. The next program was being held in a different room, with third graders.

Gracie nodded. "I don't either," she agreed.

"You're still limping," Jack commented, looking pointedly at Gracie's ankle. It was more swollen than it had been that morning, since Gracie had been walking on it, but it wasn't as swollen as it had been, and although she was still limping, she wasn't limping as badly.

At least, that's what Gracie thought, and that's what she told Jack. "Dr. Grist said that in three weeks I'll be walking normally," she reminded him. "It's only been one week."

Jack made a noise that suggested to Gracie he was unconvinced and Gracie tried not to limp as they gained the corridor.

The problem was, when she did that, she felt as though she was stressing her knee and the rest of her leg, so frankly, she thought she'd rather limp than injure another joint.

"Are you icing it, and putting it up?" Jack asked.

Gracie sighed. "You sound like your mother," she quipped. "When I can, Jack: clearly, my lifestyle doesn't exactly permit me to sit around all day with my foot on a pile of pillows, and an icepack on my ankle!" she retorted in defense.

"I just meant, in the evenings, when you're finished running around for the day," Jack parried.

Gracie shrugged. "I do, when I remember," she murmured. Mostly, she forgot.

Jack gave her a look.

"Listen, Sheriff Shermayne will probably be calling you today," Gracie said brightly, changing the subject. "He wants to use an aerial thermal imaging camera to look for the guy who shot the McGinleys, but he needs a pilot. I told him maybe you'd do it free if his office pays to rent the plane, as his budget is limited," she explained.

Jack looked intrigued. "Where'd he get the TI camera?"

"Springfield," Gracie answered.

A teacher approached them, apparently intent on escorting Jack to his next talk, with the third graders.

Gracie and Jack said a hasty goodbye, and Gracie did her best to walk normally down the hall until she turned the corner, just in case Jack watched her leave. She appreciated his solicitude, but she knew that only time would heal her sprained ankle and she had faith in her chiropractor. She would heal her own body her own way, and sometimes she felt Jack's criticisms were more annoying than helpful.

CHAPTER TWENTY-THREE

Jack stopped into the Sheriff's office on his way up to his own, once he had finished at the Elementary School. He thought the morning's sessions with the students had gone well, and had received quite a lot of praise from the teachers involved.

Gracie's tip about the thermal imaging flyover of Greylock Forest had intrigued him, and he decided to grab his favorite Italian 'grinder' from the Sub Shop, see the Sheriff, and then eat his lunch at his desk while he caught up on what would no doubt be a large pile of messages from the morning.

Sheriff Shermayne was not in his office, however, so Jack just left a message with his secretary, and ran up the two flights of stairs to the DA's suite on the third floor of the Courthouse.

Millie greeted him with a smile, and introduced him to Pamela, a new hire for the office, and a legal document specialist. While Millie was the Head Secretary, Pamela would provide backup when Millie was not there, as well as work directly with the DA's Legal Aide, Phyllida.

Jack knew Phyllida was seriously overworked, and was only too happy to see that she was finally getting some help. Jack did most of the legwork and investigations for cases in the office, but Phyllida did most of the paperwork.

Jack accepted the raft of pink message slips Millie handed him and headed for his office. The DA and Phyllida were in court, at that morning's DUI adjudications, so Jack could expect about another half hour of peace and quiet before Court broke for lunch and Popovitch returned to the office.

Jack unwrapped the sub and took a couple of bites before he began to return the phone calls.

One was from Lisa Starling, just calling to thank Jack because the problem with her husband's paperwork had been straightened out. She told Jack in her upbeat, grateful message, that she and her husband had met privately with Judge Norcross who had apologized on behalf of the county for the snafu. Mrs. Starling also told Jack that Judge Norcross had released Steven Starling from jail, noting that he had served the minimum required for his level of DUI arrest.

Jack smiled: it was nice, he thought, when things worked out well. After what he'd been through, Starling would probably think twice before driving after even having a couple of beers at a local bar, too, which was all to the good. From what he'd gathered from talking to Lisa Starling, this had been an isolated incident on her husband's part, and Jack knew that, even though he had a zero tolerance policy for drinking and driving, anyone could make a mistake.

Jack turned back to his lunch: as always, the Sub Shop had done a great job: fresh bread, fabulous Italian cold cuts and cheeses, with crisp lettuce and savory tomatoes, all brushed with garlic oil and toasted in southeast Massachusetts and Rhode Island 'grinder' style. It wasn't something he indulged in too often, as it was more calorie laden than he liked. But it was a nice treat.

He'd just started on the second half of the sandwich when he heard the scanner on his credenza go off. The tones were many, and strident. Not five seconds later, both the office phone and Jack's mobile rang.

He chewed and swallowed quickly, and answered. Two minutes later he was wrapping the remainder of his lunch and tossing it in the small fridge in a corner of his office. With a practiced move, he grabbed a chilled bottle of water from the same fridge's door rack, shut the door with his foot, and hurried out of the DA's suite.

"Tell anyone who calls, I'm on my way," Jack said to Millie and Pamela as he whisked by.

Both women nodded, then busily began fielding the calls that had started to come in rapid succession.

Gracie ran her errands—or in her case, she wryly thought to herself, she 'hobbled' her errands—and arrived home about 2:30 p.m. Since she'd grabbed a quick lunch at Whole Foods before doing her shopping and making her other stops, all she had to do was put her groceries away as well as the other items she'd picked up. Then she intended to get outside and begin the gardening she needed to do. She had no doubt that this task, like most others right now, would take her longer than usual.

The zinnias and dahlias weren't going to dead head themselves, she reminded herself as she changed into work clothes and limped to the mud room where she kept her gardening shoes, gloves and secateurs. The temptation to check her iPhone was strong, but she told herself that she would give herself a break after about an hour in the garden, and could check her messages then. After all, her paper was put to bed for the week and technically she had nothing else to cover until next week.

That was the reason that Gracie didn't hear until late Thursday afternoon about the rather awful homicide that had interrupted Jack's lunch. She spent nearly two hours in the garden, but had achieved more than she'd anticipated, despite her ankle: all the annuals had been dead headed, as she'd planned, but she'd also cut back the irises. This was a back breaking job when done by hand, which Gracie did, and she was fantasizing about a glass of pinot grigio and a relaxing soak in her hot tub—with her ankle propped up on towels at the rim, and an ice pack on it, when she finally trudged into the mud room and divested herself of her gardening gear.

As she sucked down a glass of well water—always smart to hydrate before drinking, Gracie knew, especially since lunch had been a while ago—she picked up her iPhone and accessed her voicemail. There were two messages, both from Jack.

The first noted that he was en route to a '20' in Peru Township, which was Jack-speak for a crime scene. Peru Township was east and slightly south of Gracie's house, on the border with Hampshire County. The next message was more urgent; although Jack was always careful about what he said over the telephone, and especially over mobile telephone connections, which could be very easily hacked, his voice as well as his coded police band references told her everything she needed to know.

'I am 10-23, and it's a 10-5, Gracie. I don't know where you are, but you should get here asap,' and he gave her map coordinates rather than an address. It was their way of communicating so that anyone monitoring the call—and it wasn't out of the realm of possibility that Jack's calls at least might be monitored—wouldn't know exactly what they were talking about, or where the action was.

But Gracie did: a '10-23' meant he was at the scene of a crime, and '10-5' meant the coroner had been requested. That meant some kind of suspicious death, most likely a homicide.

The police code '187' for homicide was too well known, even by the most casual interloper, so Jack usually didn't use it although the dispatchers at the county's 911 center did, much to Jack's annoyance.

The coordinates Jack gave were 42.31 and -73.18, and they popped up as Garnet Hill Road when Gracie input them into her iPhone's map app. Luckily, her Sat Nav worked on both street addresses and coordinates, so once she'd combed her hair, changed out of her work clothes, and washed her hands, Gracie was once more in her Jeep and on her way to a crime scene.

The ice pack, the wine and the hot tub would have to wait.

CHAPTER TWENTY-FOUR
CHAPTER TWENTY-FOUR

Gracie arrived at the white clapboard home on Garnet Hill Road as the coroner, Dr. Spears, and his assistant, Heather Wilcox, were bundling a shrouded gurney into the back of their van. Gracie parked and hurried to the best of her ability towards the perimeter and the bright yellow and black 'CRIME SCENE' boundary tape, but was able to see nothing. The Cheshire Fire & Emergency Services Ambulance was parked next to the Coroner's van, but no one was near it, and Gracie presumed the EMTs were inside the house.

About two dozen people were bunched at the edge of the tape: they were muttering among themselves and by listening carefully, Gracie was able to glean the fact that an elderly woman had died inside the house. It had been her body that Dr. Spears and Wilcox had been removing.

Gil Butcher of the *Gazetteer* was talking to a small knot of people, his fingers scrabbling across his notepad as he jotted down their comments. Gracie scanned the area for Jack, but did not see him. However, one of the State Troopers from the Cheshire Barracks was guarding the scene; since Gracie regarded the Cheshire Barracks as her 'local' police station, and stopped in every week for news releases for the paper, she knew many of the personnel assigned there. This Trooper, Luis DelRay, was no exception, and he greeted Gracie with a nod and a small smile as she moved towards him.

"I was wondering if you'd show up," he said to her. "What's with the limp? You okay?"

"I was in the garden so I didn't hear my scanner," Gracie replied to DelRay's first comment. Then, "I twisted my ankle at Morris Dance practice," she answered, bracing herself for the usual 'what kind of dance?' question. Pretty soon, she thought, she'd just say, 'walking' or 'in the yard' or something, since she was getting tired of giving a mini history of English Country Dance to everyone who inquired about her injury. "Can you tell me anything beyond the fact that an elderly woman is dead?" Gracie continued quickly. Maybe if they focused on the subject at hand, DelRay would forget about her ankle and any related queries.

DelRay shrugged. "She lived here. With her son and grandson, from what I heard."

"Where are they?" Gracie queried. She supposed DelRay knew the surname of the residents and the deceased, but also supposed she could find that out through public record.

"Inside."

"Uhhmmm…EMTs and the County Detective in there, too?" she queried, thinking that it was a logical question.

DelRay nodded. "Yep. Talking to the boy, from what I understand."

Gracie paused, and gave the Trooper a long look. "It's a homicide," she said. It wasn't a question. She knew that from Jack's voicemail message.

DelRay said nothing, but his silence confirmed Gracie's statement. So did the infinitesimal nod he gave from beneath his wide-brimmed hat.

"It was the boy?" Gracie whispered. Logically, that made sense: if it had been someone other than the grandson, like the son or another person, the boy would already have been removed from the scene. But since he was inside, with his father, and Jack was inside too, Gracie could only imagine Jack was questioning a person, or persons of interest. Fleetingly, Gracie wondered if Child Protective Services had been called.

DelRay swallowed. At the moment, no one else was around them, but out of the corner of his eye, he could see more people, probably neighbors, walking slowly towards the scene. Technically, he did not know for certain who had killed the old woman. What he'd heard when he'd first arrived on the scene, from both Jack and from the neighbors and friends who were gathering, was exactly what Gracie had just deduced: the grandson had killed his grandmother.

But he couldn't tell Gracie that, even though he liked Gracie: she was a good reporter, and a really nice person. A couple years back, after a horrible shooting at the barracks, she had brought home made casseroles and soups to the Cheshire station for the troopers, calling it 'comfort food.' He also knew that she'd quietly started a fund to help the families of the two troopers who had been shot, and to help pay their medical bills. Many others had contributed to the fund, but Gracie had been the one to start it, and now both troopers had recovered, in no small part because no one had had to worry about where the money to pay for anything was coming from.

DelRay also knew that Gracie lived just outside of Cheshire, and he considered her a neighbor, since he and his family lived just on the other side of Outlook Avenue. So his impulse was to help her by sharing what he'd heard. But he couldn't. It wasn't confirmed, and in any case, such chatter on his part would be unprofessional.

Still…DelRay cleared his throat and swallowed again. "You should probably talk to the neighbors," he offered, nodding at a couple of women and an older man who were several feet away. The group was the same one Butcher had just been interviewing.

"I'd rather talk to different people," Gracie murmured, and explained that her rival paper had just interviewed the individuals DelRay had pointed out. "Do you know who else lives nearby, or knew the family?" she asked DelRay.

It was possible, since Peru Township was within the Cheshire Barracks' jurisdiction, but one trooper couldn't be expected to know every resident.

"I'm not sure," DelRay answered, predictably. "But—" he glanced around and pointed out a young woman in a red T shirt, denim jacket and jeans. She had a boy of around ten by one hand, and was talking to three other people, two older men and an older woman. "She got here pretty quick," DelRay said, nodding towards the woman in red. "And her kid is around the same age as the Cooper kid," he noted. As the surname left his lips, DelRay immediately looked chagrined. But he couldn't take the name back, and anyway, Gracie would have got the name when the police released a news bulletin. But still, the trooper looked down at his shiny boots, and grimaced.

Gracie stepped over to the woman DelRay had indicated. After introductions were made, by which Gracie learned that the woman and her son were indeed neighbors of the Coopers, as were the older couple and the older man in the group, she asked them all what they'd heard, and why they were there. She had, of course, identified herself. But some instinct made her tuck her notebook under her arm and just listen: perhaps this approach would put everyone more at ease, she thought.

"I have a police scanner," the older man answered Gracie with some pride. He hadn't hesitated at all. "I like to keep up with things, and know if anything is going on in the area," he added.

"Bill always tells us if there's anything we need to be concerned about," put in the older woman helpfully. She had been introduced as Minnie Learn. Her husband was Paul, and Bill, whose surname Gracie had spelled 'Pryzowski,' apparently lived in a trailer just over their property line. The three seemed like they were close friends.

Gracie nodded as though agreeing. "So, Mr. Pryzowski, you heard…what? on your scanner?" she prodded.

"Same's you did, I expect: that an elderly woman was in need of an ambulance, at this address."

"We were concerned, because Mabel has—had—a heart condition," Minnie put in, nodding worriedly.

"So we came right over to see what we could do," Paul offered. "But the County Detective had just arrived," he went on, nodding to Jack's dark blue cruiser, parked in front of the Cooper residence. "He asked us to wait outside, so we did."

"And then the ambulance came—" Minnie began.

"About how long after the Detective arrived did the Ambulance get here?' Gracie asked, thinking that now she knew the deceased's whole name.

"Oh, 'bout four, five minutes, tops," Bill Pryzowski told her.

Gracie nodded again, and asked Bill Pryzowski to spell his name; she was surprised to find she had spelled it correctly. "And do you folks live around here, too?" Gracie asked, turning to the young woman in the red T shirt. She'd given her name as Brenda Young, but hadn't introduced her son.

Brenda nodded, and pointed to a log cabin style rancher on the other side of the Cooper house. It was just visible through the trees that separated the properties in this wooded residential area. She told Gracie she and her husband and their son lived there, giving her husband's name as Ron, and their son's as Ron, Jr., or 'Ronnie.' "We heard the commotion when the ambulance came, so we came over to—to see…" she trailed off, uncertain.

"Were you friends with Mabel Cooper?" Gracie asked Brenda, but she looked at Ronnie, who stood next to his mother, and held tightly to her hand. He was tall for his age, and had a distinct overbite where his adult teeth had come in, appearing too large for his still childish mouth. Freckles dotted his nose, and his light brown hair was mussed. He looked perpetually startled to Gracie. Perhaps that was due to what certainly had to be the unnerving circumstance he found his young self in, she thought.

"Ronnie sometimes played with Leroy," Brenda offered.

Gracie nodded again, and thought to herself that now she knew the name of the suspect: Leroy Cooper.

"Oh? What sort of games did you play?" Gracie asked, expecting to hear about some computer role playing game. Instead, Ronnie Young told her that he and Leroy had usually played in Leroy's tree fort; the child pointed to a small wooden structure in a large maple tree to the rear of the Cooper home. He explained that Leroy's father, Jim, had built the fort for his son several years before, and that Leroy considered it his private domain, complete with passwords and a rope ladder that he could retract if he didn't want anyone to reach his 'fort.'

"That must have been fun," Gracie said to Ronnie with a smile. The tree fort looked to be about 30 feet up from the ground, and Gracie hoped to herself that the structure was stable and secure, as 30 feet, even on to grass, was quite a fall. "Are you in the same grade as Leroy in school?" she asked next. She noticed that Bill, Paul and Minnie were still standing close, and listening to every word. Oh, well, she couldn't help that.

Ronnie nodded. "Yup. Just started fourth grade," he offered.

"Oh, I remember my fourth grade teacher: Mrs. Kennedy. She was wonderful," Gracie said warmly. "We learned all about geography that year, it was fascinating." She paused. "Do they still do Geography in fourth grade?" she asked Brenda, amused at the idea that school might have changed so much in the 25 years since she'd been in fourth grade.

"I think so: Ronnie's brought home a big Geography text book, didn't you, Ronnie?" Brenda replied, hugging her son closer.

The sun was behind the trees now, and even though it had not set, the day had become chillier.

"Well, it's getting late, and I'm sure you want to go have dinner," Gracie said kindly, taking all five people she'd been talking to in with her glance. "But, Ronnie, could you maybe tell me one more thing?" she asked, and looked both at the boy and at his mother.

CHAPTER TWENTY-FIVE

Brenda gave a small nod.

"How was Leroy in school, today: did anything happen to upset him? Was he okay on the bus coming home?" Gracie asked gently. She assumed they took the school bus home, as most students did.

Ronnie frowned, and looked down at his sneakers. Gracie noticed they were New Balance brand, and probably had cost quite a bit, even at an outlet store.

"It's okay, you can tell her," Brenda whispered to her son.

Ronnie took a deep breath. "Leroy got made fun of in school," he began. "The other kids teased him."

"About what?" Gracie asked, matching the boy's quiet tone.

Ronnie shrugged. "His clothes," he murmured.

"Leroy's clothes were—well, they were from the charity shop," Brenda elaborated. "And they were usually too big. Mabel always said she bought things Leroy could 'grow into' but it made him look like—"

"A ragamuffin?" Gracie suggested, and Brenda nodded.

"Exactly. They don't have a lot of money. Jim, that's Leroy's Dad, he worked at Savoy Stone," she went on.

"The place that went out of business?" Gracie asked. The stone quarry had been played out, and the corresponding stone business had shut down a few months before. It hadn't been huge news, as the quarry and the business had both been small. But it had impacted the workers, nonetheless.

Brenda nodded. "And since then, he hasn't had any luck with anything steady. And Mabel's on social security. I think they lived with her to save money," Brenda added in a whisper. "I would have given them some of Ronnie's things, but they two boys are completely different sizes," Brenda added.

Gracie looked a question.

"Leroy is very, uhm, stocky, and short. And Ronnie takes after his dad: tall and slender," Brenda answered. "My husband runs the hardware store in Worthington, and coaches the boys' basketball team at the high school," she added, sounding happy.

"Yeah: Leroy can dribble good, but he never makes baskets," Ronnie put in with a grin.

Gracie could imagine the two boys playing basketball, perhaps shooting hoops in the Youngs' backyard, and the shorter, stocky Leroy not being very good at scoring. That was probably why he and Ronnie had played in Leroy's 'fort.' Not only was it something the little boy was good at, he was in charge, since it was his 'fort.'

"I tried, a couple years ago, to give Leroy a couple of new shirts and a pair of trousers, for his birthday," Brenda continued.

"And they wouldn't accept it?" Gracie suggested. She knew people could be very proud, sometimes to the detriment of their children.

"Well, not exactly," Brenda explained. "Mabel let Leroy accept the gifts, but then told me she'd returned them to the store in the mall where I'd got them, and used the money to buy hand me downs at the thrift store," Brenda continued, low. Her face frowned and she looked annoyed. "She said she hoped I didn't mind, but the money bought a lot more at the charity shop," Brenda added, squeezing the words out between pursed lips.

Gracie clicked her tongue. "Well, that wasn't your fault, you tried," she reassured the woman.

Brenda shook her head.

"Aaaahhh—did the kids make fun of Leroy today?" Gracie asked then, tipping her head and looking at Ronnie with a smile.

Ronnie nodded, but he was uncomfortable.

"And what did Leroy do?" Gracie asked. "Did any teacher step in to help?" she asked as an after thought. Weren't they supposed to do that?

Ronnie shook his head. "No. The kids are smarter than that: they don't do it so's the teachers can see. And anyway, this was on the bus, on the way home. Driver didn't see nothing," he murmured.

Gracie wanted to ask Ronnie what kind of torment the other kids had put Leroy through on the bus on account of his clothes, but she sensed that the child had been through enough. She also knew that details like that would probably come out in the course of the investigation—certainly once Leroy 'lawyered up.'

So she merely said goodbye, and thanked them all for speaking with her. Then she headed for her Jeep.

Jack was still inside the home, apparently, and most of the neighbors who had gathered were dispersing. Gracie thought that she, too, would head home, and try to type up something about this case, from what she'd learned. It would be a challenge, since she didn't really know much, for certain. But she could try.

As she unlocked her Jeep's door, Gil Butcher approached her, apparently en route to his own rust bucket Suburban, parked a few feet from Gracie's Jeep.

"You missed everything," Butcher said, his tone sounding superior.

Gracie wanted to retort that she'd managed, thank you very much, and that she would still bet her article would be better than his. But she kept silent, biting the inside of her cheek to do so. However, she did turn to face her opponent.

"I got here right after the ambulance did," Butcher went on boastfully. "I was able to see the whole thing," he added, nodding to himself and smiling broadly.

Gracie thought perhaps he was becoming somewhat senile, although he was probably only in his 50's. But he looked like a fool, just standing there, smiling and nodding like a human bobble head. Still, she said nothing.

"Got some great interviews, too," Butcher continued. Clearly, he was talking to Gracie to try and get her worked up, and give him some kind of nasty reply which he could then complain about to anyone who would listen.

Instead, Gracie just smiled sweetly at the has-been editor. Then, she hopped into her Jeep and shut the door in Gil Butcher's face. She started the engine, and waved to him as she drove away; her reward was his expression, which went from surprised, to disappointed to truculent.

Gracie laughed nearly all the way home.

CHAPTER TWENTY-SIX

It was after dinner on Thursday evening when Gracie heard from Jack. She'd typed up what she knew about the alleged homicide in Peru Township and emailed it in to her paper. Her editor would probably send it out as a news bulletin, and possibly put it up on the paper's web page. She planned to have a longer, more informative article, for next week's paper edition.

A quick repast of grilled tilapia—she'd used Marilyn Draper's spice mix, and had been pleased—and a salad was what Gracie had made for dinner; now, she and Pumpkin were in the Oak Room, relaxing. The TV was tuned to the BBC 24-hour news channel and was on low while Gracie caught up with her Twitter and Facebook feeds, and Pumpkin perched on a low, wide windowsill and monitored the activity outside.

Most of the seasonal bird visitors had already migrated south for the winter, and any nests in the rhododendrons that flanked the windows on the west side of Gracie's house were empty. But there was still the occasional squirrel or chipmunk, busy gathering nuts against the coming winter, to pique Pumpkin's interest.

When Gracie's iPhone sounded the trumpet voluntary, she answered immediately.

"What did you think of this afternoon?" Jack asked after they had exchanged hellos, and he'd inquired about her ankle. "DelRay told me you'd been at the scene—sorry, I was inside for a while," Jack explained, somewhat vaguely.

Gracie told him she'd got his messages when she'd come in from the garden and driven right over to the crime scene. "Can you tell me anything?" she asked bluntly.

"How 'bout you tell me what you know?" Jack countered, sounding weary.

"Ok." Her article, with all the details she had thought pertinent, was fresh in her mind. "I know hearsay makes Leroy Cooper, 10, as the alleged killer of his grandmother, Mabel Cooper. They live with Leroy's father, Mabel's son, Jim, who's been out of work for a while and money is tight. The incident happened this afternoon after the school bus dropped Leroy back home, and police and an ambulance were called but Mabel was deceased—I don't know if that happened before emergency personnel got there or after, but I saw her body being carried out by the Coroner." Gracie paused. "That's about all I know for sure, for fact," she said, sounding regretful. "I imagine there will be a press release tomorrow with more details. The evening news didn't have anything more than that."

"That's all correct," Jack confirmed. "But I know you, Gracie: what else do you know, even if it's not fact?" he asked.

"Mmmm…well, a school chum of Leroy's, Ronnie Young, who lives in the log cabin type place just down the road, often played with Leroy and says the kids in school bullied and made fun of him—Leroy, that is—because of his clothes. Ronnie's mother Brenda confirmed this and said she tried to give Leroy some new clothes she'd bought, but that the grandmother, Mabel Cooper, returned the new clothes and bought second hand clothes with the money she received. She told Brenda she could buy a lot more at the thrift store," Gracie said.

Jack made a noise that was half way between a sigh and a grunt. "Go on."

"That's really all I have," Gracie finished. "Your turn."

"Well, CPS was called," Jack told her, meaning Child Protective Services. "I spoke to Leroy in the presence of his father James and Leroy confessed to killing his grandmother," he said flatly.

Gracie couldn't help gasping at the thought of a ten year old child killing someone—anyone.

"That much should be in the press release, and it'll be out tomorrow morning," Jack added.

"What was the murder weapon?" Gracie asked. "No one reported hearing a gun shot or anything," she added, mentioning she'd spoken with a couple other neighbors as well as the Youngs. "And where was the father in all of this? He doesn't work, wasn't he home?" she concluded, sounding incensed.

Jack sighed. "The boy told me he had entered into an altercation with his grandmother over the bullying he was the victim of at school," he told Gracie. "Apparently the argument escalated and Leroy lost his temper and grabbed his grandmother's cane and began to hit her with it." He paused. "These details won't be in the press release, but—"

She could hear the desperation in Jack's voice: he had to talk to someone about this, to help him process it. And Gracie was, at the very least, his best friend.

"Go on, Jack: this is off the record," she soothed, and waited.

"Mabel Cooper tried to deflect the blows but she was unsteady on her feet and she fell against the side of the kitchen counter and went down onto the linoleum floor," Jack continued.

Gracie could picture the event he described, clearly, in her mind. "And then?" she urged gently.

"And then, Leroy said he didn't know what came over him, but he just took her cane—it's one of those metal ones, with the rubber tip?" Jack put in.

"Uh-huh?"

"Anyway, he took it and pushed it against his grandmother's throat until she stopped struggling, and stopped breathing," he said.

"He was able to hold her down on the floor?" Gracie queried, trying to imagine it.

"Mabel Cooper was a small woman, and even though she was overweight, she wasn't strong. As I said, she was unsteady on her feet, and had heart issues—I'm not sure exactly what— for which she was on several medications. Leroy is a strong, stocky kid. He told me he stood over his grandmother, then stepped on the cane to force it against her throat hard enough to make her black out."

"Did he realize he'd killed her?" Gracie asked, breathless. "Did he intend to kill her? Was he remorseful?"

Jack cleared his throat. "He seemed—stunned. He said he didn't intend anything beyond shutting her up—his words. I guess his grandmother had been scolding him and going on and on about how tight things were and how little money they had and how the money they could spend on new clothes and shoes for him could buy him used stuff and still put food on the table." He paused again. "And then she said something about his dad being no good because he wasn't working, and that Leroy should be angry with his father, not with her, she was doing the best she could…" Jack trailed off, clearly troubled by what he was recalling.

"So Leroy maybe felt he was defending his father," Gracie assessed. "And in any case, he was probably very conflicted with having to choose between the two people he loved and relied on most, his grandmother and his father. And conflicted because there was tension between those two, also," she added.

Jack chuckled. "What are you, his defense attorney?" he asked, trying to lighten the mood.

Gracie sighed and shook her head. "Well, no: just trying to understand. Ronnie—that's the neighbor kid—said Leroy had a fort, a tree fort, that he'd let Ronnie play in with him. But he kinda indicated that the tree fort was Leroy's sanctuary, you know? His castle: the kid even had a password and a retractable ladder, so no one could get to him there. He felt safe there."

"Mmmm…interesting."

"So: what happens now? To Leroy, I mean? He's in custody, I presume?" Gracie asked.

Jack told her that CPS had agreed that the boy should be taken to a secure juvenile facility until he could be arraigned. That would happen Friday morning, the next day. Then, Jack continued, the family would be evaluated and eligibility for the Public Defender would be determined. "I fully expect them to qualify," Jack told Gracie. "And I also expect that Felicia Laurenti will recommend a 30 day stay at a juvenile psychiatric clinic, for evaluation," he added.

"Sounds logical," Gracie agreed.

"Speaking of which, Gracie: I need to ask you something," Jack said, his tone altering and the subject changing.

Gracie smiled into the phone. "Sure."

"Did you ever talk to anyone about that whole PD eligibility thing?" Jack asked. It had only been two days since dinner at his parents' house where Gracie had learned about the issue, but she'd said she'd check into it and Jack knew from experience that Gracie was usually determined and quite aggressive when tracking down a story.

Gracie sighed in consternation. "I tried to. Yesterday, after I got back from the chiropractor's and checking at the Pittsfield PD about the Starling incident I called Judge

Cranston," she told Jack. "He's in the Florida Keys with his wife."

"Oho, good for him!" Jack put in. The Judge was semi retired now, and he and his wife, a retired attorney, did a lot of travelling.

"Yeah, well. So then I called Lance Melling at Probation," Gracie continued, not in good humor. "I had to leave a message and he never called me back. And honestly, what with the last minute school thing yesterday and gardening today, and then the whole Cooper case, I haven't had time to call him again."

"Understandable," Jack put in.

"I also called Felicia Laurenti," Gracie went on. "And at least *she* had a minute to speak with me," she told Jack, sounding a bit happier. "She said that yes, she had thought the system had been set up with Probation doing the evals, and had not thought to question it, since it seemed to work and no one had ever suggested that it had been done as a temporary measure."

"Huh. Just what we thought the other night," Jack said, referencing dinner at his parents'.

"Exactly. Felicia did say, though, that now that the situation had been brought to her attention—I gather you spoke with her?"

"Only in general terms," Jack admitted. "Asked her what her office would charge per year to do the evals, stuff like that," he explained quickly.

"Well anyway, she's figured out what the problem is," Gracie said.

"Smart woman."

"She is. And she told me she's going to speak to the Commissioners and Judge Norcross about changing it back to being the responsibility of her office, at her first opportunity."

"That ought to be interesting," Jack chuckled.

"Mmmm…well, there's a Prison Board meeting on Monday, and of course both Felicia and the Judge will be there. I expected they would discuss the Starling incident but I wonder if Felicia won't bring up the Probation/Evaluation thing, too?"

Jack said he thought that was likely, and said he'd try to stop down for the meeting. Gracie, of course, would attend, and cover it for her paper.

It was nearly 11 p.m. when Jack and Gracie hung up, and even though the next day was a Friday, it was still a work day. So Jack took his half dog half wolf, 'Woof', out for a last constitutional, and then got ready for bed.

He stretched out between the cool sheets, and Woof jumped up and settled himself at the foot of the queen sized mattress. Within a minute, the dog's breathing slowed and he 'whuffed' slightly: Jack knew he was asleep.

Sleep didn't come quite that easily for Woof's owner, and Jack stared at the ceiling, reviewing that afternoon's quite horrible events. It had helped a lot to talk everything over with Gracie, but the whole thing still disturbed him.

He supposed that if it didn't disturb him, he would have more to worry about, and smiled grimly in the dark. What would drive a child of ten to beat and then kill his grandmother? Clearly, from what Leroy had said that afternoon, the relationship between the two had been strained. And Leroy had just come from the bus ride home from school where he'd been the victim, once again, of very nasty comments and hurtful taunts from his schoolmates.

So Jack could understand how Leroy could have been feeling vulnerable. And then he'd arrived home and when his Grandmother had asked how his day had been, and then asked why he was upset, Leroy had snapped.

Jack supposed he could understand that: people 'snapped' all the time, and did things they later regretted. Things they normally wouldn't do. But those things usually weren't murder.

He had to say, the State Police had been most helpful securing the perimeter and making sure that only authorized people gained access to the house. Also, Trooper LeRay had been the one to transport Leroy Cooper to the juvenile detention facility where he would spend the night, while two other troopers had assisted Jack with closing the scene once the Coroner and CSU had finished there.

Jack turned over and put an arm beneath his pillow. The state troopers from the Cheshire Barracks were a good bunch of guys, Jack thought sleepily. Not that the other barracks' personnel weren't, but after what the Cheshire troopers had been through—what was it now, almost two years ago?—they'd become even closer, more tightly knit and supportive, not only of each other, but also of other law enforcement personnel.

At that time, Jack recalled, two of the troopers from the Cheshire barracks had been shot at as they'd left the building at end of shift. Both had been critically wounded, but the second one had just left the rehab facility to return home a month or so before. The shooter, who had not been seen by his victims, and who had remained just out of sight of the exterior surveillance cameras on the barracks building, had not been found. It was thought he had had an escape vehicle nearby and was presumed to be long gone from the area.

Jack fell asleep, listening to the sound of Woof's breathing. He dreamt of tall trees, and black powder muzzle loaders.

CHAPTER TWENTY-SEVEN

Jack sipped his morning coffee on his front steps while he watched Woof trotting around the clearing in which their double wide sat. It was Friday morning, early: the sun wouldn't be up for another 45 minutes, but Jack could see a pinkish glow in the eastern sky, behind the tall trees bordering the clearing on his property.

Trees…he'd dreamt about trees, he recalled with a chuckle. He took another sip of the intense, dark brew. What had he dreamt, exactly? It had been a strange dream, and it seemed somehow important…

Jack frowned. Trees. And something about black powder muzzleloader rifles. And…

He called sharply to Woof to come inside, and the well trained animal obediently trotted to his side. Jack and Woof gained the security of their home, then Jack gave his drained coffee mug a fast rinse, checked to make sure everything was as it should be, and hastened out the door. It wasn't even 6:30 a.m. yet, but perhaps that was best, he thought as he revved up the engine in his unmarked navy cruiser and zipped down his driveway. Early starts often produced good results.

He'd remembered his dream. And he'd remembered why it was so important. Now, he needed to check a couple of files at the Cheshire SP Barracks and make a call or two before he could be sure that he'd gained a major milestone in the solution to the McGinley murders.

Gracie attended the preliminary arraignment of Leroy Cooper on Friday morning. The boy had been detained overnight at the nearby Juvenile Detention Center, and appeared in court with his representative from CPS and with his Public Defense Attorney, Felicia Laurenti. The PD gave

Gracie a small smile as she took her seat next to her client, and Gracie wondered, not for the first time, how some defense attorneys managed to do their jobs and sleep at night. How could you defend someone you knew was guilty, someone who admitted he or she was guilty?

She'd talked to Felicia about this once, over lunch, and the clever attorney had told Gracie that, at least for her, it was a belief and a trust in the judicial system.

'I know it's flawed,' Felicia had said, stoutly defending the system nonetheless. 'But I have faith in the concept of due process, the idea that if each side presents its best argument, an impartial jury will come to the correct conclusion as to guilt or innocence.'

While Gracie admired her friend's trust in the system, and could see how that trust enabled defense attorneys like Felicia to do their jobs to the best of their ability and let the system sort a matter out, she still thought she would have trouble being a defense attorney.

To present the police's evidence in the case, Gracie was surprised to see Trooper LeRay, and wondered where Jack was. However, since LeRay was the officer of record, it made sense for him to present the prosecution's findings to the magistrate.

In a way, Gracie was relieved not to see Jack: he'd just grouse at her some more about the way she was limping, still favoring her right ankle, which was still swollen. The fact that Gracie had an appointment for a treatment with Dr. Grist at 11 a.m., right after the hearing, probably wouldn't have impressed Jack, either, Gracie thought as she looked around the small courtroom and waited for the hearing to begin. And she was in no mood to argue with him, not for the first time, over the efficacy and relative merits of chiropractors versus regular M.D.s.

A smattering of the Coopers' neighbors, some of whom Gracie recognized from the afternoon before, were trickling in and taking seats for the hearing, as was Leroy's father, Jim. Little Robbie was probably in school, but his mother Brenda was there: she gave Gracie a tired smile.

The matter concluded swiftly, and much as Gracie and Jack had expected: Felicia asked for her client to be sent to a juvenile psychiatric facility for 30 days' evaluation and treatment, prior to determining the child's eligibility to stand trial. The evaluation would also help the court determine whether to uphold the current charges against Leroy, which named him as an adult, or to adjust the charges and try Leroy in Juvenile Court. It all depended on whether or not the psychiatrists felt Leroy had been thinking and reasoning as an adult when he'd killed his grandmother, or whether, at ten years of age, he was still too young to fully comprehend what he was doing, or its consequences.

The magistrate ruled that Leroy should spend 30 days at St. Christina's in Albany, which specialized in juvenile psychiatric disorders. Everyone seemed pleased by this and Gracie slipped away as quietly as she could while Leroy's father was hugging him and saying goodbye.

She made herself go up the inner staircase of the courthouse to the DA's third floor suite, even though she had to take the steps one at a time, two-footing it the entire way, which seemed to her to take an inordinate amount of time. She was surprised once again when Millie and Pam told her that Jack was not in the office, and sighed in frustration.

It wouldn't be so bad, she thought, if she had taken the elevator, or if she were walking normally and had just run up the stairs as usual. But the effort she'd expended to climb the two flights seemed wasted now, which made Gracie feel even more annoyed with herself, and with what she still called her 'stupid ankle.'

"He did talk to Dr. Spears this morning," Millie offered, sensing Gracie's disappointment. "I know, because I connected the Doctor when he returned what had been Jack's earlier call," she added mildly.

"And he ran out of here almost as soon as he'd hung up," put in Pam with a smile.

"So he's at the hospital?" Gracie asked; the coroner's office and suite was in the hospital's sub basement.

Both secretaries shrugged. "Seems logical," Pam quipped.

"You might be interested to know that the Sheriff just confirmed a flight with Jack next Tuesday morning, too, Gracie," Millie continued, referring to a scribbled note on her desk.

"That's when they're doing the thermal camera flyover," Gracie said, brightening, and Millie nodded. "I hope the Sheriff lets me go, too," Gracie added. Then she smiled suddenly. "I've been meaning to ask you, Millie: do you know Ms. Wolter, over at the Police Department?"

Millie's lined face broke into a huge smile. "You mean, Althea? Why of course! We were girls together, even went to Pittsfield Academy together, and then Mount Holyoke...do you know her?" Millie inquired, intrigued.

Gracie explained how she knew Althea Wolter.

"You know, you'd think that we worked, and lived, miles away from each other, because we hardly ever see each other, except at Class Reunions," Millie noted, sounding a little sad.

Gracie gestured to the telephone on the secretary's desk. "Call her up. Ask her to lunch some time," she suggested. "I bet she'd be delighted, especially since the two of you both ended up in law enforcement careers," she added encouragingly.

Jack sat next to Dr. Spears at his desk in the autopsy suite, and peered with him at the photos from the McGinley post mortem.

"You'll note the entry wounds are smaller than the exit wounds," Dr. Spears murmured. He pointed to several spots on the photos: the places where the bullets had left the body were considerably larger and more ragged in appearance, but the entry sites were comparatively neat, round holes.

"They weren't all through and throughs," Jack stated. He knew that, having been on scene, and having read the reports from both Dr. Spears and the CSU team.

Dr. Spears nodded. "Right. Some bullets remained in the body," he confirmed. The photo they were looking at was of Aaron McGinley, who had sustained nine bullet holes. Jack was grateful that the Coroner hadn't used Wyatt's autopsy photos: somehow looking at the body of an eight year old who'd been ruthlessly gunned down would have been far worse than looking at his father's.

Some of the wounds had not been lethal, but the two to the chest and the one to the head had been.

Dr. Spears showed Jack another closeup photo. "High velocity bullets cause cavitation upon entry," he explained. "They yaw when they enter a body," the coroner continued, putting one hand out in the air and twisting it as he spoke to mimic the movement of a high velocity bullet. "Their kinetic energy sheers and compresses the tissues surrounding the entry point into a hole, or cavity. The tissues rebound, but you can still see the distinctive, ovoid, entry point."

Jack nodded. "The CSU report noted that the ovoid shape indicated the shooter had been above the McGinleys, probably standing, while they had been sitting. The angle of the trajectory of the bullet made the—cavitation?—"

Spears nodded.

"Made it oval in shape."

"That's right. If the shooter had been, oh, sitting with the McGinleys around their fire pit when he'd shot them, the cavitation at the entry point would have been almost perfectly round," Spears confirmed.

Both looked at the photos again in silence for a few moments. Then:

"These entry wounds look different from ones inflicted by, say, a handgun or a pistol," Jack offered. "But those bullets don't yaw."

"Injuries from handguns and pistols are confined to any tissue or organs directly in the bullet's path, in the wound track," Dr. Spears explained. "In contrast, high velocity rifle bullets can injure tissue and organs even if they don't come in contact with them, because of the cavitation."

"Like a shock wave?" Jack asked, with a raised eyebrow at the coroner.

"Precisely!"

"What kind of pressure are we talking about, Doc?" Jack asked.

Spears tipped his head, thought for a moment, and then said, "as much as 200 atmospheres, which is enough to partially or completely disintegrate an organ."

"Ummm…what's that in pounds per square inch? I know normal pressure is around 15 pounds per square inch," he added.

"Nearly 3000 pounds per square inch," the coroner replied, and Jack whistled.

"And, many of these bullets, as their name implies, the 'total fragmentation soft point' type, shed pieces of their core as they pass through the body, which does even more damage," Spears added grimly.

The coroner selected an x ray film from the file in front of them, and stood to put it on the light box that hung over his desk. "See here, and here?" he said, pointing. "We call that a 'snowstorm pattern,' and it's typical of fragmenting bullets. I found molybdenum in the wounds, which I can only assume was the coating on the lightweight bullets, designed to allow for fragmentation."

Jack sifted through the photos in the file, and then looked at Dr. Spears. "These are not common bullets, then," he said. It was a question, despite its declarative phrasing.

Dr. Spears sighed. "Not very common, no. Law enforcement has them, of course, for use in penetrating glass and body armor. And hunters sometimes use them. But hunters and even our SWAT teams don't use such high-velocity bullets as these: their ends can be achieved with less."

"What kind of velocity?" Jack asked quickly.

"You're looking at more than 5900 feet per second," Dr. Spears replied gravely. "Probably around 3500 fps would be enough to shatter bullet proof glass or body armor. Minimum is 2500, and these wounds were produced by bullets…"

"At more than twice that speed," Jack finished, astounded.

Dr. Spears nodded again.

"Do you remember the shootings a couple years back, up at the Cheshire State Police Barracks?" Jack asked then.

The county coroner nodded, and said that he did.

"You weren't involved in that at all, because no one died," Jack continued, reaching for a manila envelope he'd brought with him and temporarily placed next to Dr. Spears' desk.

"Thankfully, yes: both troopers survived," Dr. Spears agreed, looking cheerful.

"Would you look at photos from the ER, from when those two troopers were brought in?" Jack asked.

"They were brought here?" Dr. Spears asked. It was the closest hospital to the Cheshire Barracks, so he supposed they had been.

Jack nodded. "Yes. These are records from the Barracks, though," he explained, and he withdrew several photos and a couple of documents from the envelope. It shouldn't matter that the records he was giving the coroner weren't from the hospital: the police file had the same photos as the hospital file, since they were copies.

Dr. Spears reached for the photos. He examined each one silently, turning them this way and that to orient himself to the body part he was viewing. Then he tucked the photos together and tapped them lightly on the surface of his desk, lining up the corners and edges. He looked a question at Jack, and waited.

"Doc, can you tell me if the wounds in those photographs look like the ones from the McGinley autopsies?" Jack asked bluntly. His anxiousness was clear in his voice.

"I can tell you that they are substantially similar," Dr. Spears replied, hedging. "They have ovoid cavitation present and the exit wounds are consistent with high velocity bullet injuries."

"Is it possible to tell the muzzle velocity of the bullet that inflicted those wounds, from those photos?" Jack pushed, motioning to the State Police file photos. "Was it the same as in the McGinley murders?"

"I can't determine muzzle velocity, not exactly," Spears admitted, shaking his head. "But I can tell you that the wounds in these photos," he lifted the small sheaf of pictures from the police file, "and the wounds in the photos from the McGinley autopsy," he gestured to the file on his desk, "were *both* made by extremely high velocity bullets, fired from a distance of several hundred feet."

"So they could have been made by the same gun, and maybe the same shooter?" Jack asked, knowing his query was a long shot.

Spears gave a grim chuckle. "There is no way to *know* that for certain, Jack," he countered. "Not from photographs and really, not even from direct wound examination. But it is possible, certainly."

Jack nodded, appearing satisfied with the limited declaration made by the coroner. "I also have these," he noted, and reached in his shirt pocket, bringing out a small plastic evidence bag. Inside were a few bullet fragments. "You have fragments from the McGinleys, right?"

Dr. Spears nodded thoughtfully. "You want me to compare the two," he said. It was not a question. "I did look at the McGinley fragments, of course, as part of the post mortem," the coroner went on.

"Right. But—would you be able to compare the two sets of fragments?" Jack asked directly.

"Certainly," Dr. Spears agreed, reaching for the evidence bag. He initialed the bag to preserve chain of custody. "If we're lucky, I should be able at least to tell you if the bullets in both cases were fired from similar guns. It's not a fact, it's just a likelihood," he cautioned. "But along with the rest of the evidence you've got, it certainly begins to suggest that the person who shot at the state police troopers is the same person who killed the McGinleys."

CHAPTER TWENTY-EIGHT

Friday night, Gracie made roast butternut squash bisque, crab stuffed grouper with a beurre blanc sauce, sautéed kale and leeks with cranberries, and salted caramel crème brulée for dessert. She had texted Jack, asking if he'd like to come try out a new recipe, the grouper, and asked him to show up around 6:30 p.m. if that was convenient.

Jack had texted back with a terse 'see you then,' but had followed it with a silly smiley face emoticon, which had made Gracie laugh.

Although butternut squash was not Jack's favorite, he had to admit the bisque was delicious: clearly, Gracie had done something to the squash to make it really tasty. Although Jack complimented her on the soup, Gracie didn't reveal her secrets, just smiled mysteriously and said she was glad he liked it.

The evening had turned chilly after a clear, sunny day. It was mid September, and the sun's angle was more acute, the shadows longer, and the twilight grey-blue. Although they didn't often eat in the formal dining room when it was just the two of them, Gracie had decided they would this night, and had set the table and fashioned a centerpiece made from small gourds in oranges and greens in a myriad of shapes. These sat on a blanket of yellow and just-turning-from-green fallen leaves. A scattering of acorns completed the creation, which held a central pillar candle in a large hurricane crystal. Gracie chose to use no tablecloth, to show off the polished cherrywood of the dining table, but the placemats were the pale gold of ripened wheat, with linen napkins to match.

'We're going fancy tonight?' Jack had asked as Gracie had ushered him into the dining room.

She had shrugged. 'Not really: it's just nice to use this room sometimes. And the view is so pretty from here,' she had added.

It was true: the large dining room windows looked out on the western aspect of Gracie's property: the low shrubs near the house gave way to a manicured lawn with a small Native American prayer circle beneath a tall hemlock tree; beyond this was a wildflower meadow blazing with solidago, and then the horizon, fringed with tree tops. Most of Gracie's forty acres was wooded. The sun when they sat down at a quarter to seven was just skimming the tree tops on its way to setting. The sky was clear, but the sunset would likely be spectacular.

Now, Jack and Gracie began on the stuffed grouper, which Gracie had not stuffed and rolled, but merely draped the tasty fish over a mound of stuffing. To serve it she'd drizzled the beurre blanc sauce on top. The sautéed kale and cranberries had droplets of a balsamic glaze to finish it, and Jack loved it all.

"I don't know that I've had grouper before," he said. "It's good. Has more flavor than a lot of white flat fish," he commented, and Gracie smiled.

"Makes a change, I thought, from salmon," she agreed.

She had been very careful to walk slowly, but as normally as she could, that evening. Her treatment at Dr. Grist's that morning had made her ankle feel a lot better; it was still somewhat swollen, but Gracie felt she could put more weight on it. And Dr. Grist urged her to walk as normally as she could: he had explained that by favoring her right foot, she was actually compromising the muscles, which would stiffen and atrophy if they weren't used.

Although the range of motion work she did with the chiropractor helped combat this, the best thing was for her to use her foot and ankle as she normally would, as much as she could, and to do the ankle-rolling and foot pointing exercises Dr. Grist had given her.

So Gracie was doing her best. Thankfully, Jack hadn't mentioned her ankle at all: he seemed, actually, to be preoccupied, and wasn't as talkative as usual.

Gracie made conversation while they ate, telling Jack about the preparations for the next fund raiser at Greylock Manor, the historic home on the grounds of Greylock Forest. Gracie was on the board of the Manor, and helped give tours and organize various fund raisers and events throughout the year.

The next event was called the 'Fancy Fair,' and it was just a few weeks away. Area residents scoured their attics and basements for forgotten treasures they were willing to donate, a couple of other board members who collected antiques donated some finds from auctions they'd attended, and it all went up for sale on long tables placed throughout the Manor's ground floor.

Greylock Manor dated from 1802: nowhere near as old as Gracie's house, which had originally been built in the Colonial saltbox style in 1679, with several additions in the ensuing decades. But Greylock was one of the most well-preserved examples of Federal architecture in Western Massachusetts, and unlike Gracie's home which had begun as a small two room endeavor, Greylock was, truly, a 'manor' with three floors, balconies, and even a ballroom.

As Gracie had told Jack before, Greylock State Forest Ranger Victorine Hansen was in charge of the Mansion and its environs; she had just begun a new period clothing exhibit at the House, and had asked if Gracie would possibly have time to help her.

"I don't know why she asked me, exactly, because it's not as if I know anything about old clothes," Gracie told Jack as they ate.

"But you have an eye," Jack replied immediately. "You know what looks good, and how to place things."

Gracie looked astonished, then pleased. "I do?" she asked, and Jack nodded. "Well in any case, Victorine has been collecting vintage and antique clothing for years and she's using some of her pieces for the initial display. We're hoping people in the area will donate items once they know we have the exhibit. And Tony and Jeannie go to auctions all the time for their antiques," she continued, mentioning two of the other board members at Greylock. "So now they can keep an eye out for pieces we could use, too. That way, we can change it every season, or every year, and keep it fresh."

"Where are you going to put the clothes, all over the Mansion?" Jack asked, forking up the last bite of kale.

"No, just on the top floor. We have the ballroom on the one side of the central stair, and then those bedchambers and such on the opposite side, and the wide hall. So there's plenty of room," she explained.

Jack said he thought that sounded like a good idea, and said he'd be interested to see the exhibit once it opened.

"I think it'll be ready for the Christmas Tea," Gracie noted, excitedly.

By the time Gracie served the crème brulée, the sun had finally dropped behind the trees, which still had most of their leaves. But shafts of yellow and then red light shot up from behind the darkening horizon into a sky that was going from cerulean to indigo quite fast.

They both loved the dessert.

"You don't usually do dessert, do you?" Jack queried, licking his spoon of the last remnants of the creamy sweet.

Gracie chuckled. "No, but it looks like you're glad I did!" she quipped. Then she shrugged. "I just felt like it. It's Friday, I got a lot of my garden work done, I got all the stuff for the paper written and filed, so I thought a bit of a celebration would be in order. Besides, I'll work off any extra calories this weekend: there's more gardening to do, fall cleanup, you know, cutting back perennials and ditching annuals…" she trailed off as she looked out the dining room windows at the lawn just beyond the prayer circle. "I've been thinking."

"Uh oh," Jack put in with a smile.

"Ha ha ha. No, seriously, I think I'm going to ask Larry if a couple of his guys could help me put in a labyrinth out there," Gracie replied, gesturing with her spoon to the lawn.

She had pulled the net curtains that normally shrouded the windows aside, so the view was unobstructed.

"A labyrinth?" Jack echoed. He knew better than to ask 'what for?' since Gracie was about to tell him.

"Yeah. I think it would be neat. Good place to meditate, get connected with nature, all that stuff," she replied.

Jack nodded, but looked unconvinced. "How would you make it: you wouldn't put blocks of stone up or anything, would you?" he asked, clearly envisioning monoliths in rural Western Massachusetts.

Gracie laughed out loud. "You mean, like Avebury or Stonehenge? No, those aren't labyrinths per se, they're stone circles. I don't think I want to put a new stone circle up: seems a contradiction in terms. No, I've seen some labyrinths done with circles and patterns of low plantings that fill in the ridges to about knee high," she explained. "Shrubs like viburnum would be pretty in spring and summer, since they flower, and I could intersperse them with those burning bush things that turn bright red in the fall," she told Jack.

"My parents have a couple of those in their back yard," he put in, and Gracie nodded.

"And junipers, maybe, in between, for evergreens to keep the shape even in winter." She paused. "I'll have to design it, and then see if a couple of Larry's guys can help me plant them."

"Now?" Jack asked, surprised.

Gracie nodded. "Autumn is the best time to plant shrubs, if you do it early enough. We could probably get it done in a couple of days and this way the shrubs would have a chance to establish, and then winter in, and be ready to go next spring," she continued.

Jack nodded. "Okay—when are you thinking, because I could probably help out, if you needed me to," he offered with a smile.

"Next week, if the guys are free. You never know with Larry: it depends on what jobs he's on, and if he has a full crew, or if he can spare someone for a day or so," she said.

"I'll be working, of course, but barring some emergency I could probably help out after work," Jack continued.

"Thanks, Jack: I'll let you know, after I talk to Larry," Gracie replied. Then she stood up from the table. "I'm going to wash up," she announced.

"I can definitely help you there," Jack smiled. "I'll dry," he offered.

Gracie nodded. "Ok, thanks. Then we can have coffee and maybe you will tell me what's been on your mind all evening."

CHAPTER TWENTY-NINE

Once they'd settled in the Oak Room with their coffee, Jack began to explain his new theory about the McGinley murders to Gracie. He'd brought Woof along, of course, and Gracie had fed him, along with Pumpkin, in the kitchen. Now, both animals stretched out on the rug in front of the large stone fireplace, even though there was no fire. Jack and Gracie sat on her chocolate brown sofa; Gracie had turned on the Tiffany lamps and the baby spots in the room, and the atmosphere was quiet and conducive, she thought, to conversation. And perhaps revelations.

Jack told her about his odd dream of trees and black powder rifles. Then, he said, he thought that seeing Trooper DelRay again might have subconsciously made him think about the Cheshire Barracks and recall the shooting there the year before. And so he'd thought to check to see if the two incidents could possibly be related.

Gracie was impressed with the level of Jack's intuition and told him so.

"I don't tell everyone this kind of stuff, especially the part about my dream," Jack confessed, sipping at his coffee. "I didn't tell Dr. Spears, for example," he went on. "I just asked him to compare the wounds and the bullet fragments from the two cases. And as I just told you, he agreed that from his examination of the evidence in both cases, it looks to him like the troopers and the McGinleys could have been shot by the same person. Or the same gun. But at least, from a similar gun," he finished. The Coroner had reached him a couple hours earlier with his message that yes, the bullet fragments from the McGinley site were nearly identical to the ones from the barracks attack.

"Where was I when the Cheshire Barracks shooting happened?" Gracie asked, somewhat rhetorically. "I know I didn't cover it for the paper, but I know I heard about it, so I must have been away somewhere…"

They both thought for a moment.

"You were in Boston a few weekends, and in Ogunquit a lot that summer," Jack said quietly.

Ogunquit, Maine, was where Ben Holmes, a defense attorney from Boston whom Gracie had been dating at the time, had his summer home. Gracie and Jack had begun dating the year before, but had broken up, and Gracie had dated Ben exclusively until he'd been offered a job in Washington, D.C. Ben hadn't wanted to turn down the position, as it was with the U.S. Attorney's Office, so Ben had moved and he and Gracie had grown apart.

Since then, Gracie and Jack had become closer, but they were taking the romance side of their relationship at a glacially slow pace this time around. Neither wanted to end up as painfully and angrily as they had before.

Gracie nodded, now. "Mmmm…I was. I think the shooting happened when I was away for a long weekend," she agreed. "All I know is, Dave Tiller covered it." She shrugged. "But I read about it, of course." She looked at Jack. "And Dr. Spears agrees with you that the two crimes could have been done by the same shooter?" she queried.

Jack nodded. "Yes. Well, provisionally: the fragments were just that, fragments: not enough to make a positive determination that they were from the same gun. And the wounds in both cases were similar, but there's no way to know for sure that the same person, or even the same gun, was involved in both crimes. You can't write about this, Gracie," he reminded her. He'd given a lengthy preamble before revealing his theory, and told her that what he was about to tell her was in the strictest confidence and totally off the record.

"I know, Jack, but it's exciting to think about it," Gracie replied eagerly. "But—if, say, this guy shot at the two troopers a year or so ago," she began.

"Summer before this one," Jack clarified.

"Okay, well, if someone shot the troopers then, and just shot the McGinleys two weekends ago, where has he or she been? Has he been in plain sight, walking around and no one knew he was a murderer?" she asked tartly.

"The shooting at the barracks wasn't a murder," Jack reminded her.

"Well, thank god, but don't you think the shooter intended it to be?" Gracie replied.

Jack had to agree: both troopers had been critically wounded, and had endured several surgeries and months—in one case, a year—in hospital. The gunshots had been to their torsos and heads, but for whatever reason, had not been fatal.

"Maybe he's been out practicing so he got to be a better shot," Gracie put in darkly.

"So he could shoot a banker and his little boy?" Jack scoffed.

"Well, I agree, Jack: the McGinley murders don't make any sense at all. Why kill them? Their financials came up clean. Neither Aaron nor his son Wyatt had any enemies. The mother Belinda is a sweetheart, so even though she inherited the house and their savings it's not like it's bazillions of dollars or anything, and I can't see her as a killer..." Gracie summarized rapidly, her tone heated.

"Ok, ok, don't get all worked up about it," Jack soothed.

"Well, I just don't like the thought of a nutcase running around with high powered automatic weaponry, ready to shoot at anyone who looks at him crosseyed," Gracie replied, defensive. But then she took a deep breath and calmed a bit.

Jack finished his coffee. "If I could just figure out *why* the McGinleys were killed," he said, low. "Maybe I could figure out who."

"No one ever figured out why whoever it was shot at the troopers, did they?" Gracie asked.

"Nope. That wasn't my case, though: it was handled by the State Police and their investigators, since it happened on their property," Jack put in.

"Who would want to kill—even though they didn't succeed—state police troopers, and then a banker and his son a year later?" Gracie asked. "Are there any connections between the McGinleys and the two Troopers?" she asked, just as Jack said:

"First thing Monday I'll see if I can turn up any connections between the two troopers and the McGinleys."

They both laughed at the simultaneous expression of identical theories.

"Great minds!" Gracie quipped. "I'll bet you'll find something!"

Monday morning, Gracie attended the county prison board meeting as she generally did. The three county commissioners held the meeting in their conference room, as usual. On the board were the commissioners, and all those associated with the judicial system in Berkshire County: Judge Norcross, PD Felicia Laurenti, Sheriff Shermayne, Warden Mick Jones and DA Peter Paul Popovitch.

Popovitch, of course, was not present, although everyone else was, so there was still a quorum, and business could be conducted. The county executive Andrew Gaillard was also on hand for the meeting. Gracie wondered briefly where Jack was, as he often sat in for Popovitch. Then she figured he might be out of the courthouse on one of the several cases on his desk.

The commissioners called the meeting to order right on time. After routine business was dispatched, the board members immediately went into executive session to discuss personnel.

This meant that Gracie, as well as the new stringer for the *Gazetteer*, had to leave the meeting. Gracie waited patiently in the commissioners' outer office, chatting with the two secretaries as she did. Lori and Linda had both known Gracie for years, so they had a lot to talk about. The stringer from the *Gazetteer* sat quietly and tried to pretend she wasn't listening to the conversation, but it was clear that she was.

Gracie thought that given the animosity towards herself on the part of the stringer's boss, *Gazetteer* editor Gil Butcher, the new reporter had likely been 'warned' to give her a wide berth. Still, the girl appeared reluctantly interested in the chat among the three other women.

"My daughter goes— went —to school with Wyatt McGinley," Lori told Gracie at one point. "I wish they'd figure out who killed him and his dad," she added sadly.

"You daughter is in the same grade as Wyatt?" Gracie asked, curious.

"Yep. Same home room, too," Lori added. "She thought Wyatt was the smartest person she'd ever met," Lori continued.

"How so?" Gracie queried, even more interested.

Lori explained that Wyatt had always been inventing languages and codes and doing complicated mathematical problems.

"And that intrigued your daughter?" Gracie asked, perplexed.

Lori smiled. "Julie loves math—she's not like me, that's for sure. Actually, I'm not sure who she takes after," she said with a thoughtful smile and a chuckle. "But anyway, yeah, she saw Wyatt doodling one day last year, before school ended, and asked him what he was doing, and she was really interested. I think Wyatt enjoyed having someone to talk to about what he loved."

"Is Julie—like Wyatt? I mean…" Gracie wasn't sure how to phrase the question she wanted to ask without insulting Lori: she could hardly ask if Julie's IQ were as high as Wyatt's.

Lori grinned. "Oh, Julie's smart: not up in the stratosphere, like Wyatt, but smart enough to understand a lot of what he was doing when he 'doodled' in that notebook he always had with him. And she's always been a bookworm: read since she was three years old!" Lori told Gracie proudly.

Linda smiled over at her co-worker indulgently.

"The two of them even worked out a coded language that only they could understand," Lori continued. "They used to pass notes to each other written in it: even if the teachers read the notes, they couldn't make heads or tails of them. And given that it was Wyatt who was involved, well, he was rather a favorite, so no one ever said anything."

How interesting, thought Gracie.

CHAPTER THIRTY

In the closed executive session, the prison board began to discuss the Starling incident. Warden Jones stressed the fact that all persons involved in the Jail's portion of the snafu had been disciplined, and it appeared from the discussion that the police were also fairly blameless in the matter.

"I trust you didn't go too hard on—what's his name, the trainee?" asked the Judge.

"Norman Dinkelaub," replied the Warden. "I tried to use it as a teachable moment," he responded gravely. "I suspect CO Dinkelaub will become extremely proficient in book-ins in the very near future," the Warden finished, his voice firm.

"Good," the Judge replied. He informed the board that after speaking at length with all the Pittsfield Police Department officers involved, namely officer Bondino and the Police Chief, he was satisfied that no 'egregious transgressions of policy or procedure' had been made, as the Judge phrased it. Bondino, he explained, had understandably ceded to Magistrate Robertson's wishes with regard to the commitment order, and had therefore received a stern talking to from the Police Chief, but nothing more. "The Chief wanted to give Officer Bondino a day off without pay, but since Bondino is a 20 year veteran of the force and generally an excellent officer, I convinced the Chief to just give him a warning," Judge Norcross said.

"I really think that was appropriate," put in Sheriff Shermayne. "I mean, put yourself in Bondino's shoes: wouldn't you go along with whatever the Magistrate on call said?" He chuckled. "I know I would. And Magistrate Robertson promised to have the commitment order faxed first thing in the morning. Seems reasonable enough."

Everyone murmured acquiescence and nodded.

"But—let's talk about the elephant in the room, shall we?" the Judge went on. "What are we going to do about Magistrate Robertson?" he asked.

"Well, it's not for *us* to do anything about him, necessarily," replied Commissioner Morton. She was the chair of the commissioners this year, and also of the prison board, and kept a close eye on everything she was involved with.

"No, that would be down to the Judicial Conduct Board," the Judge replied mildly. "But I think the complaint, if one is filed, would have the most 'teeth' if you will, if it comes from not just my Chambers, but the County as well."

Everyone nodded in agreement.

"We would need to have a list with summaries of this incident as well as any others where Magistrate Robertson has been—shall we say, lax in his duties?" Commissioner Morton went on. "And I'd like to review that list carefully before we proceed," she added.

"That's a good idea," PD Laurenti said.

The Judge said that he would also speak to Magistrate Robertson's secretaries in the strictest confidence about any lapses they may have observed.

"Do you think you can trust them?" PD Laurenti asked frankly.

Sheriff Shermayne's niece happened to be one of Magistrate Robertson's secretaries. The Sheriff spoke up and said that he felt his niece as well as her co-worker could both be trusted. "Stands to reason, if their boss is being lazy about stuff, they probably don't like it," he added after reminding the PD of his connection to the one secretary. "Just makes them look bad, and they're not at fault, so I'd think they'd like that attended to."

"You're right about that," PD Laurenti admitted.

"I also would hope that the, erm, *gravitas*, of being addressed by the President Judge on a matter of strict confidentiality would make some kind of impact," Judge Norcross put in wryly.

"I'm sure it will," the PD agreed. "And I guess it wouldn't really matter if Robertson found out he was under investigation," she concluded.

Judge Norcross nodded, adding that he would have one of his staff go through the magistrate's adjudications for the past couple of years to see if any cases had been dismissed for reasons that suggested errors or wrongdoing on the part of the magistrate, or if there were any other irregularities.

Everyone around the long oval table in the commissioners' conference room took a deep breath, and then opened the meeting up to the media again.

"After discussion of a personnel matter that has been brought to our attention," began Commissioner Morton, "we have decided to launch an investigation. Nothing further is being released at this time."

Gracie knew the investigation had to be on Magistrate Robertson. She also knew that, until formal charges were brought, probably by the Judicial Conduct Board, no news would be available. So she couldn't write anything on that.

She'd covered the Starling incident as far as it had gone: that the man had been brought in to the jail on a DUI but booked in, apparently, with no paperwork. Until additional information connected to the case, i.e., disciplinary action or an investigation on Magistrate Robertson, came to light, she did not need to write any updates.

The next topic, however, was not handled in executive session since it was a policy matter: how evaluations were handled in the county to qualify people for the Public Defender. Gracie busily took notes as the current practice of having the Probation Office qualify prospective PD clients was explained, along with the 'administrative fee' paid by the county—which meant the taxpayers, Gracie thought with a huff—to Probation for this service.

Then Judge Norcross explained that according to Massachusetts Law, the Public Defender's office was supposed to have the task of qualifying people for its services, not Probation.

He read aloud the relevant section of the statute, which confirmed what Gracie already knew, thanks to Jack's discussion the other night at his parents' home: that when the former PD Donald Prestwick had died quite suddenly, his job had been handed to his protégé, Attorney Constance Cowens-Mitchell. She, however, had not been looked upon as quite ready to assume the mantle of Public Defender, so as a temporary measure, former President Judge Cranston had 'farmed out' some of the tasks and duties of the office to other county entities. Qualifying for Public Defender had been one such task, and once Cowens-Mitchell had been defeated in the next election by current PD Felicia Laurenti, and Judge Cranston had retired, no one remembered to change everything back to the way it had originally been under Prestwick.

Now, of course, people's memories had been jogged and the Prison Board issued a formal recommendation to the commissioners to change things back to the way they once had been, and the way that was in accordance with the law; they settled on the end of September—the end of the current quarter—as a good time to make the shift, and PD Laurenti said she would be ready by then for the change.

"Could you tell me, please," Gracie began during a lull, "how you all suddenly remembered this statute and realized that the current practice was not in line with it?" She smiled sweetly.

"I wouldn't say we all 'suddenly' remembered," Judge Norcross replied swiftly. "The way things are being done now was brought to my attention a few days ago. I looked into it and also discussed the matter with Attorney Laurenti, and we agreed the matter should be rectified."

Gracie nodded: okay, she wouldn't mention that Jack had been the one to bring it to the Judge's attention, since apparently the Judge didn't feel that was something he needed, or wanted, to disclose.

"Has anyone spoken with Mr. Melling?" asked Commissioner Morton of the Board.

"Not directly," the Judge replied after everyone shook their heads.

"Well, perhaps we should call him down here, and let him know face to face," Commissioner Morton continued. She lifted her voice and called to Linda in the outer office to ring over to the Probation office and ask Mr. Melling to stop down. "It seems the right way to handle it," she continued with a small smile. "Followed up with a written communication, of course," she added, with a glance at Andrew Gaillard.

The County Executive nodded and made a note to himself to draft a formal letter notifying Melling of the change in policy, and copying the Judge and the PD on it.

CHAPTER THIRTY-ONE

When Lance Melling appeared a few minutes later in the Commissioners' conference room, he looked as though he didn't expect any type of confrontation at all: cheery and smiling, he came in on a gust of Aqua Velva, and took his seat at the long oval table, nodding expectantly.

Once Judge Norcross had explained what was going on, however, Melling looked thunderous.

"You can't say my office hasn't been doing a good job," he whined, defensive. "One or two oversights in hundreds of qualifications is a pretty good record, seems to me!" he protested angrily. He'd fisted his hands and was in a half crouch in his chair, as though prepared at any second to rise.

And…what? Gracie wondered. Start a fight?

"No one is saying your office isn't doing a good job, Lance," the Judge assured him, trying to pacify the Probation Director. "And the oversights you mentioned are, as you say, a rare occurrence. But the fact is, Massachusetts Law demands that the qualification be done by the Public Defender's office, not by yours." He spread his hands in an 'I can't do anything about it' gesture and looked hopefully at the Probation Director.

Melling's truculence did not subside. "So, what, you're going to just rip the files out of my guys' hands and give them to Felicia?" he asked, as though that would be tantamount to handing nuclear weapons to a child. His sneer as he said, 'Felicia,' surprised Gracie, and apparently the PD as well: her face flashed with surprised indignation, and then she recovered herself and resumed her 'poker face.' But Gracie could see that her lips were thinned and pressed together in displeasure and the tips of her earlobes were still red.

"Well, being that in a couple of weeks, we begin a new quarter," the Judge continued smoothly, and Gracie had to admire his calm, "we will do the handover then, Lance, of all the files for all the qualifications, both past and current. Everything your office has. That gives you and your Probation Officers time to tidy everything up and make it as clean a transfer as possible. And it gives the Public Defender's office a chance to get ready to accept the files and do the job," he added, with a nod to the PD.

She nodded back shortly, as though she wanted to keep herself on a very tight leash. Gracie thought she was probably still simmering about Melling's attitude, and wondered if there were some longstanding rivalry or disagreement between the two.

"And it will save the county money," Laurenti put in a moment later. Her tone was matter of fact, but there was an edge to her voice. She smiled over at Melling, but her smile reminded Gracie of an animal baring its teeth.

Felicia just couldn't help herself. Jack's confidential call the week before had piqued her interest, so she had checked the county's budget and been shocked to discover that Probation was charging $20,000 to do what she was convinced she and her staff could do for about $10,000 a year.

When Felicia had gone to the Judge about the handling of qualification, and requested that he set the wheels in motion to have the job transferred back to her office where it belonged, she'd asked him if he knew how the $20,000 figure had been arrived at. He had told her that to the best of his knowledge, it had been a figure that Melling had decreed to Judge Cranston as being an appropriate one for the task.

At Felicia's comment now, Melling's normally pale face grew pink, then turned red, then puce.

"You'll never be able to do qualification for less than we do!" he shouted. "And you don't have the staff we do to do it!" he went on. He pounded the table and Gracie wondered if, à la Nikita Kruschev, he was going to throw his shoe next.

It was true, Felicia thought: she had two secretaries and a legal aide, so with her that made four people to do qualification. Melling had assigned four of his officers, plus himself, so that was five. But somehow Felicia just didn't think that qualification would take that many people—or $20,000 a year.

Despite her wish to reply to Melling's outburst with a snappy retort, Felicia held her tongue while the Judge continued to try and pacify Melling.

Gracie wrote, and wrote, and wrote, and although she normally didn't take photos at meetings—who wants to see a picture of a bunch of people sitting around a big conference table?—she did snap a shot with her iPhone of Melling, fist pounding on the table and mouth wide open as he hollered at the Public Defender. It was a juicy shot.

A few minutes later the charged meeting was concluded, Melling swept out of the meeting in high dudgeon: his Earth Shoes could be heard stomping into the hall and through the doorway to the staircase. The rest of the Prison Board members followed quietly, talking among themselves in subdued tones.

Gracie walked carefully out of the office, down the stairs and out the door of the courthouse to finish the rest of her usual stops. Then, she had a chiropractic appointment, after which she'd head home and begin to write up the story, and this week's other news items. She thought as she walked that Jack had missed a pretty exciting meeting. She also thought that he would be pleased to know that Judge Norcross had advanced the hand over of eligibility from Jack's suggestion of January to the start of the fourth quarter, in two weeks.

She was surprised to see Belinda McGinley at the chiropractor's office.

"Belinda! I didn't know you came here!" Gracie said with a smile. Having checked in, she took a seat next to the woman.

Belinda had been on her smart phone, but looked up at Gracie's hello. "Hi Gracie: yes, Dr. Grist has been adjusting me for years. Aaron always thought it was a lot of hooey, but…" she shrugged, and gave a little smile.

Gracie shared that Jack had a similar opinion of chiropractic, and the two women laughed together.

"What's that?" Gracie asked, curious, and pointing to a page that was loaded on Belinda's phone.

"Oh—I've been looking at various cat rescue groups on line," Belinda said, low. She almost sounded embarrassed.

"Oh?" Gracie said encouragingly.

Belinda nodded. "There really isn't one here, I mean, in this area," she said, and named one or two in the southern part of the county. "Not north of Pittsfield."

"Uh huh?" Gracie said again, thinking that she thought she knew where Belinda was headed with this, and also thinking how wonderful that would be.

"But there are a lot of stray cats, and the humane society is overwhelmed trying to trap, neuter and release them all," she added, warming to her subject. "They don't have room at the shelter. There's a real need for a place that can not only assist with TNR but also provide a home for rehabilitated ferals and strays—ones who can become used to being handled and who would make good pets," Belinda explained.

"And you are thinking about—" Gracie prodded. She hoped Lindsey wouldn't call her in for her appointment just yet: she wanted to hear Belinda's plan. But it seemed that Dr. Grist was running late, so she was able to focus on what her friend was revealing.

"I'm thinking that I could convert that four car garage and loft on my property into a little Rescue," she finished, her voice still low, but her excitement unmistakable.

"Wow, Belinda, that's great: of course you could!" Gracie chimed in, nodding happily.

"And I'd network, with other Rescues," here she lifted her phone, "to find homes for my kitties once they're ready," she concluded. "And meanwhile, they'd be safe."

"Oh, Belinda, I think that's a great idea, and a wonderful thing to do," Gracie said. "Why not let everyone in Club know at the next meeting, too: maybe there's some money we could donate to the cause, or we could have a fund raiser or something," Gracie went on, thinking as the words flew from her lips. "The Winter Dance always chooses a charity, maybe this year we could choose your Rescue," she suggested.

"I won't be up and running that fast, I don't think, Gracie," Belinda replied hesitantly. "I've kept my veterinary tech license up to date, so that's all right, but there's a lot of renovation work in the garage to get it ready," she explained. "And then, if I really want to get official, I'd have to incorporate as a non profit. But I'll wait a while before taking that step," she added thoughtfully.

"But still, Belinda, maybe we could help a little with the cost of everything, to get you set up," Gracie pursued.

Belinda's smile told her all she needed to know, and Gracie determined she would raise the issue herself at the October Club meeting, if Belinda did not.

CHAPTER THIRTY-TWO

CHAPTER THIRTY-TWO

Late Monday afternoon, Gracie wrote up all of her articles for the newspaper, and then plopped herself on her chocolate brown leather sofa with her iPhone and iPad. Stuffing a couple of pillows at one end, she elevated her 'stupid ankle' and arranged an ice pack over it the way her chiropractor had shown her.

Lindsey and Dr. Grist had both admonished her for not following the 'RICE' system: rest, ice, compression and elevation. 'I can only do so much to regain range of motion, Gracie: you have to do the exercises I gave you and elevate and ice this ankle so the muscles heal,' Dr. Grist had told her, for the first time being a little abrupt. 'And wear that compression bandage,' he had ordered her.

Gracie had sighed, but had put the bandage on when she'd got home, and worn it all afternoon as she'd written her articles and done various little chores around the house. When everything had been finished, she had sat on a kitchen chair and done the exercises Dr. Grist had told her to do: roll the ankle one way, then the other; flex the foot one way then the other; bend the ankle this way, the that way, hold for a count of ten. And so on.

She didn't think the exercises did much, but Dr. Grist told her that she was favoring her ankle, so she had to do the exercises to keep the muscles from atrophying. He said her muscles would respond, and within days she would be able to use her ankle better.

When she had finished, Gracie sat on the sofa and applied the ice pack. She had to admit, it felt pretty good. She was about at the half way point of the treatments from Dr. Grist, and while she thought she'd made great improvements, Dr. Grist apparently didn't think so. Since Gracie very much wanted to be able to stop limping by the end of September, she decided to be a model patient from that moment on.

While she sat, Gracie checked her social media feeds. Belinda had been right, Gracie realized: a lot of Rescues and adoption agencies for both dogs and cats used social media to get the word out about their adoptable pets. If Belinda worked in conjunction with local vets and the humane society, and also networked with other Rescues and the like, Gracie was sure the enterprise would be successful. And, as Belinda had said, at least at her little Rescue, the cats would be safe.

Too many unwanted animals were killed every day in shelters across the country, Gracie knew. She also knew that 'unwanted' could mean anything: from a stray, to a feral, to someone's pet who had been abandoned or left behind. It didn't mean the animal was un-adoptable or in any way un-lovable.

She wondered if Belinda would let her help out a little at the Rescue, once she had it going. Gracie thought she'd like that. Also, she'd help Belinda set it up: she knew Belinda had some money from the life insurance but she also knew that a little extra cash would come in handy. And although she freely confessed herself a bit of a klutz, Gracie was pretty handy with a hammer and a paintbrush, so maybe she could help out with some of the more minor renovations, as well.

She was just about to call Belinda and make these suggestions when her iPhone's ring tone—she had changed it now to the first movement of Vivaldi's 'Autumn' from *The Four Seasons*— sounded and Jack's face appeared on the screen.

Gracie answered and Jack said he was calling to tell her that the flyover was scheduled for the next morning, Tuesday, at 11 a.m.

"Can I come?" Gracie asked bluntly. She knew the Cessna Jack normally flew held four people, so in this case it would accommodate Jack, the pilot; Sheriff Shermayne with the thermal camera; and two empty seats in the back. She'd like to occupy one.

"You writing a story about how the Sheriff's office is using thermal imaging to search for the McGinley killer?" Jack asked.

Gracie averred that that was precisely what she was planning. "I can't write about how the McGinley murder could be connected to the shooting of the troopers last year," she groused.

"Not yet," Jack agreed. He wanted to keep the fact that that seemed likely, and that the authorities were aware of it, quiet for the moment: if the shooter was monitoring news reports at all, revealing that might tip Jack's hand, although he was unsure just how.

"Did you find anything besides the ammo to link the troopers and McGinley?" Gracie asked, fast.

Jack confessed that he had not.

"Well then, seems like the thermal imaging story is the only one I've got," Gracie said triumphantly. "The public has a right to know what measures our officers are taking to find this person, and the flyover seems like a good thing to tell them, especially since it's taxpayer money that's renting the plane, even though your services are free and the camera's borrowed," she added persuasively.

After she'd got Jack to agree—grudgingly, but agree nonetheless—for her to be on the plane the next day, Gracie rang off and dialed Belinda. The time was up for the ice pack on her ankle, so while the call connected, Gracie walked slowly into her kitchen to toss the pack back into the freezer, and to think about dinner.

Belinda was delighted to hear of Gracie's offers and said she'd be happy to have the help, and the company.

"I find myself, not exactly lonely, but, well, I'm used to having someone else in the house," Belinda admitted.

"Why not go to one of the shelters down in southern Berkshire County and see if any of the kitties there appeal to you—or you to them?" Gracie suggested. Pumpkin had been adopted from the humane society in Boston, and was a wonderful companion. She thought she knew exactly what Belinda meant about having another being in the house. Another heartbeat; another soul.

Belinda told Gracie that she must be psychic, since she'd planned to do exactly that later in the week. "It'll also be a good chance to network, and to check the other shelters out," she added.

Gracie was almost ready to hang up when a thought popped into her head and right out of her mouth.

"Belinda—I wanted to ask if maybe you'd allow me to borrow Wyatt's notebook," she asked.

"His notebook?" Belinda queried. "Whatever for?"

Gracie explained that ever since she'd heard about Wyatt's intelligence, and his penchant for mathematical and linguistic puzzles, something had been nagging at her, something about his notebook. "I know he wrote everything down in there," she said gently. "You told me, it was the closest thing Wyatt had to a diary."

"That's right, Gracie: but you've seen it. And so have the police, and they thought it was nonsense. It's mostly gibberish, or math," the bereaved mother protested. "I mean, if it's not an equation or something, it's paragraphs in letters that aren't from any alphabet I know, or English words and letters that make no sense."

"I know. But—I can't explain, Belinda, but I just have a feeling. I think somehow that maybe Wyatt did have a chance to write about the camping trip and maybe there's a clue in that writing that will help us find the killer," Gracie explained honestly.

"You do?" Belinda sounded amazed. "But—the police said they had both been killed instantly." Her voice was small.

"Yes, of course, Belinda: they didn't suffer. Didn't know what had happened," Gracie hastened to reassure her. "I meant before they were shot. Maybe while dinner was cooking, after they'd set up camp, or maybe after dinner. Maybe Wyatt wrote down his impressions so far of the trip. And maybe there's something in what he wrote, maybe he didn't realize it, but maybe there's a clue there—" Gracie finished, unsure. "It's just my theory, a hunch."

"But how will you understand it? It's all in code or something," Belinda protested further. She really seemed reluctant to part with her dead son's notebook.

Gracie knew, however, that the issue wasn't that Belinda didn't trust her with the notebook. Rather, she realized that the notebook was perhaps the closest thing to Wyatt that Belinda still had, the item that retained the spirit of her son. Gracie could understand not wanting to let anyone borrow it. Also, Gracie thought that perhaps Belinda was genuinely doubtful that her son's 'gibberish' would be of any benefit.

She explained about Julie Sweetwater.

"Oh, yes, Julie!" Belinda acknowledged readily. "She was just about Wyatt's only friend, real friend, in school."

Gracie could hear Belinda's smile.

"She might help you translate one of the code languages. I think she only knew one. There were several."

Gracie laughed. "I imagine there were: codes, ciphers,

secret languages…I just thought that if Julie could help me figure out one, maybe I could crack the others and perhaps as I said, there is a clue there, something Wyatt had seen or done or remarked on at the campsite. I'd only keep it for a day or so," Gracie continued appealingly.

"Well, if you think it'll help, of course you can have it," Belinda finally agreed. "And keep it as long as you need to."

"I promise it'll be safe," Gracie told Belinda. She actually intended to make photocopies of each page, and return the actual diary itself to Belinda within a day.

CHAPTER THIRTY-THREE

Tuesday, Gracie met Jack, the Sheriff and much to her surprise and dismay, Gil Butcher, at the Pittsfield Municipal Airport.

"I had to call him," Jack murmured, low, to Gracie as he finished his pre-flight checklist and invited Butcher and the Sheriff to climb into the small plane. "If I hadn't, there would have been trouble, you know that, especially since you're here," Jack finished.

Gracie sighed. "I know. I was just hoping he was scared of heights or something and would send someone else," she whispered back.

"Oh, he's scared of heights, all right," Jack chuckled.

Gracie rolled her eyes, then opened the door on her side of the rear seat and slid in. She gave a nod to Butcher and buckled her harness. Then Jack took his seat, and after checking a couple more things, opened his side window and yelled, 'clear!' and started the engine.

While Jack taxied to runway fourteen, which was being used for takeoffs and landings this day, given the light breeze, Gracie chatted with the Sheriff, who sat in front of her in the co-pilot's seat. Although part of Gracie wished Jack had put her there, of course it made more sense to have the Sheriff with the thermal imaging camera sit up front where there was more visibility and bigger windows.

The good thing about sitting behind the Sheriff was that she could easily see the camera's LED screen and watch the images the Sheriff took without contorting herself too much. He seemed very happy to show Gracie all the bells and whistles on the camera and she even took a staged shot of him with the camera, aiming out the window. That picture would run with her piece on the continuing search for the McGinleys' murderer.

Butcher was mostly silent. The windows in the back seat weren't very large but the *Gazetteer* editor still avoided them, and kept his gaze on his knees, which were shaking. Or maybe that was the engine's vibrations?

Gracie wondered, if this was how Butcher was when they were still on the ground, what would he be like when they were airborne? She hoped the little Cessna had air sickness bags, just in case.

They reached the end of the runway and Jack did a few last minute checks: Gracie could see the ailerons move, as well as other crucial navigational elements on the plane's exterior. Then Jack asked, "everyone ready?"

Everyone nodded that they were, and Gracie gave him a big smile: this was exciting! She'd only gone for a flight with Jack once, and that had been a couple of years before, when he was still logging hours to obtain his pilot's license. For that ride, which had been just a brief tour of the immediate area, his instructor had gone along, too, even though Jack had been qualified to fly the plane himself.

Now, Jack had logged hundreds of air hours and Gracie had every confidence in him.

Jack got on the radio and announced the plane's call letters and the fact that they were about to take off on runway fourteen to fly a grid search over Greylock Forest. Since everything was A-OK they were green lighted to take off, and Jack pushed the throttle to full: the little plane roared happily.

Then they began to move forward at a fast pace and in another few seconds Gracie saw the ground remain behind her as the plane climbed gently into the clear morning.

Butcher whimpered quietly; Gracie nearly asked him why he'd come along on this ride if he was so terrified of heights, but decided not to. The man's face was the color of milk, and sheened in sweat, and his breathing was rapid.

"We'll be fine," Gracie assured him, low. "Jack's a good pilot. Try to relax."

Butcher took a deep breath, shot Gracie a surprised look, and then gave a nod.

Jack and the Sheriff had mapped out the area they wanted to survey—Greylock State Forest including the primitive and the 'luxury' camping areas, and the land immediately around it—in a grid, and so as soon as they'd reached altitude, Jack began piloting the plane along those pre-arranged lines.

It was quite pretty, Gracie thought, looking down at the swaths of evergreens interrupted by deciduous trees that had begun to change color for fall. A few had even dropped some of their leaves. She saw Greylock Mansion at one point, and remembered that she needed to get in touch with Victorine to set their first meeting at the Mansion to start mounting the new Period Clothing Exhibit.

As they flew, Gracie looked out the window, but also kept a close watch on the thermal camera's LED screen. The Sheriff was very amenable, alerting Gracie when the camera picked up a small herd of deer.

"So if the guy who killed the McGinleys is hiding in the woods, that camera should pick up the heat signature from his body?" Gracie asked.

Sheriff Shermayne nodded. "Even if he's inside, like in a deserted cabin."

Gracie thought that sounded pretty good, but she couldn't help wondering, if the killer was the same guy who had shot the troopers, had he been hiding out in the woods for so many months? If so, where? And most of all, why? Why not just leave the area, or stay in a motel or rent an apartment?

The Rangers patrolled the Forest pretty regularly, so Gracie thought that anyone living, even temporarily, in a cabin not assigned to them would have been discovered. It seemed too risky to her, especially for over a year.

It was an interesting subject to speculate on. However, Gracie's speculations were interrupted when, after a while, she spotted some familiar terrain.

"That's my property!" she told the Sheriff excitedly. She'd never seen her home from the air, and it was quite cool.

She pointed out the rocky outcropping that marked the boundary between her land and the State Forest. "I'm not really sure of just how the line goes, not from up here, though I have a map on my deed," she told the Sheriff.

"How many acres do you have?" the Sheriff asked.

"Only forty," Gracie replied...and there's my pond!" she pointed to the triangular water feature. "See the little boathouse? I keep the floats and a rowboat in there, and of course, you can change in there if you want to..." she told the Sheriff about floating on her pond in the summer.

"No wonder you always have a good tan," he commented with a grin. "So that's your house?" the Sheriff continued.

Gracie said that was indeed her house, and pointed out the terrace and the conservatory, and explained quickly about the original house and its later additions.

"It's a really nice property, Gracie," Sheriff Shermayne said.

Butcher still wasn't looking out the window much, but he was no longer whimpering, and his color was more normal. He peered over at the thermal camera's LED screen a few times, and made some scribblings in his notebook.

So far, so good, Gracie thought.

Now, Jack turned the plane around and headed back on a different tangent, doing another section of the grid. The Sheriff aimed his camera out the window once more, and everyone waited to see if the thermal imagery would show the shooter.

"Sorry it was a bust," Jack told the Sheriff a couple hours later as they said goodbye and shook hands. They were just off the tarmac, where Jack had parked the plane after landing. He chocked the wheels and tied down the tail and wings.

Gracie had watched, fascinated.

"Oh, I wouldn't say that, Jack," the Sheriff came back with a big smile. "At least we know he's not in the Forest!" he noted of his quarry.

"He could be long gone from here," Butcher put in; now that they were back on solid ground, he had recovered his voice. But Gracie thought he was being far less obnoxious to her—and in general— than usual.

"Yeah, I thought that, too," Gracie said mildly. Of course, if the shooter was the same one who had attacked the state police barracks, it was likely he was still in the area. Or had returned. Actually, it was likely that he was a local person. Once again, she wondered if she passed the man on the street in the course of his daily business: was he a 'normal' person who was hiding in plain sight?

Still, it was something of a relief to know the guy wasn't in the Forest or anywhere near Greylock Mansion, and the plane ride had been great fun.

"Maybe I'll take some lessons," Gracie told Jack as they walked together back to the Airport's office. She was still limping, and her ankle felt stiff after two hours of inactivity in the plane.

"You'd love it, Gracie: I can give you the contact info for my instructor, he's great," Jack replied happily. Then he made a face and pointed to her right foot. "Got to get that fixed, first, though," he noted. "Can't right rudder with a bad ankle."

Gracie nodded.

A few minutes later, everyone parted, and Gracie headed home for lunch. She would spend the afternoon writing up her article and emailing it in. Then, at 4 p.m. she had an appointment to meet Lori Sweetwater at the courthouse. Her daughter Julie was coming there directly from school and Lori had arranged for Gracie to speak with Julie at their home nearby, about Wyatt and his notebook.

Belinda McGinley had dropped the notebook off at Gracie's early that same morning and Gracie had copied every page, then dropped the notebook back at Belinda's on her way to the airport. Belinda had been extremely grateful for Gracie's thoughtfulness and understanding, and invited her to lunch on Wednesday. She said she wanted to show Gracie the four bay garage and loft, and get her ideas on the proposed cat rescue.

CHAPTER THIRTY-FOUR

Julie Sweetwater was a very bright girl of nearly nine years old. Clearly her mother's pride and joy, the girl was friendly and outgoing and more than happy to talk to Gracie.

"I read your articles in the *Intelligencer*," she told Gracie in admiration. "Mom says you're the best reporter around, and I think so, too!" she added with a grin.

The three of them: Julie, Lori and Gracie, were seated at the Sweetwaters' kitchen table. Lori had put out a small plate of fruit and home baked oatmeal raisin cookies and poured milk for Julie while she and Gracie had tea.

Gracie had taken out the sheaves of paper that were the copies of Wyatt's notebook pages, and Julie had delightedly agreed to see if she could decipher any of the writing in it.

"Well, the first thing Wyatt taught me was the difference between codes and ciphers," Julie began, munching on an apple. "A code has each word in the message replaced with a code word or code symbol."

Gracie nodded.

"A cipher is where each *letter* in a message is replaced."

"Which did Wyatt use?" Gracie asked.

"Oh, he used both, but mostly we used ciphers, because they're more fun and there are a lot more variables," Julie answered gleefully. "Here, I'll show you…" She turned the pages of Wyatt's notebook until she found what she wanted. She pointed to a sentence that read:

VRFDA'U UdLGQdG dODUU YDU RQ WG
SGbLRFLd VDEOG. & Pb UVpDbV VROF pU
DERpV PDFDPG yPdLG.

"Ok, now, see that?" Julie asked, sounding like a teacher.

Gracie nodded meekly. It looked like gibberish to her, all right. But with strange letters mixed in with the normal alphabet she was used to.

"That's an R-O-T-3 substitution cipher," Julie said.

At Gracie's blank look she smiled, and explained that an 'ROT3' substitution cipher replaced each letter of the alphabet with the letter three ahead of it: hence ROT3, which stood for 'rotate [forward] three [letters.].

"It's pretty simple," Julie insisted, and began to translate the paragraph.

"Oh!" Gracie exclaimed after a moment or two. "I get it...but what's with the funny letters? Those look like stuff I read in *Beowulf*, in college," she told Julie with a shake of her head.

Julie looked delighted at Gracie's perspicacity. "That's exactly right, Miss Barufaldi!" she exclaimed. "Those are some of the letters that used to be used, but aren't in our modern alphabet. There's the thorn, and the wynn, and the yogh, and the eth," she pointed to examples of each of these and explained what sounds they stood for. "Wyatt liked to use them, kind of as a shortcut."

"But how did he know where they would go in our alphabet?" Gracie asked. "I mean, if he's using ROT3, they'd have to be inserted in some kind of order, wouldn't they?" she asked.

"Yes: Wyatt always put the thorn after the T, the wynn after the W, the yogh after the Y and the eth after the E. So his alphabet had more letters than ours does."

Gracie nodded again.

"Can you read ROT3 pretty easily?" she asked Julie.

The girl nodded. "We used that mostly so yeah, I can read it well."

"Did Wyatt use other ciphers? And did he ever use codes?" Gracie queried. She sipped at her tea and gave Lori a smile.

Lori just shook her head slightly and smiled back: her daughter was amazing, and she was extremely proud of her.

"Like I said, he didn't use codes much. He liked ciphers. He did sometimes use the Vigenère cipher, which uses a code word, like 'cat' or 'philosophy,' or anything you like. Then you use a Vigenère square that you have to write out, to figure out the cipher. But first, of course, you have to figure out the code word, and it could be anything," Julie explained, as though it were really quite simple.

Gracie said she thought that sounded very complicated, and did not ask Julie to explain what a 'Vigenère square' was.

"He used ROT3 with me, because I knew it well: that's why I was able to pick it out here, in his notebook." The girl looked again at the copied pages. "But there are other ciphers in here…ones I don't know, or don't know well. And, of course, Wyatt was working on his own alphabet to use, and I see some of that in here, too."

"His own alphabet?" Gracie asked, feeling momentarily stupid.

Julie nodded enthusiastically. "Yes. He wanted to create his own language, too, but I don't think he'd got 'round to that yet," she commented matter of factly, as though she were talking about homework, or chores. "But he liked the Vinča alphabet, and I think he was trying to simplify that one and adapt it to use with English, for a start."

"Mmmm…" Gracie didn't know quite what to say to all of that. She had no idea what the 'Vinča' alphabet was, so she asked Julie, who told her.

"But he didn't use that with me," Julie admitted.

"Could you talk me through a couple of ROT3 messages, so I can learn how to do it?" Gracie asked humbly. "I'd like to be able to at least scan some of what Wyatt wrote in here, particularly the last few entries."

"You mean, in case he wrote down something about the camping trip that might help you find the killer?" Julie asked, her gentle brown eyes huge behind her light blue-framed glasses.

Gracie nodded.

For the next hour, Julie translated and Gracie watched, and then Julie watched while Gracie translated a few of the sentences from Wyatt's notebook. The final entries, the ones Gracie wanted to focus on, were not in ROT3, but in what Julie said was Wyatt's version of the ancient Vinča alphabet, so she was unable to help there. But she cheerfully made sense of the ROT3 entries in some of the rest of the notebook, and Gracie got an idea of what Wyatt had written about in his journal.

By the time Gracie was able to stumble through most of the ROT3 entries, Julie was thrilled and Gracie had a headache.

"You know I've really missed having someone to write to in code," Julie told Gracie as they said goodbye. "Maybe you could email me sometime, in ROT3!" she suggested.

Lori laughed. "Oh, I think Miss Barufaldi has too much to do, to do that," she told her daughter, who looked abashed.

Gracie smiled. "Well, I tell you what, Julie: if I find anything in Wyatt's notebook that helps the investigation, I'll email you to let you know, but I'll write it in ROT3, ok?"

When Jack called Gracie on Tuesday evening to say goodnight, Gracie answered with a moan.

"What's wrong?" Jack asked quickly, thinking her ankle had got worse.

Gracie explained about Wyatt's notebook and the cipher lesson she'd had from his school friend Julie Sweetwater. "My head is going to explode!" Gracie said in protest, adding that she'd been hard at deciphering the copies of the notebook pages since dinner time.

"Have you made any headway?"

Gracie sighed. "I'm getting pretty good at reading ROT3 by now," she groused. "But mostly it's been entries about school, or about other projects he'd been working on." She paused. "He got bullied a lot, at school," she murmured. "By some of the older kids, I guess. Wyatt confessed in his notebook entries that he was frightened of them. Called them monsters." She paused. "He had an extremely active imagination," she went on, "and he wanted to invent his own language," she continued, sounding a bit awed. "He was also fascinated by the Vinča alphabet and was working on adapting that to use with English."

"The what?" Jack asked with a chuckle. "I thought vinca was a vine. My mother grows that on her patio, I think."

"This is 'Vinča,'" Gracie explained, "it's pronounced a bit differently, and I had to ask Julie what it was," she admitted. She filled Jack in on the ancient Southeastern European language that had been discovered but not translated, and that predated Egyptian by thousands of years. "But Julie doesn't know how Wyatt used that alphabet, and unfortunately the entries at the end of the journal, the ones I want to look at, are all written in Wyatt's adaptation of Vinča."

Jack whistled. "Wow: that kid must have really been something," he commented. "I'm so sorry he was bullied," he added, thinking of Leroy Cooper. "Maybe if that anti-bullying awareness initiative had started a couple of years back instead of this fall, Wyatt wouldn't have been bullied. Or Leroy Cooper."

"Yes, you're right," Gracie agreed sadly.

They talked a bit more and then disconnected. Gracie promised Jack that if she found out anything from Wyatt's notebook, he would be the second to know. "I promised Julie, since she'd been so helpful, that I'd let her know first," Gracie explained.

She didn't mention that she'd promised to write in code to the girl.

Gracie read Wyatt's notebook well into the night: even though it was hard going, she couldn't seem to put it down. The boy's mind was amazing, and reading what she could of the notebook was allowing Gracie a much better understanding of the young genius. She thought what a shame it was that he wouldn't live to fulfill his potential, because who knew what he might have become, or what he might have discovered or cured.

The entries in what Julie had called Wyatt's 'simplified Vinča' script looked completely mind boggling, and Gracie wondered exactly how it was supposed to be a simple writing system. She concentrated on the ROT3 entries, things she had a shot, at least, of understanding.

She went to bed about 1 a.m. and slept deeply. Pumpkin woke her on Wednesday a little after 8 a.m., with an insistent orange paw on Gracie's cheek and a not-so-gentle 'miau!'

"It's late, past your breakfast time, hey, puss-cat?" Gracie asked the large orange tabby. Pumpkin twined herself around Gracie's ankles as the latter shrugged into her terrycloth robe and made her way downstairs.

She realized what had made her cat so insistent she get up: not only was Pumpkin out of food, but Larry's crew had arrived to start work on her labyrinth. Gracie could see Charlie and George out on her west lawn, marking out the spiral shape; a peek out at her driveway confirmed their pickup truck jammed with viburnum, yew, fire bush and junipers.

"They must have bought out every nursery in a ten mile radius!" Gracie murmured to herself, giving the guys a wave from the dining room window. She'd go out and say hello properly once she'd had coffee and dressed.

Before she brewed her coffee or even had juice, Gracie filled clean bowls for Pumpkin with cold water and the cat's favorite organic kibble. She put two treats atop the kibble and watched with a smile as the cat dug in happily.

Gracie sighed. If only people could be so pleased with so little.

She set up her coffee maker and switched it on, then poured herself a small glass of organic carrot and apple juice and washed her vitamins down with a few swallows. While the coffee brewed and Pumpkin ate, Gracie washed out the cat's soiled bowls: one said 'Purrfekt' and the other said 'CAT' in different languages.

Gracie examined the bowl in the soapy water: GATTO, KATZE, CHAT, KISSA, KAT...most words for 'CAT' were descended from Indo-European and so looked very similar.

Gracie shook her head.

All the words looked similar. Hmmm...

If she could figure out what, perhaps, a simple word like 'camp' or 'tent' might look like in Wyatt's version of the Vinča alphabet, maybe she could find that word in his notebook. And then maybe she could translate the entry.

Julie had said that Wyatt was using the Vinča alphabet as a simple polyalphabetic substitution. She had said he had simplified it to use with English words; because Vinča had never been translated, however, Wyatt would have had to have assigned English alphabetical correspondences randomly to the Vinča letters or symbols he used.

But simple, short words like 'camp' and 'tent' only had four letters. Surely they wouldn't be too hard to pick out of the Vinča entries in the notebook. And if Wyatt had written anything about the camping trip in his notebook, it was almost certain he would have had to have used one of those words!

Gracie poured herself a large mug of coffee, added organic half and half, and brought it to the kitchen table. Then she dug out the notebook pages and flipped through them until she came to the last few pages, where the Vinča lettering began to appear almost exclusively, interspersed with mathematical equations. She flipped to the last entry in the journal, and began to work backwards: it stood to reason that anything about the camping trip would have been among the last things Wyatt would have written.

She sipped at the coffee and scanned the lines of peculiar letters. Whenever she came to a group of four letters or symbols, she circled it with a pen. After about three pages, Gracie thought she'd probably done enough to encompass any entries made during the camping trip, so she stopped, dashed upstairs to throw on sweats and sneakers, checked on Pumpkin, who had gone through her cat flap out onto the screened porch, and then went out to greet the landscapers.

CHAPTER THIRTY-FIVE

After just a few minutes, it was clear Charlie and George knew exactly what Gracie wanted. She brought them each a steaming mug of coffee, poured a second one for herself, and went back to her task with Wyatt's notebook.

She wrote all the circled letter groups down on a fresh piece of paper; before Gracie had written half a dozen, she realized that already, one had repeated. She continued writing, however, copying the circled letter groups from the last three pages of the notebook.

Then she studied the list of what she presumed were words once again. Two groups of four letters each repeated: one three times, the other twice. The two groups of four were completely different:

Y I IIIII I=   and   H T IIIII H

Gracie thought that since the first and last letters of the second group repeated, that word could very well be 'tent.' If one were writing about a camping trip, the word 'tent' was bound to come up!

If this were so, the H symbol was a 't,' and the T symbol and the IIIII symbol stood for 'e' and 'n' respectively. She looked at the first group. If IIIII were 'n', then maybe the IIIII in the first word group was 'm' and if that were so, this first word could be 'camp.' That would mean Y was 'c' and I was 'a' and I= was 'p.'

Feeling accomplished, Gracie smiled. That was great! But what did it mean? It meant that she could use the eight letters she thought she knew to fill in where ever they appeared in the rest of the text. It would be like a giant crossword puzzle, with only one or two letters known in each word, but she could try.

Too bad she'd never liked crossword puzzles.

While she gobbled down a plain Greek yoghurt cup and an apple, Gracie diligently placed the eight letters she knew inter linearly through the text for the last entry in Wyatt's notebook: might as well just try one entry, to see if her theory made sense.

Then, she looked hard at any words that had even one letter in them identified. She looked at the placement of the word within the sentence—thank god, Wyatt had used punctuation, she thought. And she tried to get a sense of what Wyatt had written.

Instead, she got her headache from the evening before back.

Gracie popped a couple of ibuprofen, brought Pumpkin in from the porch, and checked her time: it was just 10 a.m. She had said she'd be at Belinda's at 1 p.m. for lunch, so she still had two hours before she needed to shower and dress quickly for her afternoon of civilized company. Meanwhile, Gracie took a deep breath and returned to her list of crossword puzzle words as she had come to think of them, to see if she could get anything intelligent out of them.

She got plenty of 'words:' wonderful ones like '_a_,' '_at_e_,' and 'm_n_te__.' She studied '_ent' for a moment: it wasn't 'tent' because the first letter was different from the last: it looked like a short railroad track. 'T' looked kind of like railroad track with one tie in the middle, like the english letter H. So maybe this railroad track symbol was a letter next to 't' like 'u,' Gracie wondered. That seemed logical, but she had no idea if that was the value Wyatt had assigned to that symbol.

However, 'uent' wasn't a word.

Aha, but the letter before 't' was 's' and if the railroad track symbol meant 's' then that word was 'sent.'

Gracie chuckled and filled that in on her 'translation.' She felt as she had when she'd been translating Caesar's *Gallic Wars* in prep school, and jotting down the words and phrases in English, in between the Latin lines.

All right: if that was 'sent' and the railroad symbol was 's...' Gracie busily filled in all the other 's' symbols she could find. The word 'm_nste__' she noted once she had added the 's' to the middle of the word, appeared twice in the entry she was looking at, the last one Wyatt had written.

It still didn't make much sense to her: all she'd pieced together in the first sentence was:

'd_d sent me t_ _at_e_ _____ ___ ___ camp ___e.'

The last word could be 'site' but the first letter wasn't an 's.' Camp...what? Camp site, camp ground...too many letters. Camp spot? No, no one said that...camp, camp, what else was at a camp?—camp—FIRE!

Quickly, Gracie filled that in. If that were the word 'fire' then she could fill in 'f' and 'i' and 'r' wherever they appeared. Now the first sentence read, '_a_ sent me t_ _at_er _in__in_ f_r __r camp fire.' Logically, Gracie thought, if Wyatt and Aaron had been the only two camping, then if Wyatt had been 'sent' it had to have been by Aaron. Could that first word be 'Dad?'

If so, then '_in__in_' became '_ind_in_.'

It made sense that after the phrase, 'sent me' the next word, 't_' was 'to.' If she filled in the other 'o' symbols, she got , 'Dad sent me to _at_er _ind_in_ for o_r camp fire.' She thought 'o_r' was probably 'our.'

But what had Aaron asked Wyatt to do with regard to their camp fire?

Gracie sat back and closed her eyes, and tried to imagine going camping as Wyatt and Aaron had. Her own camping days were long past, but Gracie could recall setting up the tent and getting firewood for the fire ring. She had always been obsessed with having enough wood and had always worried until the kindling had caught and the larger logs were being licked with flames...

Kindling. That '_ind_in_' word had to be kindling!

Aaron had sent Wyatt to gather kindling!

And...what? Hastily, Gracie filled in all the other letters she thought she had identified, then stared at the sentence before her. She sat back in her chair, hard, and her stomach clenched.

The puzzle reminded her a little of the things that appeared every so often on social media feeds, words written with numbers instead of letters and reversed letters that said, 'if you can read this...'

Gracie could always read them.

Just as she could read this.

What Wyatt had written on the afternoon of the day he and his father had died read, "Dad sent me to gather kindling for our camp fire. I did really well until I saw that monster in the woods.'

"Jack, I figured it out!" Gracie announced breathlessly a few minutes before noon. It had taken her until then to finish guessing and piecing together all of the last entry in Wyatt's notebook.

Completed, the translation read, "Dad sent me to gather kindling for our camp fire. I did really well until I saw that monster in the woods. He came up out of nowhere, like he'd materialized from the shrubs and trees. Then I dropped everything and ran back to the campsite. Dad doesn't believe me. He says there are no monsters, but he doesn't go to my school. We have enough wood now and the tent is pitched, and looks very cosy. We are having Dinty Moore stew for dinner, with green beans. Dad says we can eat out of the tins. Mom would be horrified!'

"Figured what out?" Jack asked. Her call had come through just as he had been pushing away from his desk and thinking about lunch. She'd called on his mobile, though, and so he'd answered.

Quickly, Gracie read him Wyatt's last entry. "He *saw* someone, in the woods, that last day," Gracie crowed. "That must have seen the guy who killed Wyatt and his Dad."

"But why kill Wyatt and Aaron, just because Wyatt saw him?" Jack asked. Then he answered his own question. "Unless whoever it was didn't want to be seen."

"Right. He was hiding," Gracie returned.

"But we checked the woods," Jack came back. "We've had Rangers with canines out in force, and we even did the thermal imaging camera, and nothing: no one's hiding in those cabins in the Forest," Jack said firmly.

"But Jack, listen to what Wyatt wrote," Gracie insisted, and read from her translated text again. " 'He came up out of nowhere, like he'd materialized from the shrubs and trees.' " She paused. "See? 'came up' he says. Maybe the guy was hiding underground!"

Jack started to laugh, and then turned it into a not too convincing cough. "Hiding underground?" he echoed.

Gracie pretended not to have heard Jack's aborted chuckle and continued in a serious tone. "If it's the same guy who shot at the troopers, maybe he's been hiding out in a series of underground caves and tunnels or something," she said.

"For more than a year?" Jack asked doubtfully, but at least he matched Gracie's serious tone.

"Maybe," Gracie insisted. "Maybe he used the cabins during the winter. I'm sure the Rangers don't patrol that assiduously when there's three feet of snow or more on the ground," Gracie insisted.

Jack had to admit that she had a point, and it was a possibility, even if he thought it was a far fetched one. "How on earth did you translate that, anyway?" he asked as he moved through the outer office on his way downstairs.

Gracie airily told him it had been a simple process of polyalphabetic substitution, and once she'd figured out a couple of letters, it had come very quickly.

Jack answered, reassuring her that he would contact the Greylock Forest Ranger station and ask them to start a ground search, examining each quadrant of the Forest for hidden underground entrances, caves or similar hiding places. "It will take quite a bit of time: the Forest is hundreds of acres," he noted as he reached the outside. It was a lovely autumn day. He headed across the street to The Docket for their usual Wednesday special.

"I know, " Gracie returned. "But the sooner they start, the sooner they might find something."

"Yeah, and their search might tip him off, too," Jack said, then, sobering.

"Maybe. But maybe it'll flush him out and they can get him!" Gracie said.

"I wish I'd been able to find something connecting the troopers to the McGinleys," Jack said, low, as he entered The Docket. He saw numerous people he recognized, including several on duty and off duty law enforcement personnel. A smattering of courthouse staff were also there and no wonder:

The Docket's Wednesday lunch special was a prime Angus beef burger with truffled mac and cheese.

Although Gracie had sampled the latter and whispered to Jack that she thought they used portobello mushrooms and truffle infused oil, not actual truffles, it was still incredibly yummy. Whenever he was able, Jack tried to get to The Docket for lunch time on Wednesday.

Now, Jack paused while the hostess seated him at a table to one side of the main dining room, then continued his call, "but you discovering that entry by Wyatt kind of takes the pressure off."

"What do you mean?" Gracie queried as she ran upstairs: she only had 45 minutes to shower, do her makeup and dress, and get to Belinda's house.

"Well, if what we think is true, based on Wyatt's entry, everything happened because he saw that guy, in his hiding place, in the Forest," Jack explained, purposely using general terms and keeping his voice low. He didn't think anyone was paying him the least mind or eavesdropping on his half of the conversation, but you could never be too careful.

"Or one of his hiding places," Gracie put in.

"Yes, okay, Gracie, one of them. Anyway, if that's true, there doesn't have to be a connection, if you see what I mean," Jack finished.

"Oh, yes, of course: the McGinleys weren't targeted, their murders were crimes of opportunity," Gracie finished.

The waitress came to take his order, even though she knew what he most likely wanted to eat. Jack and Gracie said quick goodbyes and Jack told the waitress what he would like.

Gracie jumped in the shower, stuck her hair up in a ponytail, tossed some makeup in the direction of her face, slid into a cotton sweater and jeans, and evaluated herself in the mirror. She dug one of her favorite Hermès scarves out of a drawer, and knotted it around her neck. A fairly new one, it was called 'Bouquets Selliers,' in shades of grey, crimson, white, and black, with patterns of bits and bridles.

Her black blazer and black slip ons completed the outfit, and Gracie dashed out to her Jeep, and headed for Belinda's.

CHAPTER THIRTY-SIX

Belinda showed Gracie the four bay garage after lunch. A roomy area, the garage boasted an upstairs loft as well, that Belinda said could serve as an open space cattery.

"I'm imagining that once a stray or an abandoned cat is brought in, I'll check him or her over for immediate issues then bring the cat to one of our local vets," Belinda began, "for a checkup."

Gracie nodded. "I use Doctor Zjanek, right in Cheshire," Gracie said. "She's very good, and she might be willing to work with you," she suggested.

Belinda smiled. "I'll go and ask her!"

They were standing in the loft at the moment: large windows looked out on both sides. Belinda's yard was in one direction, and a wooded area in the other. The loft had a wooden floor in fairly good shape, and the ceiling was open to the roof.

"I'm going to put insulation and a drop ceiling in here," Belinda pointed above their heads. "We had the roof done about five years ago, when we had the roof on the house done, so it's fine."

"Mmmm…" Gracie nodded. "What about the floor?"

"Oh, it's sound, but I thought I'd get some of that indoor outdoor rugged carpet. Would be good for the cats, and it's easy to clean if anyone has accidents…"

Gracie nodded again and walked the length of the loft. There was one door, on the opposite end, which opened onto the staircase that led to the lower level and the bays originally meant for vehicles.

They returned to the ground floor and Belinda explained that she had thought one or possibly two of the bays could be quarantine areas with large cages. The bay nearest the door, she said, would be for supplies. All they would have to do would be to create a hallway that accessed the bays, and install doors and front walls.

"I'll keep the concrete floor here, but have plywood and linoleum put down, which will make it warmer and cushier," Belinda explained. "And shelves and cabinets for the storage area. Large cages for the quarantine/intake bay, and maybe an exam table."

So—you'll have one bay free?" Gracie asked, wanting to see if she was visualizing Belinda's dream correctly.

Her friend nodded. "Maybe two, make another one into a nursery because I'm sure I'll get kittens and I wouldn't want them in with the adult cats until they were bigger. Why?"

"Well, of course, it depends on how many cats you have and how many you would have in the quarantine/intake cage area but that last bay," Gracie replied, pointing to the far end.

The two walked down to the bay in question.

"What if—you could put another staircase here? Maybe one of those metal spiral ones? Just so that there is another mode of egress from the loft?" Gracie suggested.

"Oh! You mean, cut through the roof of the ground floor?" Belinda asked.

Gracie nodded. "Yes. You wouldn't need a lot of space for a spiral staircase. You might not even use it that much— but the cats would, if you turned this last bay into part of the open cattery," she continued. "You could even install a fireman's pole and cover it with sisal or carpeting and it would make an amazing scratching post—and some of them might even use that instead of the staircase to go between floors. I've seen special ramps, too, and hammocks, in addition to the usual cat trees and condos—" Gracie continued, her imagination in top gear.

The two women enthusiastically started to dream up more and more amazing furnishings for Belinda's Rescue.

"But, Gracie: simple basic renovations I can do with the money I have," Belinda said as they walked back towards her house. She had promised Gracie coffee and pound cake after the cattery tour. "What we've been talking about, well, that'll all be really pricey!"

Gracie smiled. "If you like the idea of putting in that spiral staircase, I'll help you with that cost. And as for the ramps and hammocks and stuff, a lot of that I think we can do ourselves. And I'd like to help with that, too. We could get a bunch of our friends together, maybe even some of the women from Club, and make a work party out of it!" she suggested enthusiastically.

Belinda opened the back door to her house and ushered Gracie into her kitchen. Then she turned and Gracie saw she had tears in her eyes.

"That would be great, Gracie. That would just be so amazing!" Belinda said with a catch in her voice.

A few minutes later, the two were sitting at Belinda's kitchen table—lunch had been more formal, in her dining room, but by now Belinda felt so comfortable with Gracie she asked if the kitchen would be okay. Of course, Gracie had said yes. They each had a mug of coffee and a large slice of pound cake in front of them.

Gracie took a bite of the cake. "Wow, Belinda this is great!" she enthused. "How do you get it so moist? Every time I've made pound cake it's always dry."

Belinda smiled and told Gracie that she used coconut oil in place of butter in the recipe. "So it's healthier, too!"

Gracie said she'd have to try that.

"I'm almost afraid to ask…have you looked at Wyatt's journal?" Belinda asked then.

Gracie grinned, and told her about meeting with Julie Sweetwater.

"Oh yes, Julie: she's a darling girl. Wyatt's only real friend at school," Belinda replied. "She is a lot like Wyatt, too. I think they felt if there were two of them they wouldn't get picked on as much, you know?" Belinda said.

Gracie nodded, and said that her friend Lori, Julie's mother, hadn't mentioned that Julie had had a problem in school with being bullied or picked on. But she supposed that could be due to the fact that Julie had a couple of other friends besides Wyatt in school: she kind of bridged the gap, Gracie explained, between the 'geeks' and the 'normal kids.' Then she told Belinda about the anti bullying initiative, and then about the Cooper murder.

"I heard about that on the news!" Belinda replied, sounding shocked. "It sounds like a horrible crime. You're covering that?" She looked at Gracie as though she thought that a very challenging task.

Gracie smiled. "Yep. Goes with the job. And it's not a mystery or anything as to what happened: Leroy Cooper killed his Grandmother. He told the police, confessed, explained what had happened to him at school earlier that day, what his Grandmother had said, and told them he'd just 'snapped.'" She sighed. "The thing will be to explore Leroy's psyche, now, and see if it was a one time situational thing, or if he will always be a danger to himself and others."

"That's why he's being evaluated, isn't it?" Belinda asked.

Gracie told her she was correct. "But to answer your question, yes, Belinda, I did manage to translate quite a lot of Wyatt's notebook," Gracie replied.

"You did?" Belinda responded, and her eyes filled again. "Oh—what does it say? What did he write?" she asked, and her voice broke.

Gracie reached out a hand and clasped Belinda's firmly. "I should have thought to bring my copy with me, and read it to you," she murmured, chagrined.

"Oh, no, Gracie—you only got it yesterday!" Belinda replied sweetly. But Gracie could tell, the idea of knowing what her son had written was irresistible. As well it should be: Wyatt's notebook was the most intimate talisman Belinda had for her dead son. If she could actually read and understand what was in it, even some of it, it would be a real gift, and a comfort.

"I promise I'll come by this weekend and translate everything I can for you," Gracie replied feelingly. "OK? But meanwhile, he talked mostly about school," Gracie began, summarizing. "And about some mathematical problems he was working on, his Vinča alphabet, and stuff like that. He does mention being teased for being an 'egghead' by some of the other kids at school, but mostly it's commentary about things in his classes at school that intrigued him, or things he did with you and Aaron, you know—there was something about a trip to a museum?"

"That was just four weeks ago," Belinda replied, looking both happy and sorrowful. "We went to Boston for the day, to the Science Museum."

"Well, Wyatt had a lot to say about that, especially about the Planetarium," Gracie recalled with a chuckle. Then she explained that she had wanted to see if there had been anything in the notebook about the camping trip, and so had actually started from the back of the book, from Wyatt's last entry, and therefore hadn't read much of the earlier topics the boy had written about.

"And, was there anything in there about the camping trip?" Belinda asked hesitantly.

Gracie nodded. "There was." Then she told Belinda what her son had said, about seeing a 'monster' in the woods. "My theory is, and Jack agrees with me I think, is that the person Wyatt saw in the woods didn't want to be seen," she explained. "And that's why Wyatt and Aaron were killed." Her voice was gentle.

But Belinda looked at her, dry eyed. "But—why? Who was the person Wyatt saw?" Belinda asked.

A good question, Gracie thought, but one she wasn't quite prepared to answer yet. "We don't know. We are still looking in the Forest, though. But this new information might change the way we do the search. Or, the Rangers do the search," she amended.

"How?" Belinda asked.

"Because if Wyatt saw someone 'come up' from the ground or the shrubbery, which is how he phrased it, maybe that someone was hiding out in the woods. For whatever reason. But maybe long term," Gracie said, trying not to say too much. It wasn't for her to tell anyone the theory Jack and she had about the shooter being the same man who had attacked the state police barracks, and it wasn't her place to tell anyone that Jack had discovered that the ballistics in the two cases were similar. "So now the Rangers are going to be looking for different types of hiding places," she finished, somewhat vaguely, but with enough information that Belinda smiled and nodded.

CHAPTER THIRTY-SEVEN

"Hey, Jack, how's it going?" Sheriff Shermayne asked. He and his Deputy, Cal Shubert, had also been having lunch at The Docket, and stopped by Jack's table on their way out.

"Good, Ned," Jack answered. He was only two bites into his bison burger and had yet to touch his mac 'n' cheese. "Hiya, Cal," he smiled at the Deputy.

"You got a second, Jack?" the Sheriff asked, dropping his voice.

Jack put his burger down and wiped his mouth with his napkin. "Sure." He motioned to the empty chairs at his table, and both Shermayne and Shubert seated themselves, perching on the edges as though they would not be seated for long.

"You catch a break in the McGinley thing?" Sheriff Shermayne asked, his voice barely audible.

Jack frowned at him. "What makes you think that?"

Jack was all for sharing info among law enforcement agencies, but in this case, it was too soon to tell anyone about the ballistics being similar in the McGinley murder and the attack on the barracks, and way too early to start explaining about the 'monster' Wyatt McGinley allegedly saw in the forest and how that person might be the shooter in both cases.

The Sheriff shrugged. "We kinda heard you talking on your phone—to Gracie—when you first sat down," he admitted a bit sheepishly.

"We weren't intentionally listening, or anything," Deputy Shubert hastened to explain, and Jack smiled and nodded. "But we heard 'Wyatt' and our ears perked up."

"Ah, well…" Jack tried to remember what he'd been talking to Gracie about, specifically, as he'd sat down. About Wyatt's notebook entry indicating that the McGinleys had been killed because of something Wyatt had seen, not because of any connection to the trooper shootings. "Gracie's been examining the boy's notebook," he answered, his voice still low. No reason to inform everyone else at The Docket.

"That one with the gibberish and all the math?" Sheriff Shermayne asked, surprised. "What for?"

Jack shrugged. "You know Gracie: she's kind of a geek, like Wyatt was, and she's been trying to translate the stuff he wrote," Jack replied.

"She thinks maybe the boy wrote something down that could be a clue?" Deputy Shubert asked, looking interested. He'd caught on fast, Jack thought.

Jack nodded again. "Anyway, she did manage to work out some of it, and it seems that Wyatt may have seen someone, or something, he wasn't supposed to have. In the woods, in Greylock Forest," Jack murmured.

The Sheriff and his Deputy both knew Jack wouldn't reveal any more details until he was more sure: this was still a theory, albeit a promising one.

"So—you going to search the Forest again?" Deputy Shubert asked. He sounded eager, and his voice was a conspiratorial whisper.

Jack nodded. "Yes. As a matter of fact, when I finish lunch I'm headed for the Ranger station to discuss that," he added, realizing as he spoke that that was precisely what he intended to do.

"Well, if you or the Rangers need any more manpower, you've only to ask," Sheriff Shermayne said gravely. "We've got four full-time and six part-time deputies, all happy to help out," he reassured Jack.

At the Greylock Ranger Station atop the mountain, adjacent to the Veterans' War Memorial that crowned the highest point in Massachusetts at 3400 feet, Jack met with Ranger on duty Steve Smithson. Smithson appeared intrigued by the idea that the suspect in the McGinley murders might be hiding out in the Forest, but underground.

"It certainly would be an original plan," he commented after Jack had explained his theory. Then he looked at Jack with sudden inspired recollection. "Hang on a minute. I seem to remember—" The trim older man got up from his desk and strode towards the office door. "Come with me for a few minutes," he encouraged Jack. The Ranger led Jack across the station's main floor to a locked door on the other side.

Smithson opened the door and Jack found himself in a large storage area. He looked askance at the Ranger, and wondered what he was doing.

"Just let me find the plans for the campground," Smithson told Jack and moved away, searching on the ordered shelves until he found, apparently, what he wanted.

He brought out a long roll of what looked like blueprints, then escorted Jack back to his office.

Fortunately, the Ranger Station was not busy on a weekday afternoon in mid September, and Smithson and Jack had time to peruse what the Ranger had retrieved.

"The Forest was the state's first State Forest, way back in 1898," Smithson told Jack. "For the first few decades it was just that: forest. Then people started to want hiking trails, so they started putting those in. But then in the 1930's, the WPA came in and built proper trails, and built the camp grounds: first the cabins, then the areas for people with tents and campers, both the primitive sites with just one pit toilet and later the so called 'luxury' sites with the showers and flush toilets," he explained, rifling through the blueprints until he found the sheet he wanted.

As the Ranger spread the sheet out on top of his desk, Jack could see that the blueprint showed the entire campground: the dozen cabins in one area, and the 'luxury' and primitive areas elsewhere, all clearly marked.

"Aha!" Smithson said triumphantly. "Look: here," he told Jack and pointed to some lines on the blueprint map.

They extended out a short way from the kitchen areas of all twelve cabins and Jack was at a loss to say what they were, so he asked.

"Well, originally, they were meant to be root cellars, for provisions. The cabins were built to mimic the way early settlers in the area had built their homes, you see," Smithson explained, one finger still on the peculiar feature on the map.

"And early settlers had root cellars," Jack nodded.

"Right." Smithson shook his head. "I can't see someone living in a root cellar for months at a time, though," he put in doubtfully.

Jack replied that his theory was that the person 'came up' periodically, maybe even as often as once a day. But the discovery of the root cellars had given him another idea.

"Can we go look in these root cellars?" Jack asked Smithson.

"They're all locked up," Smithson hedged. "We wouldn't want little Johnny to get stuck in one on a family camping trip or anything," he chuckled.

"You must have a key?" Jack pushed. Maybe Gracie had been right! Maybe the guy who attacked the troopers had gone to ground here, in the Forest, using the root cellars of the cabins as hidey-holes. It wouldn't be that hard, Jack thought, to rotate among the dozen hidden spots; he could have even come up once or twice every 24 hours to use the primitive latrines and in the warmer weather, the showers. That was assuming he had stayed in the Forest for the past year or so.

It was, of course, quite possible that he had only used the bunkers periodically, when he had really needed to disappear. Perhaps, as Gracie and Jack had discussed, the man who shot at the troopers last year was walking, most days, among them: hiding in plain sight.

Smithson admitted that there was a key, and walked over to the key locker, opening it with a key from his ring. He scanned the short rows of keys, each neatly labeled. Then he turned to Jack with a frown.

"What is it?" Jack asked, knowing, somehow, what the Ranger would say.

"The key for the root cellars," Smithson replied, his voice grave. "It's not here."

Thursday morning, Jack knocked on Popovitch's open office door. "Got a minute?" he asked, making his tone as deferential as he could. Since he didn't think his boss deserved any deference, it was a challenge; however, since Popovitch was quite thick, he didn't notice Jack's struggle.

The DA looked up from whatever he'd been gazing at on his desk, and grunted.

Jack took this as assent, and stepped in.

"I've got some news about the McGinley murders," he began.

Popovitch exhaled a gusty sigh. "About time, Jack," he responded with a smirk.

Jack gave a tight smile. "And it involves a cold case," he went on, and explained his curiosity about whether the shooter in the McGinley case could have also been the shooter who ambushed the state police barracks the year before.

"What made you wonder that?" Popovitch sneered. "I mean, one's a murder, the other's not, one's a father and son, the other's law enforcement: I don't see a lot of similarities,

Jack." Popovitch shook his large, shaggy head and looked amused.

Jack explained how seeing Trooper DelRay just the other day at the Cooper murder scene prompted him to recall the details of the barracks attack from the year before. "I remembered the way the bullet wounds looked in the trooper case," he said. "And I thought they reminded me of the bullet wounds in the McGinleys' bodies," he added quietly.

"Yeah, yeah, Jack but don'tcha think that if the shooter who killed the McGinleys could shoot that well to kill them from what—100 yards away or something?—he would'a killed the troopers, too?" Popovitch retorted. "But he didn't. He missed."

"He missed vital organs and a head shot, thankfully," Jack corrected Popovitch. One trooper had made it to rehab fairly quickly, but the other had been hospitalized until very recently, undergoing more than a dozen surgeries. Jack shrugged. "Maybe the barracks attack was the shooter's first try. Maybe he's been practicing in the time since, and he's got better. But I still don't think he's that great a shot: look how many times he shot at the McGinleys. A good sniper, a good shooter, wouldn't have had to riddle their bodies with bullets," Jack finished, clipping his words and making his tone hard. "It would have been one between the eyebrows, and done."

Popovitch smoothed a chubby hand over his yellow and maroon striped tie that stopped several inches short of the massive belt around his waist and his bulging belly. He didn't say that Jack made a good point, he was merely silent, which for him meant concession.

"What else?" Popovitch growled. "I gotta be in court at ten," he added, sounding much aggrieved. Did he think that being a District Attorney meant he never had to appear in court or argue a case?

Jack told him he'd asked Dr. Spears to compare the bullet wounds in both cases, as well as shell fragments collected in both cases, and that although no guarantee was possible, Dr. Spears felt it was extremely likely that the same type of gun was used at the two crimes. "Possibly even the same gun, though the fragments are too, well, fragmented to allow us to look for striation matches," Jack added. "But possibly, therefore, it was the same shooter."

"But I still don't see why the two cases would be connected!" Popovitch whined.

Jack took a deep breath. Popovitch genuinely and deeply disliked Gracie, and had from the day they had met. But it was Gracie's decoding of Wyatt's notebook that had given the clue that had really made the connection between the two crimes a possibility. So Jack would have to find a way to tell the DA that.

"You remember Wyatt's notebook, don't you?" Jack asked in a slightly more jocular tone.

The DA nodded and made a face. "Yeah, filled with math stuff and nonsense, wasn't it?" he asked dismissively.

"Mmm...well, Wyatt was kind of a geeky kid, you know the type?" Jack put in.

The DA huffed. "The annoying kind who's always asking questions and who's always way ahead of everyone else, yeah, I know the type," Popovitch answered in a tone full of resentment.

Jack recalled that it had taken Popovitch five tries to pass the Massachusetts Bar, and suspected that the DA hadn't been any brighter in law school than he was now.

"Well, I guess it takes a geek to know a geek," Jack said.

Popovitch looked up, puzzled.

"Gracie knows Wyatt's mother, and asked if she could examine the notebook more closely," Jack began, and was not surprised to hear his boss mutter a disparaging word or two under his breath when he heard Gracie's name. "And she managed to figure out what Wyatt had written in the last part of the notebook: his last entry."

Popovitch didn't look impressed, but he did look interested in spite of himself. "Yeah? What?" he growled reluctantly.

Jack told him Gracie felt that Wyatt might have written something in his ever-present notebook about the camping trip, something that might provide a clue. Then he told the DA that Gracie had figured out that Wyatt written about seeing someone in the woods as he'd been gathering kindling, and that that someone had frightened him.

"Kid was probably a wuss," Popovitch muttered in response, looking ready to discount the theory.

"But you see, Peter, if Wyatt saw someone in the woods, someone who was hiding in the woods, who didn't want to be seen..." Jack pushed on. Then he waited.

It took two or three seconds more than it would take most people, Jack thought, but finally the DA caught on. "Oh! So you think that's why Wyatt and his Dad were killed? Because the kid saw someone in the woods he shouldn't have?" Popovitch asked. For the first time, he sounded interested in the conversation.

Jack nodded. "People kill people all the time because of something they've seen or heard that the other person didn't want them to," Jack replied. "The similarity of the bullet wounds in the McGinley case to those in the trooper shooting last year, coupled with the theory that it was someone who was hiding in the woods, who didn't want to be seen, leads me to the conclusion that the person who shot at the troopers was also the person hiding in the woods, the person Wyatt saw, and who then killed him and his father," Jack finished.

Popovitch frowned as he listened to his Chief Detective, as if trying to work it all out in his head. "It's a kinda iffy theory, Jack," he told him.

"I know it's tenuous," Jack rephrased with a self deprecating smile. "But I'm working on getting more supporting evidence. We aren't sure if the shooter has been hiding in Greylock Forest the entire time since the barracks attack, but we're checking into that. I'll be working with the Rangers on it. And I'm going to bring the State Police Cheshire Barracks Commander in on the theory, too: maybe they can shed more light on the subject, you never know. But I wanted you to be apprised," he concluded.

The DA nodded and assumed a very businesslike demeanor. He cleared his throat. "That's excellent, Jack. Good." Then he waved a hand as though brushing away an invisible feather in front of him. "Well, carry on," he dismissed Jack, and returned to whatever document was on his desk.

CHAPTER THIRTY-EIGHT
CHAPTER THIRTY-EIGHT

Ranger Smithson, along with most of the rest of the available Rangers assigned to Greylock Forest, and with help from the Sheriff's office, the State Police and local law enforcement, began their intensive search of the Forest on Thursday afternoon. They focused on the twelve cabins and their root cellars; even though the key to the cellars was nowhere to be found, the hasps on the padlocked cellar entryways were easy enough to break with bolt cutters.

While they began that search, Jack met with the Cheshire SP Barracks commander and filled him in on his theory about a connection between the McGinley murders and the barracks attack. Corporal Krieg gave Jack much more encouragement and a much more enthusiastic hearing than the DA had given him.

"Frankly, Jack, the attack on our troopers has stumped us for more than a year," Krieg admitted tightly when Jack was finished. "An unsolved case involving our own is not something I want on my watch. I'll look into just about any idea that seems to have even a tiny bit of merit. And yours has a lot more than that: it's a credible, plausible theory, at least in my opinion."

Krieg provided as many troopers as he could to assist the Rangers with their search, and Thursday afternoon Jack got a call from Smithson, asking Jack to drive over to the Forest.

The Ranger had given Jack a location in the cabin section of the campsite area, so Jack identified himself to the Sheriff's Deputy standing guard, parked his navy cruiser and entered the cabin.

Smithson was inside and greeted Jack happily. The two other Rangers in the cabin also looked somewhat triumphant and, Jack thought, relieved.

"Come take a look at this," Smithson urged, and led Jack to the root cellar entryway of this particular cabin. Since the cabins were electrified, there was a single bulb in the doorway, which dimly illuminated a small, subterranean space and a few shallow stairs accessing it.

Jack stepped down at Smithson's invitation, taking the offered flashlight.

In the original root cellar, all was bare except for some piles of dirt against the perimeter and a very small kerosene heater. More interesting was a shadowy opening along the far wall. It was no more than a couple feet high and about the same wide: big enough for a slender person to crawl through quite comfortably. It had clearly been shoveled from the packed earth.

Jack whistled. "Jackpot," he murmured. "You been down there?" he asked Smithson, gesturing to the tunnel.

The Ranger shook his head. "We waited for you. And I've sent a couple of my guys to get supplies and more flashlights. They should be here in a few minutes, and then—"

"We go in!" Jack finished, sounding excited.

The discovery of the tunnel in the root cellar was more than what Jack could have wished for. He had expected the Rangers to find evidence of the shooter having holed up in one of the root cellars: a broken lock, perhaps remnants of food or other items. But a tunnel that someone had apparently shoveled out laboriously over the course of several weeks was a gift, Jack thought. And depending on where the tunnel actually went, it might fit very neatly with Wyatt's tale of having seen someone in the woods.

The kerosene heater indicated that their quarry had likely used the tunnel during the coldest months, perhaps sleeping in the underground chamber as well. With the access door to the root cellar open, it had been safe enough, and with any light from the heater being underground, no one patrolling the area would have seen anything. Jack knew the campgrounds were usually only driven through once a day in the off season: a clever person could hide out and have his presence go unnoticed, if he was careful.

The Rangers returned with a spool of high tensile fishing wire, extra radios, and flashlights. Then two of them, plus Jack, began to crawl along the hand hewn tunnel. They had to crawl on hands and knees, but moving that way, the passage was adequate.

The spool of fishing wire was in the hands of the Ranger who was stationed in the root cellar; the lead Ranger of the small exploratory party held the end, looping it off as they progressed. The idea was that, even if the flashlights should somehow fail or if there were a cave in, the wire would help them find their way out, or be found.

Jack had his service revolver, and since the Rangers were not armed, he was glad he did, because no one knew what or whom they might encounter down that tunnel.

They'd crawled for several hundred feet, which was easy to estimate because of how much fishing wire had been expended, when they came to a wider, but still small, hollowed out chamber. Periodically along the corridor the path had widened a little bit to allow for more piles of dirt, and in this wider chamber, it was the same. Whoever had dug the tunnel had clearly deposited the excess earth in piles along the way.

Now, Jack shone his flashlight around the earthen walls of the little space. There was just room for him to stand up, although not very comfortably: Jack was six foot two, and his head just brushed the ceiling of the chamber.

But more interesting than the chamber itself was the detritus inside it. On one wall a small declivity had been hollowed out and in it sat a little bar light with battery powered LED bulbs in it. One Ranger experimentally turned it on, and it lit the entire space.

"Handy," he commented laconically.

A large dark green garbage bag was the only other object in the room. Clearly having been left by someone who had 'holed up' there for a time, the bag contained empty water bottles, empty pop top cans of beans, spaghetti and similar food items, candy and pastry wrappers, used wet wipes, and what appeared to be (and smelled like) used adult diapers and some toilet paper.

One of the Rangers radioed back to Smithson, who had remained in the root cellar, and related what they had found. After noting that they would bring the bag of evidence out with them on their return, the exploratory party went on.

The tunnel continued for a short distance past the chamber, and then stopped. Jack and his two companions shone their flashlights around the bare walls of the tunnel and found only piles of dirt again, at first.

"Aha!" the laconic one said a moment later, and fixed his light on a rope ladder that dangled against a side wall of packed earth.

They looked up to the top of the ladder, but it seemed to go into darkness.

"It's covered over somehow," murmured Jack, and he began to climb up the ladder.

At the top of the twelve foot ladder, Jack found a large, flat piece of plywood over what looked like a hole about the size of a manhole cover. He shone his flashlight on the beige surface, and was rewarded with the discovery of two metal handles.

"Hey, give me some light up here!" he called down to the two Rangers, who immediately trained their flashlights up towards the very top of the ladder.

Jack holstered his flashlight, gripped the two handles on the plywood and pushed up, testing to see which way the cover would most easily lift off. It ended up being a push-and-slide sort of action that moved the plywood enough so that filtered daylight came through a pile of branches that had apparently been scattered on top of the plywood as camouflage.

These had been slightly dislodged by the movement of the makeshift cover, and Jack shoved the rest of them out of the way. Wishing he'd worn gloves, he clambered out of the hole cautiously, stopping every few seconds to listen in case their quarry were near. He heard nothing besides the usual woodland sounds on an early autumn afternoon, and so he exited the tunnel and stood, trying to figure out what part of the Forest he was in. Greylock Lake was a few hundred feet to his right, but that was about all he could tell.

Once the other two Rangers had followed him to the surface, one radioed back to Smithson while the other one looked around him.

"Can you tell where we are?" Jack asked.

The Ranger nodded and pointed to his left. "That way, about a quarter mile, is the service road and the primitive campsites," he told Jack. "And of course, there's the lake," he said with a nod to the right.

The primitive campsites were that close? Jack thought for a moment, recalling the translation Gracie had given him for Wyatt's notebook entry. The boy had said that the 'monster' had 'come up' from some bushes.

Jack looked around where he stood: there were trees, of course, and lots of bushes and underbrush in the area. But the hidden entrance to the tunnel, camouflaged by fallen branches, was behind one grouping of three bushes. Could this be the spot where the 'monster' had appeared who had so frightened Wyatt? Even though Jack's exit just now from the tunnel had not been at all graceful, he supposed that if one knew how the plywood cover worked and had entered and exited the tunnel this way several times, one would do it much more quickly and easily.

Therefore, it was entirely possible that the man who had been hiding out in the tunnel had exited his snug and inadvertently startled Wyatt when he'd climbed from the hole and stood up.

Jack looked out over the lake, visible through the deciduous trees that surrounded him. He felt certain that they had discovered the shooter's retreat. He also felt certain that the person who'd been hiding had been doing so, either continuously or on and off, since he'd shot at the troopers the summer before last. And, Jack felt certain that that was the same man whom Wyatt had seen, and who had been the cause of the McGinleys' deaths.

CHAPTER THIRTY-NINE

"If you look at this map of the Greylock Forest Campgrounds, it's easy to see," Jack said carefully. He had decided it was time to tell Belinda what he and the Rangers had discovered. They hadn't solved the murders of her family yet, but they were close, Jack knew. They'd sent some of the items from the hidden garbage bag off to the lab in Springfield for testing; with the 'rush' they'd asked for, Jack hoped preliminary results might be back the next day, Friday.

Now, Jack pointed to the double half moon of cabins on the map. "See, this one? It's at the end of the back row, nearest the forest, and farthest away from the rest of the campsite," Jack pointed to the cabin whose root cellar had been tunneled out, and told Belinda and Gracie what had been discovered earlier that day.

Jack had asked Gracie to meet him at Belinda's because he felt that having a friend there would help Belinda when she heard the news. Additionally, it was a good way for Gracie to learn what had gone on in the Forest that afternoon, without Jack having to tell her directly, and therefore be honor bound to tell the *Gazetteer* as well.

Both women's mouths fell open at Jack's tale, and Jack had to admit that he had been as stunned as they now were when he and the Rangers had come upon the tunnel and then the little room with the bag of leavings.

"He could have got the shovel anywhere," Jack continued, pointing to the pencilled-in line on the map that approximated the tunnel's path from the root cellar to the camouflaged exit. "We never found it."

Gracie was frowning. "Well, if he had that bag of rubbish—things he'd used, as you say, he must have a stash of supplies somewhere, too: isn't that logical?"

Jack shrugged. "Maybe he just buys what he needs as he needs it: food and—so on," he countered. "It would be easy enough to pinch rubbish bags from the housekeeping shed in the campsite," he continued. "It's just got a plain lock, which I'll bet this guy could jimmy or pick, and one or two garbage bags now and then would never be missed."

Gracie and Belinda both nodded. It was comforting, at least at first, to take refuge in the contemplation of minutiae. But the more pressing details about what the Rangers had uncovered now had to be faced.

"How long is that tunnel?" Gracie asked next.

Jack told her the rough measurement was 1200 feet.

"That's nearly a quarter mile!" Belinda exclaimed.

"He dug all that out with a shovel? How long did it take him?" Gracie asked, amazed.

"Depends on how much dirt he could shovel and how fast, and for how long he could keep at it," Jack explained. "But he could have done it easily in a couple of months." He paused and flipped the map over and consulted some notes he'd scribbled on the back. "Ranger Smithson printed out the reservation list for the cabins for the past two years. Cabin number twelve, the one in question, was occupied on and off until the campground was shut for the season last October. The campground was shut until Memorial Day weekend this year, then open for the season. Cabin twelve was occupied through the summer months on and off," he continued, "especially on the weekends, of course."

Everyone thought about what Jack had just shared.

"So that means this person could have hidden out in the underground tunnel and the chamber and the root cellar, coming and going through the hidden entry in the forest, and perhaps using the cabin itself—carefully—when it wasn't rented out," Gracie summarized.

Jack nodded.

"And you think the person who did this," Belinda began, pointing to the pencilled in tunnel route on the map, "who dug the tunnel and hid out here was the person who attacked the troopers at the Cheshire Barracks and then killed Aaron and Wyatt?"

Jack nodded. "I do. There is too much similarity between the bullets and the type of wounds to discount," he explained. "The State Police never saw the shooter and any traces of him completely disappeared after the attack. If you know the location of the barracks, you'll realize it backs up right onto Greylock Forest."

Gracie pictured her hometown police barracks in her mind's eye and knew Jack was correct.

"So the shooter could have just—melted away into the trees," Gracie breathed.

"He could have," Jack confirmed. "I realize it sounds a little wacky, but we're not dealing with a rational person here," he reminded them.

Belinda nodded. "So—you think the—person—who shot at the troopers probably dug that tunnel and made his preparations before the attack?" Belinda asked.

"Clearly, the tunnel and the cabin was his escape plan," Gracie chimed in, "his hideout: he would have wanted to have had that ready before he shot at the troopers."

"Exactly," Jack agreed.

"So maybe it was that spring, before the cabins open on Memorial Day weekend. Maybe that's when this guy decided to shoot the troopers, and chose Greylock Cabins as his bolt hole," Gracie added. "He would have had time to work on the tunnel and the escape hatch because, as you say, the cabin was unoccupied until Memorial Day weekend. And then—" she consulted the copy of the reservation list again. "Then not again for three weeks. Then a week and a half empty, then it was rented for a couple of weekends, and then a week, and then…" she trailed off.

"He could have easily managed that," Belinda said firmly, and nodded.

Jack gave a grim smile. "That would have been enough time for him to shovel the tunnel out. Especially once he got away from the cabins: no one would have heard him once he was out of the root cellar itself, especially during the day, when it's noisier in the campgrounds."

"But wait a minute: how did this guy live?" Gracie asked, sounding annoyed. "I mean, you found food and stuff: he couldn't have stolen all of that, not for over a year," she protested. "He had to have had a job somewhere, doing something."

Jack didn't answer.

"And how did he stay warm in the winter?" Belinda asked. "That little kerosene heater? The cabins are only heated with fireplaces, and he couldn't have risked that."

"Yes, I think the kerosene heater was his main source of warmth," Jack told them. "And remember, the tunnel and chambers are all underground so it was going to be sheltered to start with." He looked at Gracie. "But you make a good point: the guy had to have got money somewhere, somehow, so a job is a likely scenario. And, in the cold months, a job would have provided him with a warm place to be for part of the time, anyway," Jack concluded.

"I wonder why he left the garbage bag behind?" Gracie murmured a minute or so later.

"Maybe he planned to remove it," Jack answered. "It was all bagged up, and he must have removed his trash periodically," he theorized.

"I wonder what he did with it?" Gracie queried.

Jack shrugged. "Could have tossed it in any dumpster, maybe even at his job, wherever that was," he added. He'd have to hope the tests on the garbage they had confiscated gave them a name. Then they could find out if the guy worked, and where, and possibly find the man himself.

"Well, if he didn't remove it, but it was ready to go, that could mean he was spooked: something made him vacate his hidey-hole ahead of schedule, and abruptly," Gracie replied.

"Maybe he saw the Rangers checking all the cabins," Belinda suggested.

Jack allowed as how that could have happened; even though they had been discreet about the search, there had been so many Rangers, Troopers and Deputies, it would have been clear to anyone that something was afoot. As a matter of fact, the few campers who were around that week had been quite curious about all the activity, especially the ones who had been asked to vacate their cabins so they could be searched.

"But I wonder where he's gone?" Gracie murmured, frowning.

Friday morning, Gracie had another appointment with Dr. Grist, and he was happier with her progress than he had been.

"You're doing your exercises," he said approvingly, knowing that Gracie was.

She nodded. "And look what I can do!" she crowed, standing in front of him and rotating her ankle slowly, but quite fully. Then she flexed it up and down. "I couldn't do that last week."

"And it'll get easier and easier," Dr. Grist assured her.

After her treatment, Gracie was driving past the courthouse on her way back home when she saw Felicia

Laurenti walking purposefully towards the courthouse's front doors. The Public Defender's office was conveniently located right across the street.

Gracie beeped her Jeep's horn lightly and gave a wave as Felicia turned to her.

The PD smiled, and then made a beckoning gesture that had Gracie signaling somewhat abruptly and pulling over to the curb. Fortunately, traffic was light.

"You going somewhere?" Felicia asked.

Gracie shrugged. "Just home. Why?"

Felicia got a wicked smile on her face. "Well, you didn't hear it from me, and if anyone asks, this chat we're having was you trying to get me to join your Junior League Club again," the PD began in a rush. Gracie had extended more than one invitation to Felicia over the years, but the PD had always said she was too busy.

"Okay," Gracie agreed, mystified.

"Lance Melling's resigned," Felicia said, low. "There's an emergency meeting of the Prison Board, with the Commissioners and the Judge, to decide what to do until a new director can be hired," she finished.

"Now?" Gracie asked.

"Now."

"It's an open meeting?" Gracie quizzed the PD.

"It should be," Felicia replied. "I'm on my way. I thought you should know." She paused. "And I really am too busy to join Club," she added apologetically.

Gracie smiled in resignation and shook her head. Then she found a parking spot in the next street and hastened back to the courthouse.

Lance Melling's resignation was issued as a news bulletin by the *Intelligencer* on line, and Gracie was tasked with doing an article for the next print edition on the search to find a new Probation Director, leading off with a recap of the resignation.

The meeting on Friday had been cut and dried: what they could say in open session was limited to the reception and acceptance of Melling's letter of resignation, and his intent to take his remaining vacation and personal days right away. This meant that although he was giving the requisite minimum two weeks' notice, he would be on vacation for those two weeks, not at work, and thus leaving Probation very abruptly and without a leader.

Also in open session, a small committee of three was selected to find a new Probation Director, and notice of the vacancy would be posted.

Gracie had to laugh to herself when they appointed Popovitch to the search committee. He wasn't at the meeting, of course, so it seemed only right that they give him extra work! She would have to be sure to ask Jack what Popovitch said when he found out about the search committee.

It was also decided in the meeting that the most senior Probation Officer would temporarily head up the department; that officer, Tina DiGiacomo was at the meeting herself to represent Probation's interests. The board no doubt thought DiGiacomo would apply for the position.

Although she had been one of the officers who had done the PD evaluations under Melling's directive, she and the other three had been spoken to and cleared of any wrongdoing or complicity in the scheme. It was clear that Melling had set the system up to benefit himself. Although the Probation Officers who actually did the work of evaluating were compensated, they had been told it was just another part of their yearly salary, and that the evaluations were part of their jobs.

After the meeting, Gracie headed home to write up the bulletin. She also wrote up a carefully phrased, quite short piece on the Greylock Forest Rangers' discovery of a hideout in the campgrounds. At Jack's request, she gave no specifics, and did not mention the tunnel. She also did not mention the theorized connection between the trooper attack and the McGinley murders: Jack would announce that when he had more evidence, or was more certain. He had talked to the State Police Barracks Commander, though, and Gracie knew Corporal Krieg had thought the idea had merit. But it was for Jack to pick the time to reveal the connection, a time when such a revelation would not compromise the investigation.

Gracie grabbed a quick lunch after she sent in the two bulletins, then spent the afternoon cleaning the house and going through her closets, weeding out anything she hadn't worn recently or no longer liked. These items she folded and bagged, to be dropped off at the local charity resale shop the next time she drove into Pittsfield. She put the filled green garbage bag in the front foyer, so she wouldn't forget to load it into her Jeep.

Her ankle still troubled her, but it hurt very little now, and she could maneuver better than she had been able to in weeks. Her gait was still a little off, but much better.

She had invited Jack for Friday night dinner again, so Gracie also had some prep work for that to do. The evening's menu was fairly simple: broiled salmon with a couple of huge shrimp on top and a spicy sriracha based salsa type sauce; fresh green beans with gorgonzola and balsamic vinegar; and an autumn salad of field greens dressed in sage infused butternut squash oil and blackberry balsamic, topped with Cortland apple slices and whole smoked almonds.

Jack was supposed to arrive at six o'clock, but he called at ten after to say he'd been detained and would be late. He finally drove up Gracie's driveway at a quarter to seven and parked at the side of the house, next to her Jeep. Gracie went out her back door and around the west side of her house to greet him.

"I'm sorry I'm late," Jack told her, giving her a hug and a quick kiss.

"Where were you?" Gracie asked, curious.

Woof, who'd been riding shotgun, hopped out of Jack's truck and padded over to where the two of them stood. He whined a bit, wagging his tail, and looked out past Gracie's garden, towards her pond.

"We got an ID on the guy in the campground bunker," Jack answered hastily. "I was talking to his foster mother and to the teachers over at the school this afternoon," he continued.

"Oh! Who—" Gracie began to ask more questions but Woof whined again.

Jack looked down at the dog. "Aw, poor guy, he was cooped up all day. When I went home to change before coming here he did go out, but he probably needs to stretch his legs," Jack explained.

Woof looked appealingly at the two of them.

"I promise to tell you everything over dinner, but right now—" Jack went on.

"Why don't you take him for a run in the meadow?" Gracie interrupted with a grin. "Sun won't set for a few more minutes, so go on: I'll be in the kitchen when you're done," she laughed.

When Woof and Jack returned, Gracie had a bowl of fresh water and another filled with kibble for the dog, and a glass of Jack's favorite bourbon and branch for the human. She herself was sipping on the wine they would have with dinner: a robust white burgundy from Henri Boillot that started out with green apples and ended with what Gracie called 'round fruits and a creamy finish.'

While she was assembling dinner, Jack sipped at his drink and watched amusedly as Pumpkin tried to steal some of Woof's kibble. She was not successful.

"The rabbits must be getting ready for winter already," Jack said, apropos of nothing.

"Huh?" Gracie asked, confused.

Jack grinned. "Woof. He was going nuts out there over by the pond? Nose to the ground like he was going to follow that scent to the ends of the earth."

Gracie laughed. "But he came when you called, right? He's a good boy." She opened a cupboard and reached into a tin, pulling out a bag with organic dog treats inside. She selected one and slipped it into Woof's bowl. He had nearly finished the kibble, but paused to grab the treat with a glance up at Gracie she was sure meant, 'thanks.'

"So we got a hit with the fingerprints on some of the stuff in the garbage bag," Jack began again. He admired Gracie's restraint in not bugging him to share the new information until he'd washed up, sat down, and had a few sips of his drink.

"Who is he?" Gracie asked as she blanched the green beans.

Jack explained that the fingerprints matched those of an Edward Felton, a graduate the year before from Pittsfield High School.

"How'd they have a kid's fingerprints?" Gracie queried, draining the beans. "He have a record?"

Jack shook his head. "No—they've started fingerprinting kids who are in foster care," he explained. "Makes them easier to find if they run away, and that demographic has a high incidence of that kind of behavior," he said.

Gracie nodded. "Makes sense. So this Edward Felton was in foster care?" she asked. "What happened to his parents?"

Jack said that according to the records he'd been able to obtain, Felton's mother had died of a drug overdose when the boy had been three. There was no record of who his father had been. The police had raided the flop where Felton's mother and her infant son had been living, and the child had been put into the foster care system and had never left. After several different homes, including group homes with other foster children, Felton had turned eighteen a couple of months before high school graduation. "His last foster mom, Doreen Tremont, says he just picked up and left two days after his birthday," Jack finished. "Never went to graduation, never actually finished school last year. Just left." He finished his drink.

"He just disappeared?" Gracie quizzed, turning from the range top where she was now sautéing the green beans.

Jack nodded. "He'd been a very troubled kid, I guess, from what I heard today," he went on, rinsing his glass out at the sink. He told Gracie that early on, Felton had had behavior issues, never accepting discipline, and had been prone to violence, especially against people or things he perceived as helpless, or more helpless than himself.

Gracie moved to her indoor grill where the salmon and shrimp had been 'resting' after she'd turned off the flames, and plated the fish. Then she went to the range top and placed the green beans at the side of both dishes. She spooned the hot red sauce over the fish, sprinkled gorgonzola crumbles and almonds on the green beans and drizzled the balsamic on top.

"Wow, that looks amazing," Jack said of the dinner, which Gracie placed on her kitchen table. The salad already waited at each setting. She added to her wine glass and poured a glass for Jack, and they sat.

"I think it'll be good," Gracie noted of the food she had prepared. "I tried to capture the flavor of cocktail sauce in the dressing for the fish," she explained. "But used sriracha instead of horseradish. I hope it's not too hot?"

Jack already had a mouthful of the salmon, shrimp and sauce, so he just nodded and gave Gracie a thumbs up as he chewed.

"So—tell me more about Edward Felton," Gracie urged. She tasted her green beans and the fish as well, and was pleased with the way the flavors and textures played together. "You went to the school, too?"

Jack made a face and took a sip of wine. "Yeah. Mrs. Tremont wasn't too talkative about the kid. Said, basically, she was glad he'd run off and since he's eighteen now, she doesn't have to do anything about it or worry about him." He paused. "Her words were, 'I'm glad he isn't my problem any more.'"

Gracie shook her head.

"She did say she will miss the check every month, but that she planned on getting another foster child—she has two more, as well—and hopes her next one is better behaved than Felton was."

"Did she characterize this bad behavior? You said he was violent?" Gracie asked.

"Yeah: Mrs. Tremont said Felton had an unpredictable and quick temper, that only got worse as he got older. He was very aggressive, too, especially towards her other foster kids, and even to her and her husband. Said he was always reading warfare and weaponry type magazines and making his own primitive arms. He liked to torture things, too, which is why the family no longer has a pet," Jack added, low.

Gracie looked horrified. "What a monster!" she whispered, looking fondly over at Woof and Pumpkin, who were sitting a couple of feet away from the kitchen table: polite and quiet, but alert for any food that might accidentally drop to the floor and need to be cleaned up.

"That's what Wyatt called him, and I don't think he was far wrong," agreed Jack.

CHAPTER FORTY

"I went to the high school," Jack continued, "Because I wanted to get a more objective and complete picture of Felton. Spoke to the guidance counsellor and one of his teachers, and the principal. The picture I got matched the one Mrs. Tremont gave."

Gracie looked a question. "Go on."

"Felton was truant as often as he could be, and liked to see how far he could ignore the rules before getting caught," Jack went on, and gave a couple of examples. "He was constantly on detention, bullied the younger kids and even assaulted a couple of teachers the past year. His grades were good, though: surprisingly, because the school staff said he never appeared to study."

Gracie frowned. "So he was smart? But had anger and authority issues," she murmured, finishing up her fish. She should have added lemon, she decided, to the sauce. Next time, she would.

Jack nodded.

"You said he was three when the police raided the flop house where he and his mother lived?" Gracie recapped.

"Yes. Apparently, she had died some hours before, in the night, but of course Felton didn't know that: he'd been asleep in his crib, according to the records," Jack recalled.

"So even if he was later told the truth about what had happened that day, in his three year old mind, everything was fine until the police came and raided his house and took his mother away from him," Gracie said.

Her eyes met Jack's.

"No wonder he hates authority," Jack said softly. He'd been so busy gathering the facts in the case and learning what he could about Felton, he hadn't stopped to look at it from that perspective.

"Yes, but you can't make excuses for him," Gracie returned, her voice equally soft, and sad.

"I'm not. But you're right: it makes sense. I wonder if, instead of shunting the kid into foster care and trying to control him, someone had taken the time to counsel him about what had happened back when he was younger, maybe he wouldn't have turned out the way he did," Jack put in.

Gracie shrugged and gathered the plates, taking them to the sink to be washed. "I don't know. He may have always been troubled, but perhaps he wouldn't have been so—vicious. So violent," she shuddered, still thinking of the remark Jack had made about Felton liking to 'torture things.'

Jack came up and stood next to her, and sighed. He took a tea towel and prepared to dry the dishes once Gracie had washed them.

"It's interesting, isn't it? I mean, two sides of the bullying issue," Grace went on. "You have Edward Felton, whose early trauma and subsequent neglect may have precipitated him into becoming an aggressively mean bully and then a killer. And you have Leroy Cooper, who was a victim of bullying, not the perpetrator, but who also became a killer."

"I don't think you can equate the two," Jack put in.

"Well, no," Gracie admitted. "But it's very interesting that both the bullied and the bully can become killers. I can understand both paths to the same end."

Jack put the dried dishes away and tucked the silverware in its proper drawer. Gracie was staring out the little greenhouse window over her kitchen sink: the back garden was deeply shadowed now.

Jack hung the tea towel on its hook: this one was from Brazil.

"So, have you found him yet?" Gracie asked. "I mean, he ran away from the Tremont home last spring, right? And apparently planned to attack the barracks and then hide at the campground: fairly well thought out, if a bit juvenile," she assessed.

"Well, he *was* only eighteen," Jack reminded her. "Nineteen, now. And yes, we learned that he had a part time job at one of the fast food places out on Route 8, so he had some money, but not a lot: he had to look for somewhere cheap. Or free."

"Has anyone gone to the place he worked?" Gracie queried. "Do you know which one it is?" she added, recalling that there were at least three or four in the area Jack had specified.

"We have people going to those places now with Felton's school photo: Mrs. Tremont didn't know which restaurant employed Felton," he added in a tone that chastised the absent Mrs. Tremont for caring so little about her foster son.

"Right," Gracie said. "So, Felton does his thing at the campground while it's unoccupied or sporadically occupied, digs the tunnel, figures out how he can hole up there and then he attacks the troopers. Where'd he get the gun?"

Jack sighed again. "We've come up empty on that," he admitted, adding that they'd canvassed gun dealers in the area and no one had sold a high velocity black powder muzzleloader rifle to anyone, let alone an eighteen year old. "But he could have got it in New York State, or New Hampshire, or online even. He had a driving license, but he didn't have a car, but he could have used public transportation."

Gracie hummed an agreeing sort of noise. "Okay, well, he goes to ground, literally, once he's done the attack, and he lays low at the campground. And he's been basically living at the campground in Greylock Forest ever since. But he's not there now, so where did he go?" she asked. "And if you're right, and he left in a hurry, why?" she continued.

"I think Belinda's idea about him getting spooked by all the Rangers searching the campground is probably right," Jack told her. He sounded tired.

"Well, they say that the simplest solution is usually the right one," Gracie agreed with a smile.

"We've got a BOLO out for him, and the roadblocks have been strengthened and the curfew is still in force," Jack added.

"So that'll make getting around more difficult for him," Gracie put in thoughtfully. "Especially if he's got the gun with him. Of course, he could have stashed it somewhere, even somewhere in the woods," she finished.

"I'm hoping he's at his job," Jack said.

Gracie looked doubtful. "I don't know, Jack: if I were on the run, and knew people were looking for me, I wouldn't go somewhere where I was known," she offered. "He left his garbage, that means he left in a rush. But now he has to have realized that if the Rangers are looking for his hiding place, they will find the garbage and test it, and ID him. Eventually. So, no, I don't think you'll find him flipping burgers at his job," she finished firmly. "It would be too easy to trace him there."

Jack sighed.

"Coffee?" Gracie asked then, and Jack nodded.

"But no liqueur in it for me," he told her. Gracie often put a bit of Rumchata or another liqueur in their coffees after dinner, calling it 'fancy coffee.' "I'm—I'm headed back to the office," Jack admitted. "I want to see if I can make any more sense of all of this, maybe go out myself and look for Felton," he added.

Gracie smiled. "Okay, Jack. Just be careful," she admonished him, concerned. "And why not leave Woof here? Then you won't have to worry about him and you can take as long as you need at work."

Deputy Cal Shubert entered the garishly lit fast food joint a little before eight p.m. Friday evening. He'd been to two such places: one with faux country decor and another done in preschool brights. Neither had known an Edward Felton.

The manager of this third establishment with its pseudo Mexican embellishments was at one of the cash registers and greeted Deputy Shubert with a tired smile.

"What can I help you with, Officer?" he asked. He pushed his straw sombrero back from a sweaty forehead and waited.

Deputy Shubert explained that he was looking for someone who might work there, and showed the manager Edward Felton's picture.

The manager squinted at it and then said, "Yeah, that's Eddie. Didn't show up last night, or again tonight for his shift, so I gotta stay late, plus which I gotta pay a kid overtime to work his hours," he informed the Deputy, his tone aggrieved.

After ascertaining from the manager that Edward Felton had worked at the fast food eatery for the past year and a half or so, generally worked a nearly full week, and always worked the late shift so he could get a share of any leftover food, Deputy Shubert left. In response to Shubert's request to see Felton's job application, the manager had provided it. Shubert had noted that Felton had given his foster home as an address, along with a phone number that probably was the land line for that residence. He got into his cruiser and radioed in the details he had just learned.

Then, because he'd missed dinner due to being called in to participate in the manhunt, he called The Docket and ordered takeaway. Their sandwiches and fries were among the best, and they were open late, which made them a favorite for law enforcement on stakeouts or late patrols.

The Sub Shop closed at six p.m. and while there were many fast food places from which late night eaters could choose, Deputy Shubert preferred quality over quantity and so ordered the Docket's organic turkey on sprouted whole grain with local swiss cheese, micro-greens, tomato and mustard. He splurged and got the sweet potato fries as well: it might be a very long night of searching for Edward Felton.

When the Deputy stopped in to the Docket to pick up his order, on an off chance he dug out the photo of Felton and showed it to the hostess.

There was a BOLO, of course, and Felton's photo would be on the 11 p.m. news, but meanwhile, it couldn't hurt to canvass any place in the area where their quarry might have been.

The hostess shook her head, but then passed the photo to a couple of servers, and then to the cook. None of them recognized Felton.

Deputy Shubert was just about to put the photo away and leave with his order when another server came out from the back kitchen area. She was going off shift, but the Deputy stopped her and showed her the photograph.

"Oh, yeah: he's in here about once a week," she said, snapping her gum and fixing the Deputy with a curious stare. "Always gets the tuna salad—cheapest thing on the menu— and never leaves a tip," she informed him. "I work the lunch shift so I know," she finished, adding that she'd worked overtime tonight to help out.

After thanking her, Deputy Shubert returned to his cruiser. He dutifully radioed in this further information before beginning his 'dinner break.'

Gracie settled down in the Oak Room once Jack had left, and put on the television. It was Friday night, so probably nothing worth watching would be on, she thought as she flicked through the channels.

She settled on a marathon of 'Too Cute' on Animal Planet and was amused when Pumpkin, who was on her lap, and Woof, who had commandeered the remainder of the sofa, both watched the kittens and puppies on gamboling on the screen with interest.

Gracie mulled over the Felton situation, trying to integrate the new information and mentally compose a timeline for what Jack theorized had happened.

As they had discussed at dinner, Felton clearly thought he needed to avenge what he perceived had been done to him by the police when he'd been just a toddler. He'd probably been honing his skills and preparing for this most of his life, at first subconsciously but then certainly with conscious, clear intent.

When he'd been old enough, he'd left the home of his hated foster family the Tremonts, got a job, and saved some money. He'd put his plan into action with the campground root cellar tenancy, and then with the shoveling out of the tunnel. Then, he'd got a gun, and attacked the barracks.

He hadn't succeeded in killing the troopers. Maybe he would have decided to try again; Gracie didn't know. But meanwhile, he'd hidden out, obviously content with the way he was 'hiding in plain sight' and deceiving everyone into thinking he was just a regular aimless teen, working in a dead-end low-paying job until something better came along. He'd retreated to his 'home' in the campground every evening, and managed to survive remarkably well.

Until one afternoon everything had changed. Perhaps Felton had been coming to the surface to go to work, perhaps he'd had other errands to run. The reason was less important than the action: he'd come up out of his camouflaged hidey-hole and surprised a little boy who was gathering wood for his camp fire.

Unable to allow the possibility that Wyatt might describe him to or tell someone about him, Felton had apparently watched the child, followed him back to the campground where his father waited, and then shot them both to death later that evening.

Since then, he'd stayed hidden, using his subterranean retreat as his base, and working at the fast food place.

It all made sense, Gracie thought.

CHAPTER FORTY-ONE

Gracie had invited Jack to return and spend the night whenever he was finished at work. However, by eleven o'clock she was tired enough to head for bed and not wait up for him. He had a key, so he could let himself in, whatever time he got back.

She got to her feet, dislodging Pumpkin, who jumped down in annoyance and stalked off towards the kitchen, tail high with disapproval. Switching off the television, Gracie rotated her ankle, which became stiff when she didn't move for a while. Then she beckoned to Woof.

"Let's go for a walk," she invited the dog, who trotted out to the foyer with her, nails clicking lightly on the parquet floor.

Gracie saw the bag of clothing by the front door. She could take the bag out to her Jeep while Woof took his constitutional, she thought, grabbing her keys as she unlocked the front door. The dog could have a wander around the site of her soon to be labyrinth in the west garden, and she'd load the bag of clothing into her Jeep so it was already there for the next time she drove into Pittsfield.

Woof followed Gracie out the front door and turned left, on her heels, as she headed for the side of her house where her Jeep was parked. Someday, she thought, she would extend the driveway and put up a small garage for her vehicle. Not this year, but maybe next year.

She unlocked her Jeep with the remote on the key fob, and Woof growled.

"It's just the unlocking thingy, Woof, don't worry," Gracie reassured the dog. Funny, she thought, Jack's truck and his cruiser worked the same way: why should unlocking her Jeep spook Woof?

She opened the rear door and hefted the bag inside. Who would think clothes could weigh so much? Then she slammed the door shut and re-locked the Jeep. It made the usual quick bleep.

Woof growled again.

"What is it?" Gracie asked, looking at Woof as though expecting an answer.

She scanned her garden beyond the Jeep: it was where Larry's guys had been excavating for her labyrinth, so small piles of dirt were interspersed with newly-planted shrubbery. It was quite dark, with just a quarter moon in the west. It would be setting in another hour. Gracie had relied on the lights from her house to provide enough illumination to see by, and it had been fine for the walk to the Jeep. She had walked slowly, too, and carefully because of her ankle. The last thing she wanted to do was re-injure herself, now she was nearly all better!

Woof's answering growl was low, menacing this time, and instinctively, Gracie backed up: not from the dog, but from whatever he'd alerted to. It was probably just a fox, but it could be a bear or even a mountain lion, though the last were rarely seen.

"Woof, come!" she ordered the dog. But he stood his ground and didn't budge. Something was out there: he had scented it, and this time it wasn't rabbits, if indeed it had been rabbits before.

She leaned down and grabbed Woof's collar and began to drag him towards a little used access point on the west side of her house. It wouldn't have been easy to drag a 75 pound half-dog half-wolf under any circumstances, and Gracie's ankle made it a challenge, but her stern tone coupled with the repeated command to 'come' eventually worked: Woof allowed himself to be reluctantly moved the few feet to the side of Gracie's house.

Originally a 'coffin door' in what had been the house's parlor in one of its former incarnations, the over-wide entry had been retained when Larry had done the renovation to Gracie's kitchen a few years before. Now, the old coffin door led directly into Gracie's butler's pantry, between the kitchen and the dining room. It was handy when she'd been gathering flowers and wanted to bring the cut stems directly into the pantry for arranging. And also, since it had been an early, though not original, feature of the house, she hadn't wanted to destroy it.

Now, although Woof was still growling, he wasn't growling at her, and Gracie gained the coffin door in a matter of steps. She had her keys, and so unlocked the door, and quickly deposited herself and Woof inside. Then she slammed the door shut, and turned the lock.

Woof scrabbled at the door, and continued to growl.

"No, Woof, we're not going out there," Gracie said. "Whatever's out there, thank you for warning me, but we will stay inside now, where we're safe."

She moved carefully out of the pantry into the dining room, testing her ankle to see if she had re-injured it. It appeared to be okay, however, and Gracie breathed a sigh of relief.

It was most certainly a bear or some other animal who was marauding out in her garden, she thought to herself, and she would discover the destruction they most certainly had wreaked once the sun came up in the morning. Surprises like that occurred frequently when one lived in the country, as Gracie did, and in such close proximity to the forest.

But the incident, and Woof's growling, had unnerved her, and now he was at the Oak Room threshold, staring out the windows and still growling. Instinct told her to protect herself, even if it seemed silly. And she supposed that it could be a prowler, not an animal. Better safe than sorry!

So Gracie went to the alcove in the center of the main floor, reached into a drawer of her spinet desk, and pulled out her gun. It was loaded, as it always was. When company came, Gracie locked the gun in her safe, but normally it sat in her desk drawer, just in case.

In case of situations like this.

Gracie next stepped down into the Oak Room to get her iPhone and noticed that Woof was now looking out the front windows. Whatever — or whoever, maybe—it was, was still out there, and seemed to be moving around her house's perimeter. Did bears or mountain lions behave that way? She didn't know.

Gracie punched '911' and when the operator came on, gave her name and address and told him she thought there might be a prowler on her property.

"Did you see someone?" the dispatcher asked calmly.

"No, but my dog alerted," Gracie replied. "He growled."

"We only have you down as having a cat, Miss Barufaldi," the dispatcher said, mangling her surname. "If you've gotten a dog, it's important to update us, in case of an emergency…"

"This IS an emergency!" Gracie said as sternly as she could. "Please, could you just send a cruiser to my house?"

A sound in the front hall made Gracie drop her iPhone back on the sofa cushion and stand up. Silently, she moved out of the Oak Room and into the foyer. Woof stood, right in the center of the space, teeth bared, growling at the front door.

As though in slow motion, Gracie saw the latch depress and the door open. Of course, she'd closed it but not locked it when she'd taken the clothing bag out to her Jeep and walked Woof, since she'd planned to go back inside the same way she'd gone out.

Now, the door swung wide and Edward Felton stepped over her threshold.

"Don't move and put that thing on the floor," Gracie ordered, bringing her gun up in the two handed stance she preferred. Woof, at her side, growled more loudly as if in support.

The face she'd seen in the photograph looked back at her: he seemed surprised. He held a large, long, quite nasty-looking rifle in his hands, and he did not put it down.

"I said, put it down," Gracie repeated. She flipped the safety on her gun to off.

"You won't shoot me, you don't have the nerve," Felton told her archly. His voice was normal: neither fraught with evil, nor wimpy, nor rough. "Although you're smart, I'll give you that, Miss Barufaldi." He pronounced her name correctly. "Very smart, figuring out what that boy put in his notebook," Felton commented. "I didn't even know he had a notebook, but when I heard about it, I heard it was all in some kind of code, so I didn't worry about it. And anyway, I wasn't sure he'd written anything in it about me," he went on. His tone was conversational, and Gracie had an eerie sense of surrealism. "But you—you figured it out. And you put your Detective friend on my trail." He paused, and slightly altered the aim of his rifle until it was pointing at Woof. "Now—you put *your* gun down," he ordered Gracie.

By her side, Woof met Felton's gaze unflinchingly, as did she. She had no doubt that he would shoot the dog, and then shoot her.

"No," Gracie replied, steel in her voice.

He took a step forward, then, perhaps to frighten her, perhaps to assert himself, perhaps even to reach Gracie or Woof, or take a better stance to fire, but Gracie did not wait for explanations.

He had come into her home uninvited. He had aimed his gun at her, and at Woof. She had told him to put his gun on the floor. He had not. He had stepped towards her. That was enough.

Thanking the training she'd taken and the practice she still engaged in on a fairly regular basis at the local range, Gracie tipped the nose of her gun down fractionally, and shot Felton in one knee.

He dropped with a howl that was part anguish and part surprise, but he still held his rifle. "You bitch!"

Gracie aimed again, and shot his opposite shoulder this time, and then, Felton dropped the rifle. He began to wail. Gracie was sure the pain was excruciating.

On cue, Woof ran to the gun while Felton was writhing on the floor, grabbing his shattered shoulder with one hand and his mangled knee with the other. Woof grasped the rifle butt in his teeth and dragged it over to Gracie.

"Good boy," Gracie said warmly, meanwhile wondering if Jack had taught him that trick, and if so, why. Then she caught herself wondering about such a mundane thing and smiled. But she still had her gun trained on Felton.

In the distance, she heard a siren: more than one. Good.

A few minutes later, during which time Gracie's arms started to ache and the seconds seemed to go by very slowly, Jack, along with two Cheshire police officers and Deputy Shubert, all ran through Gracie's open front door. While Deputy Shubert cuffed Felton as the two Cheshire officers aimed their guns at the perp, Jack stepped over to Gracie.

"What the hell happened?" he asked, sounding mystified and annoyed.

"He was going to kill Woof," Gracie said, flat, and finally lowered her gun. She engaged the safety, and let out a sigh of relief.

"What?"

Quickly, because she knew she'd have to repeat everything for her formal statement, Gracie filled Jack in on what had happened since he left.

"I was just leaving my office to come back here, when I heard the 911 dispatch to your house over the scanner," he said, his voice a mix of astonishment and relief.

"I was finished with my patrol for the night," began Deputy Shubert, "and was going to lock up the cruiser and head home when I saw you come running out of the courthouse and take off. So I followed you."

"We got the 911 dispatch, as we were on duty," noted one of the Cheshire officers with a smile for Gracie, whom he knew.

Gracie realized that, when she had heard Woof growl in her foyer, she'd dropped her iPhone on the sofa, but the connection to the county's 911 center had still been open. Doubtless, the 911 dispatcher had heard the exchange between herself and Felton, and had acted accordingly.

Felton was now securely bound in handcuffs, and an ambulance had been called. He was still moaning, and bleeding, but not so much that Gracie thought she'd hit an artery. Still, the damage was sufficient and had achieved Gracie's end.

She knelt down now, and gave Woof a huge hug. "This guy was my savior," she said brightly. "He kept growling, and growling, and I knew something...bad...was out there. Not rabbits," she added with a chuckle. "I thought it was a bear, or a mountain lion, but then something made me call 911," she said. "Woof was stalking whatever it was as it made its way around the house. It seemed odd to me, odd behavior for an animal, I mean: wouldn't a bear or whatever just trundle off back into the woods?"

Jack nodded somberly. "Probably. Maybe it wasn't rabbits Woof smelled earlier tonight, either," he said then as a realization struck him. "Maybe he scented Felton in the woods: your property abuts Greylock Forest. He could easily have walked here."

"Felton said he thought I was smart," Gracie murmured, mostly to herself. "He knew I had figured out Wyatt's notebook! And he knew I'd told you, and that you were looking for him," she told Jack.

"How could he have known all that?" Jack asked with a frown. "I mean, yeah, I think he knew law enforcement was looking for him, but the notebook stuff?" He shook his head.

"Well, we'll find everything out once we question him," Shubert noted. Felton had been Mirandized, then bundled onto a gurney and into the ambulance that had arrived.

Realizing that the Cheshire officers had left, Shubert now tipped his hat and said goodnight, closing Gracie's front door behind him.

"My brave girl," Jack said to Gracie, and kissed her.

"Your brave dog," Gracie countered, with another hug for Woof.

At this point, Pumpkin came sauntering out from the kitchen with a look on her face that said, 'what's all the excitement? what did I miss?' She tiptoed over to the area in the foyer where Felton had lain and scented the air, making the *flehmen* face that looked so peculiar. Then she sniffed the floor, and turned abruptly and streaked upstairs.

"Gonna be hard to get that blood out of the parquet floor," Jack commented dryly.

Gracie shook her head. "I don't care. I'll call Larry, and he'll sort it out. At least it isn't Woof's blood. Or yours. Or mine!"

EPILOGUE
EPILOGUE

Once in custody, Edward Felton explained everything to the police, refusing counsel and noting that he would represent himself.

He had, indeed, planned the barracks attack, creating the subterranean hideout ahead of the shooting so he would be able to literally 'go to ground' and disappear, just as Jack had said.

His reason for wanting to kill members of the State Police was as Gracie and Jack had thought: Felton had held a grudge against all authority figures and institutions from the time he was a small boy. He particularly despised the State Police for what he thought they had done to him: taken his mother away.

Felton had continued to work at the Mexican-themed fast food place, presuming—correctly as it turned out—that no one would connect him with the shooting. His 'home' was the little root cellar and the adjoining tunnel and chamber, where he stayed when the cabin was occupied.

It had been easy to stay fed because of where he worked. He'd also cadged a couple of garbage bags from the restaurant every week to handle any remains from his underground lodging.

Cleverly, he had not changed his routine much, even once he'd accomplished the shooting. He went to work, he patronized local stores for his meager supply needs, and once a week, just as the waitress had told Deputy Shubert, he ate at The Docket. He also used the men's room there to take an ersatz shower and wash his hair, which he cut himself. In the summer, he risked blending in with the other campers and using the 'luxury' toilets and showers at Greylock campsite. But in the off season when there were fewer people, or during the colder months, he resorted to The Docket's amenities.

When asked how he had learned of Gracie's solution to Wyatt's coded notebook entry, Felton told police that he had been at The Docket for his weekly lunch and ablutions when he'd overheard Jack talking to the Sheriff and Deputy Shubert. He heard Jack tell them that 'Gracie' had figured out enough of Wyatt's code to learn that the boy had seen someone or something he shouldn't have, in Greylock Forest. Because Felton knew exactly what it was that Wyatt had seen: himself, exiting his hidden tunnel behind a stand of shrubs, he felt he had to get rid of this 'Gracie.' Without her, Felton had erroneously thought, the theory would lack credibility.

That had been on Wednesday. By Thursday, Felton had worked out who 'Gracie' was, and learned where she lived. But that afternoon, the Rangers and other law enforcement had descended upon Greylock campground to conduct the intensive search.

So Felton had skedaddled, leaving behind the garbage he had planned—just as Jack had surmised—to bring with him to work and toss in the restaurant's handy dumpster. Felton admitted that leaving the garbage had been a mistake, and a costly one, because analysis of the items inside had led to his identification and apprehension.

Afraid, therefore, of showing up at work where he might be located and taken into custody, Fenton had merely hidden out in Greylock Forest on Thursday and Friday, all the while making his way towards where he had learned Gracie lived. Friday night, of course, had been the scene of the dénouement between him, Woof and Gracie, and that had been the end of his story.

Felton passed through his criminal arraignment and waived his preliminary hearing. A psychiatric evaluation was ordered for him, and he was sent off. If it was determined that he was of sound enough mind to stand trial, that event would likely be scheduled for early the following year.

Meanwhile, Belinda McGinley, grateful that the murders of her husband and son had been solved, proceeded apace with the establishment of her little cat rescue. As Gracie had suggested, Belinda adopted two cats from the local humane society, a brother and sister, to have as her own house mates.

Belinda called the male cat Boris: he was white with grey tabby-striped splotches and bright green eyes; the female, a grey tabby with a few caramel colored splotches and golden eyes, she named Natasha. Because of Aaron's allergy, Belinda had been without feline companionship for several years. Now that she had cats in her daily life once again, she realized just how much she had missed them.

She, Gracie, and several of the women from Club and their significant others, all held a work bee at Belinda's and made great strides in transforming her four bay garage and loft into a well appointed cattery and clinic. There would be more to add and some equipment to buy: large quarantine cages, an examining table, and the like, but the basic flooring was installed and the painting was finished.

Because Gracie had told Larry about the spiral staircase she and Belinda wanted to put in the Rescue, and had asked him for an estimate, he was aware of that part of the project. Not long after the renovations at the future Rescue had begun, Larry contacted Gracie to explain that while fixing up an older home near Mount Holyoke, they had ripped out just such a spiral stairway. "I don't know if it's the right size, or height, but I can come take a look at the space in the Rescue, and if it fits, it's yours," he had told Gracie cheerfully.

The spiral stair was a little taller than they needed but since it would mostly be used by the cats, that hardly mattered. Belinda seemed amazed at the serendipity of Gracie's contractor coming across the very sort of spiral staircase that she wanted. When Larry said he'd install the stairway free of charge, Belinda was truly overwhelmed.

In honor of her husband and son, Belinda named her rescue, 'The McGinley Feline Rescue' and Gracie gifted her with a sign for the building and a sign for the end of her driveway. Club held a special fund raiser to furnish the Rescue with cat beds, cat trees, hammocks and litter pans, and to get Belinda started off on the right paw, as it were, with a good supply of kitten chow, cat chow and litter. At their October meeting, Club also decided that the proceeds from that year's Winter Dance would go to Belinda's Rescue.

She expected to be ready for her first 'boarders' in November. "In time for Thanksgiving, and this year, I'll have a lot to be thankful for," Belinda told Gracie late one afternoon as they finished working for the day and took a long look around the nearly finished Rescue space. "I didn't think I would, either," she added quietly.

Gracie gave her friend a hug. "And you'll have kitties here by then, so they'll have something to be grateful for, as well," she reminded her with a smile.

Gracie's labyrinth was finished quite quickly, and though winter was drawing near, the shrubs Charlie and George had planted nearly all took successful root.

Her ankle healed completely, although slowly, and Gracie continued to see Dr. Grist on a bi weekly basis, just to stay in top condition. Jack still considered chiropractors marginally legit, but he was more relieved than he let on to anyone that Gracie was well again. He was also extremely guilty about the part his overheard conversation at the Docket had played in Felton's assault on her and her home.

Gracie told him many times that his intent had not been to expose her to danger, that he had merely been sharing information with colleagues, and that he had been circumspect about what he said and how he had said it. She assured him that she didn't hold him at all responsible. But still, Jack felt that it had been his fault, and worse yet, felt he'd let Gracie down.

Finally, the only way he could live with himself was to vow to do better in future, and learn from the experience. If he had been careful before about what he said where, and to whom, now he would be ever more vigilant.

"Would you have shot him dead, if he'd kept coming?" Jack asked Gracie one early October evening as they were enjoying the last of the sun's warmth on her screened porch. The days were noticeably shorter now, and once the sun dropped below the horizon, the air chilled rapidly.

Gracie looked over at Jack, and took a sip of her cider and rum cocktail. Dinner was ready, and it was time to go inside. "Yup," she averred. "The Castle Doctrine says I have no duty to retreat from my home if it is attacked, and that I may use any level of force, including lethal, if I think I am in imminent danger of serious bodily harm," she reminded him.

"I'd say having an assault rifle pointed at me was imminent danger of serious bodily harm," she smiled.

Jack returned the smile, and they both got up and headed for the kitchen, and dinner.

"It's well named," Jack noted as they stepped inside. Dinner smelled wonderful: Gracie had made a bison ragout, with sun dried tomato-corn muffins, and a salad dressed in butternut squash oil and blackberry vinegar.

"What is?" Gracie asked.

"The Castle Doctrine," Jack replied. He looked around her kitchen: at the crockpot simmering on the counter, the muffins cooling on an aluminum rack, the herbs in her greenhouse window, the filled wooden salad bowl on her scrubbed barn board table that was set with cheery autumnal themed placemats and napkins, and at Woof and Pumpkin, curled companionably in front of the gas fireplace that warmed the room pleasantly. "This house, this home: it's your Castle," Jack told Gracie.

Gracie nodded, and smiled. "Yes," she agreed. "It is."

—33—
FINIS

www.ingramcontent.com/pod-product-compliance
Lightning Source LLC
Chambersburg PA
CBHW050701290626
47170CB00016B/2562